"With all due respect, sir," she said to the rector, "I find that your lips say one thing, but your eyes have been saying another."

He stopped and turned to face her, putting his hands on her shoulders. "And just what have these treacherous orbs been saying to you, Lily?"

Lily swallowed, her mouth suddenly dry. Striving for coolness, she said, "Why, sir, the very thing they are saying now."

He pulled her closer, and smiled in a way that made her heart skip a beat. "That I find you distractingly lovely? That I would like above all things to show you how much? But eyes alone are not so eloquent."

Suddenly she was wrapped in his arms, and their faces were so close she could see the tiny flecks of green in the blue of his eyes. It took no more than an instant for his lips to close the tiny gap between them. His arms tightened around her, and she shyly put her hands up on his shoulders, enjoying the feel of them under her fingers.

It was a long moment before the danger of her situation was brought home to her. In fact, it took no less than Mr. Vernon's hands beginning a slow, caressing journey down her body to awaken her to the fact that she was being compromised, and with her own complicity. . . .

THE BEST OF REGENCY ROMANCES

AN IMPROPER COMPANION (2691, $3.95)
by Karla Hocker
At the closing of Miss Venable's Seminary for Young Ladies school, mistress Kate Elliott welcomed the invitation to be Liza Ashcroft's chaperone for the Season at Bath. Little did she know that Miss Ashcroft's father, the handsome widower Damien Ashcroft would also enter her life. And not as a passive bystander or dutiful dad.

WAGER ON LOVE (2693, $2.95)
by Prudence Martin
Only a rogue like Nicholas Ruxart would choose a bride on the basis of a careless wager. And only a rakehell like Nicholas would then fall in love with his betrothed's grey-eyed sister! The cynical viscount had always thought one blushing miss would suit as well as another, but the unattainable Jane Sommers soon proved him wrong.

LOVE AND FOLLY (2715, $3.95)
by Sheila Simonson
To the dismay of her more sensible twin Margaret, Lady Jean proceeded to fall hopelessly in love with the silver-tongued, seditious poet, Owen Davies — and catapult her entire family into social ruin . . . Margaret was used to gentlemen falling in love with vivacious Jean rather than with her — even the handsome Johnny Dyott whom she secretly adored. And when Jean's foolishness led her into the arms of the notorious Owen Davies, Margaret knew she could count on Dyott to avert scandal. What she didn't know, however was that her sweet sensibility was exerting a charm all its own.

An Easter Bouquet

THERESE ALDERTON

ZEBRA BOOKS
KENSINGTON PUBLISHING CORP.

ZEBRA BOOKS

are published by

Kensington Publishing Corp.
475 Park Avenue South
New York, NY 10016

First printing: March, 1991

Printed in the United States of America

Chapter One

Lord Vyse stared at the enameled snuffbox he held open in one palm, the other well-manicured hand poised to extract a pinch of its fragrant contents.

"Well, Quentin, what shall I tell Thorpe? Is it a wager or not?" his friend, Sir George Hollister, demanded.

Despite this urgent question his lordship still stared into the snuffbox, as if expecting to find the answer he sought in its depths.

Sir George persisted. "Will you or won't you? Never taken you so long to accept a wager before."

Lord Vyse raised his glance at last. "I have never been offered such an absurd, yet at the same time tempting one before." He snapped the box shut without taking any snuff and neatly slid it into his pocket. His handsome features were creased in amusement.

Quentin Vernon was the epitome of fashionable elegance, though his careless air made it obvious that once he had put on his clothes he never thought of them again. He was above average in height, with

5

long, muscular legs on which his stockinette trousers fit like a second skin. His broad shoulders supported a dark blue coat obviously cut by a master tailor, and his neckcloth was tied with care but without foppishness. On his well-shaped head he bore a thick crop of curling, dark blond hair that stubbornly resisted falling forward into the current style of casual disarrangement, instead waving back from his broad white brow. His deep blue eyes were set far apart over a strong, perfectly straight nose, and his mouth, though shaped generously, was unusually determined. His perfectly square chin was accented rather than diminished by a dimple.

Women of all kinds from housemaids to countesses were much affected by these looks of Lord Vyse, and though most of the time he relished his amatory success, of late his easy conquests had begun to trouble him.

A stocky, much less elegant Sir George tapped a booted foot impatiently, strode across the room, and threw himself into a chair at Lord Vyse's side. "Why'd you put away your snuff without offering me any?" he asked plaintively. "Especially when you didn't take any yourself."

Even without the snuffbox in hand, however, Quentin was abstracted. "What? Oh, you know that snuff is a mere affectation with me. I mostly like to take it in front of Thorpe and drop it on those immaculate buckskins of his. But here," he said absently, producing the box again. While his friend was engaged in partaking of its contents, Lord Vyse stood up and put on his tall beaver hat.

Despite the hat's casting its shadow over his physiognomy, Quentin Vernon knew that nevertheless when he ventured out in public he would be the object of feminine stares, some of them discreet and some quite bold. Though the admiration of the fair sex made his friends envious, Lord Vyse occasionally liked to remind them that the pleasure was not always worth all the trouble his popularity caused.

He frowned at the thought, certain that by next week he would surely find himself in yet another tangled love affair, having only recently and with difficulty extricated himself from a deep flirtation with the young wife of an elderly and jealous husband.

Women were the delight and plague of his existence. In fact, it was both his current mistress, a terpsichorean performer of no small talent, previously the exclusive companion of Lord Thorpe, as well as his dalliance with an heiress whose face and fortune had also attracted Lord Thorpe's attention, that had brought on that troublesome viscount's unusual wager. Although the odd terms of the wager would leave the field clear for Thorpe with both females, Lord Vyse had tired of the chase.

It would be as well, he thought, to remove himself from his present set of temptations for a while, and be perfectly safe from amorous scrapes. Why not accept Thorpe's challenge to pose as a rector in a country village? Should some unsophisticated country girl throw herself at him he would be safe in his guise as a clergyman and would not be tempted to begin a flirtation that, in such a rustic place, might be taken dangerously to heart. For all the trouble they caused him, at least the ladies of the ton and the demi-reps knew how to play the game.

Hat jammed well down onto his forehead, he offered his tan-gloved hand to Sir George. "All right. Tell Thorpe that I accept. I'm sure I can pull it off. I daresay I will look very natural praying in a cassock, don't you think?" He simpered experimentally and George hooted with laughter.

"Thorpe didn't think of that, I'll wager. He just assumed you wouldn't be able to last a week pretending to be a clergyman without getting into a scrape and everyone seeing through your disguise. By the way, just how are you going to arrange it?"

His lordship, on his way out the door, turned. "It's quite simple. Thorpe knows that the living I hold at Mickleford lies open and that I need to appoint a rector to replace the late incumbent. It's there he means me to go."

George looked shocked. "Your own property? Isn't that a bit risky?"

Vyse shrugged unconcernedly. "Not at all. I'm not going to flaunt my title, you know, and as I've never lived in Mickleford, the people there have never laid eyes on me, or even heard of Quentin Vernon. I shall simply appear there myself as the new rector. By the time Thorpe arrives to observe my progress at Eastertime I shall be well on the way to winning." He smiled with anticipation. "That racing curricle of his is worth the trouble, and I'll be damned if I'll forfeit my grays for want of a bit of play-acting. Besides, I shall thoroughly enjoy confounding that devil Thorpe."

Sir George prepared to follow his friend outside, looking unconvinced. "I don't know that it will be as simple as you think. For one thing, do you know anything about services, or sermons, or running a parish?"

They stepped out, having donned their greatcoats with the help of the attentive club servants, and strolled out into the damp February air.

In reply to his friend's anxious question, Lord Vyse shrugged. "I daresay I can read the sermons out of a book. Clergymen aren't always obliged to write their own, are they? As for conducting the service, you and I will question our churchgoing acquaintances or even . . ." he gave a slight shudder, ". . . appear in St. George's one Sunday morn to observe how it is done. Nothing could be simpler."

Sir George brooded. "I shall go with you into Cheshire," he declared suddenly. "I don't think you have a clue as to just how awkward it could be for you."

Lord Vyse smiled. "I appreciate your loyalty, but surely I'm old enough to do without a nursemaid."

"I shall be your curate—a rector needs a curate, don't he?" asked the irrepressible Sir George.

"My dear fellow, anyone looking less like a curate could not be imagined. You will expose me as an impostor at once!" Quentin chuckled. It would be amusing, he thought, to bring to Mickleford as his curate a man who resembled nothing so much as a prizefighter of strangely aristocratic bearing, and see what the good parishioners of St. Peter's thought of it.

But Sir George, besides being loyal, was determined not to miss a moment of this peculiar adventure, so barely a fortnight later the two set out, suitably disguised, as they thought, for Cheshire.

* * *

Miss Lily Sterling, jolted from a pleasant reverie by the sound of hoofbeats on the lane not far away, straightened up reluctantly from her contemplation of the remains of a pocket of snowdrops thrusting their way through a thin crust of frost. She began to trudge along the lane to the village, her gloved hands laden with blooms that she knew would not last but which she could not resist bringing home to brighten the wintry atmosphere. She smiled at her own foolish optimism. Before going home she had to stop at the rectory to see the housekeeper, and then to visit some village folk laid up with illness. By then the poor snowdrops might be nothing but a memory.

The middle of February always marked the beginning of her gathering expeditions, and as usual she was heartened, after weeks of dreary weather and dull days at home, by the brave flowers that gave promise of spring at last. But now the hoofbeats, wheels, and creaking springs grew louder, and when they sounded as if they might be almost upon her she drew to the side of the lane.

The tall hedges rose on either side of the lane, and she pressed herself against the spiny branches, bringing her hands, with their bouquet of snowdrops, up beneath her chin while she waited for the vehicle to pass. But the hoofbeats began to slow and finally she saw a post chaise round a bend. It eventually drew up beside her, with a great noise of creaking and jangling and a shout from the postboy. The door was flung open and a gentleman stepped down.

Lily was stunned for a moment by his appearance, though she should have been well-prepared by the vehicle itself, for it, like the gentleman, was of a type that her little village rarely saw. He was tall, with easy, graceful carriage, fair, with large, almost startlingly blue eyes that seemed to seek her out as she huddled against the hedge. When they met her glance she felt strangely short of breath for a moment, and she even imagined that her heartbeat intruded its faint sound on her ears as a drumming noise, a new and strange sensation.

The stranger's first glance was definitely admiring, and Lily knew that the pink the cold air had already brought to her cheeks was being augmented by her consciousness of his continued scrutiny. Isolated as Mickleford and Squire Sterling's family was, his third daughter had much experience of being admired by gentlemen and she knew the stranger's gaze at once for what it was.

Though she chastised herself for silliness, Lily was at the same time glad that though she wore only an old wool gown, she had put on her new fawn-colored cloak with the braided trim, and that she had tossed back its hood so that her gold-tinted brown hair, piled on her head in a new style she had only assumed the day before, showed to advantage.

Meanwhile, the vision from the post chaise spoke to her. "I wonder if I might trouble you for directions? We were on the way to Mickleford, but seem to have mistaken the road. Delightful though this country ramble has been . . ." the stranger gazed about him with a wry smile, "I suppose it is time we were arriving at our destination."

His voice was low-pitched and even and his accents refined. Lily just stared at him for a moment, taking in his well-tailored wool greatcoat and beaver hat, the

11

pantaloons that stretched down to shining leather shoes. Each article was sober and plain in itself, but even Lily's unsophisticated eye could see the exquisite quality and workmanship in each of them. The whole added up to the picture of a wealthy, fashionable town dweller.

A bit irked by his patronizing tone, she replied civilly, but with an undertone of disdain, "I hope you will not be too disappointed, sir, when I tell you that have mistaken your mistake! You are on the road to Mickleford still, and not more than a mile from it." It was not in Lily's nature to be shy, even with strange gentlemen, even when they looked at her the way this one did. Besides, she was curious to see how he would react.

The gentleman smiled straight at her, and again Lily felt that faint, unfamiliar catch in her throat. He was really quite extraordinarily handsome. A gentleman, she thought a little resentfully, ought not to be allowed to be so handsome.

"Are we really!" he said in tones of amazement. "Why, I was sure we had wandered off into the wilderness quite a quarter of an hour ago. But I am rude. If you are going that way yourself, you must permit us to take you up."

Another man had got out of the chaise, and though he was by no means as good-looking as the first, he was dressed with equal taste and care. He grinned and bowed to her. "Please do," he added to his companion's invitation. "Been a dull journey. Would be delighted to have a lady's company."

While Lily was gratified that neither of them was so witless as to take her for anything but a lady, though she *was* wandering the country lanes alone, head uncovered and with mud on her petticoats, she was not certain that it was quite safe to go with them, respectable as they seemed. True, the grin of the second man held nothing but relief and open friendliness, but the admiration of the first man was rapidly developing into what Lily's experience told her was a decided inclination to flirt. And how better to flirt with a strange female than enclosed in a post chaise?

The blond man's stepping towards her, hand extended, decided her. The thorns of the hedge prickled through her cloak at her back as she involuntarily drew away. "I thank you, but no. Besides, you hardly have need of my guidance, gentlemen. Continue along this very lane and soon you will be in Mickleford itself."

She paused, tempted to ask what was their errand there, for it was a quiet place, rarely visited by strangers, and outside of Sterling Hall, there were only two occupied houses of any importance in the immediate neighborhood, neither of which, Lily knew, were expecting visitors of this caliber. She turned, ready to disappear up a path that she knew wound through a meadow and would return her to the lane farther on, but the gentleman surprised her by blocking her way in one or two quick steps. He was only inches away, and she could see the white curls of his breath in the air between them.

"Ah, but my wood sprite, would you vanish so quickly?" he asked, smiling down at her in a way that made her feel his charm as a palpable thing, pressing itself against her will. In spite of a sudden feeling of alarm and excitement, Lily noticed that the tall man's companion had come to his side and was glancing worriedly at him, apparently trying to convey some silent warning.

"I fear I must, sir." Lily attempted to keep her tone light, but her lips felt stiff with cold and it came out woodenly. Involuntarily she shivered. "I—I am expected elsewhere."

"Ah, but you feel the cold!" Swiftly, before she could prevent him, he took her hand in its thin glove and held it between his. Though his hands were bare on this chill day, Lily still felt warmth through the fabric of her glove. He smiled down at her.

Utter confusion reigned in her breast and mind. Experienced in the sometimes heavy-handed flirtation of her local admirers though she was, Lily Sterling had never yet been so put out of countenance by a gentleman. Hurriedly she extracted her hand, as he said, "I insist that you allow us to take you up and drive you to your destination, be it in Mickleford or not."

He let her take her hand back but before she was prepared for yet another onslaught of his attentions he reached over to her and drew her hood gently over her head, tucking in her stray curls and retying the bow beneath her chin with as much delicacy as a ladies' maid, but with a more lingering and deliberate touch, saying, "There, we must not expose your fresh complexion to the rigors of the February wind, my dear. I should be repaying you ill for your kindness by neglecting to protect such loveliness."

"Oh, really, sir, you must not!" cried Lily, undone at last. "I cannot . . . I really must go."

She wriggled away and managed to set foot on the

path, but behind her she heard the second man say, "Have a care, Quentin, the gal may be one of your flock, after all!"

Lily was out of sight, but not out of hearing yet, and at this interesting remark she felt compelled to stop. She was rewarded by a long sigh from her erstwhile flirt. "I daresay you are right, George. What a clunch I am to begin so badly. And I thought I'd be safer in the country. Not nearly safe enough from my own folly. But, you must admit, she was a delectable bit."

Lily felt her cheeks burn in embarrassment and indignation, and she fairly flew along the path, not going back to the lane which would lead her to the village until she heard the hoofbeats pass far ahead of her. Whatever could those two town dandies be doing here? And how, she thought, could she explain satisfactorily to herself her own reactions, the temptation to respond to the blond man's expert flirtation? Even now his compelling features flashed before her eyes. Distracted, she was almost at her destination, the rectory, before she realized she had crushed most of the snowdrops in her anxiety and had dropped the rest in her headlong flight.

Chapter Two

The arrival in Mickleford of two elegant young men in a post chaise caused some sensation in the village, and by dinnertime every household in the neighborhood was wondering at it. At Sterling Hall—the residence of Sir Richard and Lady Sterling, their numerous brood, and related hangers-on—the vast dining room table was noisy with chatter as usual. But for once the perennial argument between the squire and his younger brother John, regarding the latter's spendthrift ways, was pushed aside by the ladies of the family. They were eager to move on to a fresh and fascinating topic, to wit, the new rector.

"Oh, do give over, Uncle John," cried Arabella Forbush, the squire's niece, "and save the tale of your gaming losses for when you and Uncle Richard drink your port. Olive and I have something *much* more interesting to tell everyone!"

"Oh, yes, Papa, we're tired of hearing you and Uncle John argue," agreed Olive, one of the squire's daughters by his first wife, "Our news is much more important—it's the new rector—he's arrived and he's brought a curate with him!"

Her plump but pretty face was creased in an expression of delight, and she nudged Violet, her elder sister, to ensure her attention to the topic at hand. Violet, who affected to be above such common gossip, frowned, but nevertheless fixed her cool gray gaze on Arabella, who was announcing, "It was the most exciting thing! Olive and I were driving home in the gig to change for dinner, and we saw them outside the church, at least it must have been them because the sexton seemed to be showing them about."

Gratified that all eyes were now turned towards her, she continued, "We thought they were both very handsome, and dressed very fashionably for clergymen. They actually *stared* at us as we drove past, so we smiled at them, and waved . . . just a little." She giggled, abandoning her usual air of simpering propriety, and meeting her gaze, her cousin Olive joined her.

"They seem very promising," said Olive, when her mirth had subsided. "I must say that we were hard pressed to decide which was the rector and which was his curate — they neither of them looked much like churchmen." She tossed back a dark curl that dangled down the middle of her forehead. "I think they will add some distinction to St. Peter's."

Her sister Violet frowned as she put down her soup spoon. "It hardly matters what they look like, Olive. If they serve the parish half as well as old Mr. Barton did, *I* shall be satisfied. And besides, it is unbecoming in a lady of your age to be so silly and flighty over a gentleman," she added, for unlike her sister who was the younger by two years, at six-and-twenty Violet was completely resigned, if not dedicated, to spinster-hood, and had taken to wearing a cap some years ago, which the family thought a shame, for it covered her lovely blond curls.

"Stuff and nonsense! I'm not too old to enjoy a gentleman's company, Vi," said Olive, with another toss of the wayward lock.

" 'Deed not, Violet. Musn't close up shop before all the custom have been in to see the merchandise, m'dear," said Uncle John the debtor, eyeing his freshly filled wineglass with satisfaction.

Violet huffed at such vulgarity but Lady Flora, the mother of Sir Richard and John, gave a guffaw of approving laughter. Though she had been an earl's daughter and was said to have married beneath her, her sense of humor was as broad as her mind was keen, and she often professed impatience with the mincing manners of modern folk. Her family some-times cringed at the hearty jokes she liked, but Olive was not one of these poor creatures, and she smiled.

She turned to her half sister Lily, who seemed to be the only member of the family taking no interest in the subject at hand. "You ought to have come with us, Lily, you might have caught the new rector's eye. Soon Violet will be accusing *you* of being too old to flirt, if you keep ignoring your suitors the way you have been doing." She pouted. "It isn't fair the way the gentlemen cluster round you at balls when you never make the slightest push to engage anyone's interest."

"That will do, dear," said kindly, vague Aunt Poppy. Even she had come out of her gentle abstraction to hear about the new rector.

"Yes, you will be giving Lily ideas," asserted Aunt

18

Hyacinth, a regal-looking woman with a tight mouth. "Though I daresay she enjoys tormenting her admirers," she said bitterly.

"Hmmph!" said old Lady Flora in response to her daughter's remark, her spoon tinkling against her glass as her hand trembled. "You ought to be thankful. If Lily hadn't ignored that foolish Watson fellow he wouldn't have offered for your Arabella." She looked up irritably as a gusting draft blew her streaming cap ribbons under her chin and tangled them with her spoon. "Haven't you found the source of that draft yet, Dickey?"

Uncle John grinned at his brother, for as Sir Richard began to reply his sister Hyacinth broke in irately, "That's nonsense, Mama. Mr. Watson was never very taken with Lily. She was hardly ever here when he came to call!"

Arabella smiled. "That's true. She used to run away when she saw him ride up. But he wasn't troubled by that for very long, for he soon fell in love with *me*." Though Mrs. Forbush deplored her daughter's lack of pride, it troubled Arabella not at all to know that she was Mr. Watson's second choice. She knew that she and not her unreliable cousin Lily was more suited to be the mistress of his establishment, the second largest estate in the neighborhood of Mickleford.

Meanwhile that delinquent beauty and object of the scolding smiled apologetically at no one in particular and relapsed into her dream. In it a handsome, stalwart hero was riding to the rescue of a fair maiden trapped in a rambling castle filled with peculiar people lying under a strange enchantment, and when he had looked tenderly into her eyes and swept her away into his post chaise — no, that wasn't quite right . . .

But to Lily Sterling's dismay, attention had now been drawn to her presence and the dream faded. What was more, a certain gentle rebuke she had been hoping to avoid fell upon her at last. She didn't care what Aunt Hyacinth thought of her but she hated to have disappointed Mama, and that's exactly what she had done by being so late that afternoon. Of course it wasn't her fault, but she could scarcely mention that shocking flirtation in the road, especially in view of later events.

"Oh dear," Lady Hortense Sterling was saying softly. No one but Lily paid much attention, for this was a habitual phrase of hers and could signify almost anything, from a lamentation that the hens were laying badly, to the fact that Baby had colic. Today it meant that her daughter Lily had wandered off again just as she was wanted to look after her little brother William.

Lily, who was the second Lady Sterling's eldest child, guiltily perceived a different note in her mother's voice when she repeated, "Oh, dear," and knew exactly what it meant.

Having built up momentum by two repetitions of her favorite phrase, Lady Sterling continued, "Now I recall what I wanted to say to you, Lily. I do wish you would tell me before you take it into your head to run off to the village, my dear. Since you had promised to look after William I sent him out to find you, only to discover him hours later at the bottom of the garden, covered with mud."

Lily's words rushed out. "I'm sorry for forgetting, Mama, truly I am. I meant to be back sooner but I went out to the meadow and got some of the early snowdrops—" She paused in confusion, remembering what had happened to the fruits of her gathering, but went on. "And there are a great many people down with catarrh in the village. But first I went to the rectory to see poor Mrs. Philpott—she's terribly anxious about the new rector and afraid of being replaced by a younger housekeeper, you know."

Trying not to look conscious as she remembered what had taken place at the rectory, Lily glanced up experimentally and took in the various reactions. Her mother's face wore only an expression of gentle disappointment, but her half sisters were thoroughly disapproving. Although they regarded her with affection most of the time, it was frequently tinged with annoyance that Lily, with her dreamy ways, so often managed to escape the tasks assigned to her, while they felt they did more than their share of the work at Sterling Hall.

Aunt Hyacinth was frowning, but that meant very little as it was her most usual expression. Aunt Poppy, the younger of Sir Richard's two sisters, was leaning doubtfully over her soup and fishing with her spoon, while Uncle John, a faded version of the robust dark-haired baronet, was already on his third glass of wine and seemed to have lost interest in the new rector and everything else.

Next to him, blond, pink, and white Arabella Forbush daintily ate her soup and looked superior. *She,* still glowing with the delight of her recent betrothal, could do no wrong, her expression seemed to say. Teague, her brother, ignored the others and drank and ate determinedly but with little evident pleasure, no doubt hoping to put on flesh and health so that his

21

mama would agree to send him to school with his absent cousins, the squire's two elder sons. His paleness, thinness, and coughs gave Lily little hope that he would accomplish this aim.

"And while you were at the rectory, my girl, did you happen to see anything of this Mr. Vernon?" inquired Lady Flora, who sat at the table's head. As usual, the sharp-witted matriarch came to the important point before anyone else. Just as the ne'er-do-well Uncle John was her ladyship's favorite child, Lily was her favorite grandchild, and she enjoyed distracting the others from the girl's minor wrongdoings. "My shawl at once," she called to a passing manservant. "Demmed drafty barn, this place," she muttered. "Well, did you?"

Fortunately Lily had prepared herself for a question like this. Blithely ignoring her first informal introduction in the lane to the new rector, she replied, "Why, yes, Grandmama, I did. I was coming out of the rectory as he was getting down from his carriage."

As expected, the attention of the family turned from Lily's neglect of her duties to her good fortune in actually having seen up close the object of everyone's curiosity.

Olive exclaimed, Arabella squealed, and even Uncle John stopped in mid-gulp, winked at his niece, and said, "That's our Lily."

In truth, until that accidental meeting in the lane, Lily's interest in the arrival of a new rector had been minimal. Although she was a friend of the rectory's housekeeper, she had never, like some others, especially the widowed and spinster members of the Ladies' Church Society brusquely headed by her Aunt

22

Hyacinth, considered any unmarried male resident of that structure her personal property. Nor was she particularly devout, for though she dutifully attended St. Peter's of a Sunday, Lily reserved her deepest expression of worship for Nature itself, and when she was not to be found about the village or the Hall, she was usually out in the meadows gathering wildflowers, taking long walks in all weathers, reading, or dreaming under a tree. But now, to appease the family, she willingly described her second encounter with Mr. Vernon, reserving the first for her own solitary contemplation.

"As I came out of the rectory the post chaise drew up at the gate," she began, enjoying the sudden interested silence at the table. "The new rector is tall and fair and handsome enough, I suppose," she said with assumed casualness, "though he seems very solemn." As she paused she heard a disappointed sigh from Arabella. "His curate was handsome, too, though he had a rather red face and his nose appeared to have been broken at some time. And, Aunt Poppy, you will not have the pleasure of feeding him up because he was very stocky, not at all thin and worn as the last curate was."

Uncle John chuckled, Aunt Poppy made a tiny sound, and Sir Richard, who had been preoccupied with his meal and his thoughts, cocked a skeptical glance at his third daughter. "You could tell all this from the doorway?"

Lily laughed. "No, Papa, by that time they had come in and Mrs. Philpott was introducing them to me."

A minor bustle of excitement broke out among the

females at the table, except for Lady Sterling, who was again mumbling "Oh, dear," but in a more optimistic tone.

Lily recalled the curious sensation she had felt upon being formally presented to Mr. Vernon after their recent encounter. For it had become apparent at once that the new rector was none other than her recent disturbing admirer. She had barely recovered from their last meeting, and the shock of his second appearance and his identity was to be followed by another. He behaved as though the flirtation in the lane had never taken place, indeed, as though he had never seen her before.

Though anxiety and excitement had made her heart drum and her face heat up, Lily had been totally unprepared for the mortifying fact of his indifference. From Mr. Vernon's solemn demeanor, one would assume the whole interlude had been a mere figment of Lily's overheated imagination. Faced with this startling and unexpected circumstance, Lily had been able to do nothing but pretend likewise. The curate, Mr. Hollister, had flashed her a friendly glance before visibly controlling himself, but the rector, after a long, unsmiling glance at her, had simply said, "How do you do?" appearing singularly unimpressed with the information that she was the squire's daughter.

Usually this awakened the interest of Lily's male acquaintances, especially if they appeared taken with her looks. Perhaps Mr. Vernon was a serious man of God and was repenting his previous frivolity with her, although she could scarcely believe it.

Her long silence obviously puzzled the others. "Do

go on, Lily. What else happened?" her cousin demanded.

"N-nothing." Lily came back to the present with a start. But she was secure in her belief that the family would suspect nothing. She often daydreamed and had to be brought back to the point. Conscious of disappointing her audience, she added, "I daresay they are both very agreeable."

"Now," said Lady Flora, nodding to the servant who had brought her shawl, "perhaps there will be an end to all this speculation about the new rector."

"I daresay it is only the beginning, Mama!" offered Aunt Poppy cheerfully. As one of the several spinster ladies of the Church Society, she looked forward to doing good works for the new bachelor inhabitants of the rectory.

Lily turned to her father. "Perhaps we should invite them to Sunday dinner?" She could not help being as curious about Mr. Vernon as the others were, especially after her peculiar encounters with him.

Rolling his eyes in mock dismay, Sir Richard said, "Will I never be free of this female interference? Very well. I suppose I must, as a courtesy, call on the fellow and I will invite him then."

Lady Flora pulled the shawl closely around her aged but straight shoulders and bestowed an approving nod on her granddaughter. "I believe at heart you are actually quite a sensible girl, Lily, in spite of not always being about when you are wanted. Dickey, where *is* that draft coming from?"

Sir Richard subsided into his fish plate. "I'll have it seen to, Mother."

Uncle John sighed and put down his wine. "I'll do

25

it." He bestowed his charming smile on Lady Flora. "Can't have dearest Mama catching a chill, you know."

Lady Flora looked pleased. "Do you see, Dickey? I can count on John to look after me. So I'll have no more nonsense from you about his trifling debts."

Sir Richard seethed silently, the girls giggled, and Uncle John smiled his triumph.

"Oh, dear," sighed Lady Sterling.

Dinner proceeded along the usual lines, with the predictable tiffs, quarrels, and accusations. Uncle John's latest incursion into the family fortune was defended by Arabella and Aunt Poppy, and frowned on by Violet and Aunt Hyacinth; Lily's failings were detailed gently once more by Lady Sterling; and Teague was adjured to eat more and sit up straight or his lungs would never settle. At last the matriarch rose and gathered her shawl about her, muttering one last imprecation against the draft. "It's a wonder everyone at the Hall hasn't joined the villagers in a bout of catarrh!"

The ladies of the family followed her regal progress to the drawing room, where a well-tended fire at last silenced her ladyship's complaints. Wrapped in rugs, she beckoned her favorite grandchild to her side.

"Well, young lady, I hope you realize that we shall have no peace about this place until you marry."

"Grandmama, how can you say such a thing! As if *I* can be blamed as the chief destroyer of your peace." Her infectious laugh brought a smile to the old woman's lips.

"You've a point, as usual, child. Your aunts and uncle and cousin and your papa, too, are all fools. Your mama's a saint, but no more clever than the rest. As for your sisters, they can be sensible when they need to, though much good it's done them in finding husbands! But they at least agree with me that it is time you left off these daydreams of yours — and don't deny them, I know you too well — and accepted one of the local lads who've been hanging about since you turned sixteen."

"Oh, Grandmama, I've tried to like them, I really have, but they seem so . . . unromantic." Lily sighed. "I know there are no knights in armor, or gallant officers, or even bold highwaymen lurking about Mickleford, but the local young men are so dull, and since Papa will not take us to London, how can I meet anyone else?"

"What about that trip to Harrogate? And Cheltenham last year?"

"Oh, Grandmama, there were hardly any young gentlemen there, and most of them fancied themselves ill and spent their time bathing and drinking those dreadful waters. And now Olive and Violet will expect me to fall in love with the rector, of all people." She felt her face grow warm, remembering his quick, summing-up look and the cool greeting he had given her after the promising beginning they had had.

Lady Flora was watching her intently. "Ah," she said triumphantly. "I take it he did not accord you the usual homage."

"Well, no, he didn't," said Lily, knowing it would just fuel her grandmother's speculation if she told the complete truth about her brief acquaintance with the new rector. "He kept his nose up in the air and treated me as though I were just a — a bumpkin! But I don't care, really I don't. When the others meet him on

Sunday and see how indifferent he is towards me, they'll soon abandon their matchmaking schemes."

Sunday arrived, and the early morning saw a yawning Quentin and an anxious Sir George making their way along the path to the church.

"Do you remember what to do?" the latter asked. "Do you think the sermon we chose will be all right?"

Quentin entered the vestry unconcernedly. "Of course. Now stop fidgeting, George. You will make everyone suspicious. Besides, you don't have to do anything but mumble along with me. I'm sure the congregation know all the prayers and I've memorized as much as I can. Thank God I know the hymns — learned 'em in the nursery and haven't forgotten 'em. Now come along."

The Ladies' Church Society, mostly well-meaning spinsters who, invigorated by the acquisition of two such promising young men, had besieged them all week with visits and offerings of food, had descended on the church and left everything in order, so there was little to do but wait for the congregation to file in.

Soon all the pews were filled except for the most prominent, that of the squire's family from Sterling Hall. Quentin had been honored by a call from Sir Richard and found that gentleman genial, but rather impatient, not much interested in his new rector. He was more concerned with the possibilities of some late hunting if the frost held and the state of his farms. And today Quentin and George were invited to dine at the Hall, where he would meet the first family of the village, including the beguiling child he had encountered on his first day.

He did not know whether to be relieved or sorry

that although he had been in Mickleford almost a week, he had failed to see Miss Lily Sterling again. It had been a close thing, he admitted to himself, the day he arrived. For a few minutes that day he had forgotten the wager, his good intentions, and everything else. Luckily, before he had committed more than a mild indiscretion, she had gone, and then he had recalled just how close he was to his destination and the likelihood that the girl would be a member of his congregation. He had hoped he would be able to ignore her in the crowds he assumed he would draw to the church.

But he had been startled when, on his arrival at the rectory, he had been faced with her again, not half an hour after their brief encounter. Fortunately she had been unaware of his initial rapt scrutiny, and by the time Mrs. Philpott had called to her and she had walked into the sunlight on the rectory porch he had been able to control his reaction.

For Miss Lily Sterling was a sprite, a fairy, a delicious, delicate morsel that might have been sent by the Devil himself, or, more likely, by his representative on earth, Lord Thorpe, to tempt Quentin into tossing away the wager and behaving in a very unclergymanlike manner. Her hair was like floss or spun gold in the sun, barely confined by a blue silk ribbon, her green eyes were wide and trusting, her skin like buttermilk, her mouth . . . but even now the remembrance of it distracted him. George, at his side, coughed loudly.

"They're all here," he whispered.

"All right, then," said Quentin. He took a deep breath and peered out at his congregation. The Ster-

29

ling pew was filled from end to end with a bewildering assortment of faces, frocks, and hats. In addition to a daunting string of females, there were two little boys, a tiny girl, and an infant in arms. It regarded him placidly, thumb in its cupid-bow mouth, and then, yawning with abandon, settled down to sleep on the shoulder of a green, fur-trimmed pelisse, the brim of a green velvet bonnet bent over it. When the wearer of the bonnet looked up, he saw that it was none other than Miss Lily Sterling, and that she had noticed his observation. Even in the dimness of the church her eyes appeared to gleam. He stared at her, and it seemed she gave him a tentative smile.

Not wanting to become too lost in admiration he hastily pulled back his head and nodded to George, who signaled the organist. Fortunately, a familiar hymn jogged Quentin's memory and he managed to make his way through the service without too much stumbling.

The congregation stared hopefully up at him while he began to read his sermon, a very serious homily on the meaning of the Lenten season, which he had chosen from one of the books of sermons in the late rector's study. Soon he saw his little band of spinsters looking enraptured, a few servant girls toward the back giggling and nudging one another, which he took to be a compliment, and most of the rest of the congregation looking either bored or resigned.

For a moment he was annoyed, but then he reflected that on the few occasions he himself had attended Sunday services he had no doubt worn the same expression, and mentally forgave them, which made him feel more like a churchman. Occasionally he sneaked a glance at the Sterlings and found that Sir Richard, an elderly lady, and the infant were all asleep, while the others, except for Lily, were hanging on his every word.

The object of Quentin's interested glance sat with a dreamy smile on her face and was patently quite far away from the church and his dull sermon. He envied her, at the same time wondering what lovely fantasy distracted her. Did she have scores of suitors? Was she dreaming of her lover? He realized that he had stopped in the middle of a prayer, and hastily resumed. To his relief, it was soon all over and he was outside greeting his flock, the faithful George by his side, more like a hulking bodyguard than a curate.

Most of the females simpered at both of them, plainly struck by the way Providence had smiled upon them in the form of two handsome single men in the rectory. The men of the congregation appeared indifferent, but it took Quentin a long time to assure his brigade of spinsters that they could sort out such duties as polishing the church silver, embroidering altar cloths, and arranging flowers among themselves. Their eager attentions disconcerted him so much that he was relieved when he saw three of the Sterling ladies approach and the spinsters move deferentially away.

Lily presented the gentlemen to her sisters, and they proceeded to give their opinions on the new rector's first performance. "I just wanted to say that I thought your sermon was wonderful, Mr. Vernon," said Olive Sterling, flushed in her tight pink silk costume and a plumed bonnet. "Your sentiments found a very familiar echo in my heart." She pressed a plump

31

hand against the spot where she supposed that organ to reside.

Violet Sterling, attired in muted blue, greeted the rector and his curate more quietly, and added, "I, too, enjoyed hearing that sermon once again. It was a favorite of the late Mr. Barton."

Quentin was startled, as the satirical look in her eye made him wonder if his inadequacies as a clergyman were already becoming obvious, but hid his anxiety under a bland smile. "Thank you so much, Miss Sterling. I wished to reassure the parish that traditions would be upheld, and that they should not fear any abrupt changes."

He paused, and sought the glance of the fair one whose charms tempted him to throw away his clerical manners and engage in a furious flirtation in his usual style. "Do you not think it a good idea, Miss Lily Sterling?" he ventured.

Relieved of the burden of the infant she had held in church, her slim, graceful figure showed to advantage. She was taller than her sisters, and as the three had moved towards him, Quentin's eye had singled out her graceful walk at once. Now she glanced up, her green eyes soft in the morning light, the fur under her chin contrasting with her creamy skin.

"Since you have asked my opinion, Mr. Vernon, I hope you will not be offended if I say that I think we have heard that particular sermon one too many times. I hope you will soon be giving us the benefit of your own *original* sermons." Thick lashes briefly veiled her eyes and her rosy mouth was pursed. "I am sure they will be quite riveting."

Vixen, thought Quentin. Would he be able to resist

her allure till Easter and Lord Thorpe's arrival? To his relief, Sir Richard called to his daughters that the carriage was ready, and with the assurance that he would join them at the Hall that afternoon for dinner, Quentin bid the ladies farewell.

"The youngest one is a beauty, ain't she?" George commented as they returned to the rectory. "If she came to town she'd have a string of admirers that would put all the reigning belles to shame."

"Just my confounded luck to find *her* here," grumbled Quentin. "Not that I apprehend any danger from that quarter. She's probably betrothed or at least being courted by some local swain, and I don't think she's very impressed with her new rector."

George grinned. "She cut you neatly down to size, didn't she, she and Miss Sterling? I shall make it my practice not to get into any theological conversations with *that* lady. Her eyes are far too sharp." He gazed after Violet with amused respect.

Quentin nodded. "Yes, let us hope that we can direct the conversation onto safer ground at dinner. Perhaps we can induce Sir Richard to tell us something more of local matters that a rector should know. He seemed little enough interested when he called on us, but maybe today he will make an effort."

But this hope proved to be too sanguine. Not that Sir Richard would not have graciously answered any questions his new rector might care to put to him, but the conversation, from the time the guests were shown in, remained strictly in the hands of the ladies of Sterling Hall.

Lily wanted badly to laugh at the dismay on the faces of the rector and his curate when the entire family was assembled in the dining room with its usual noise and commotion. She knew she had been naughty to comment that way on Mr. Vernon's sermon, to which she hadn't even listened, but his superior air had raised her ire. Now she watched him trying to absorb the immensity of the Sterling family. By the time the joint was served he seemed rather flustered, his starched cravat was a bit limp. Mr. Hollister's face was even redder than before.

"Of course, Mr. Vernon, the villagers are in pretty fair condition, except for a few of the old and indigent," Sir Richard was saying, as the ladies had subsided for a moment.

"Oh, but we do our best for them," his wife added. "Especially Lily, who—" but she was distracted by the nursery party, consisting of Steven, William, and two-year old Blossom, who were permitted on Sundays to eat in the dining room. All three had suffered a sudden lapse in table manners and were mashing peas into the cloth, shouting gleefully.

"Oh, yes." Olive, ever alert, picked up where her stepmother had left off. "Lily knows the village better than any of us, even Papa, and she could tell you anything you wanted to know about your parishioners." She smiled encouragingly at her sister.

Lily glanced up at the rector, but he appeared unmoved by this information. Next to her Mr. Hollister had been entertaining her with a wholly fictitious but believable account of his last parish, assuring her that this dinner at the Hall was the finest ever offered him, which brought pleased smiles from Aunt Poppy at his other side, who had been urging more food on him notwithstanding his burly physique.

However, despite Mr. Vernon's apparent lack of interest in her, no sooner had the gentlemen rejoined the ladies after dinner than Lily found herself in conversation with him. How it had happened, she did not know, for he had seemed completely occupied fending off an interrogation on his family connections by Lady Flora on the one hand and the theological assaults of Aunt Hyacinth on the other, but as she picked up a much-tangled piece of needlework and began trying to discover where she had left off in her stitching, she found him beside her.

"Perhaps, Miss Lily, you will be able to tell me whether any of my parishioners are currently in need of any assistance I can render?" he began.

"Spiritual or secular, sir?" she asked, without looking up at him. To look at him would render her careful attempts at mockery useless.

But the warm chuckle she heard made her look up involuntarily. "Both, of course." He was regarding her with slightly more interest than before, and she wondered if it was because he had been piqued that she did not fuss over him the way her sisters and the ladies of the parish did.

Nor did she intend to do so, if she could help it, despite the little thrill that ran through her as she looked into his eyes, which seemed remarkably blue, bluer than any summer sky or spring flower. She did, however, feel flustered, not only because he was not at all what she had expected in a clergyman but because of the observation she felt from her sisters and aunts.

Carefully, she replied, trying to ignore the new rector's dizzying smile, "Well, there are several families whose fathers spend a lot of time much the worse for

35

drink, and the mothers must work very hard to clothe and feed the children. Then there are a few very old people who often are ill, but overall I would say Mickleford is a rather prosperous village. There is almost always work here for everyone who wants it. We are very lucky, you know, and Papa is an excellent landlord, if a trifle absent-minded."

Lily was surprised at the gradual seriousness that replaced the smile on Mr. Vernon's face. For a moment he had looked at her as though he had no idea of what she was talking about. She wondered what sort of parish he had been in before — or perhaps this was his first. Wondering if her frankness would be taken the wrong way, she continued, "As for the church, most people go because it is expected of them, although I doubt you will again see it as full as it was today. You see, everyone was consumed with curiosity about the new rector."

"Ah, so that is what I owed my vast congregation to today," replied the rector.

Lily saw him quickly hide a smile, and was relieved.

"I suppose that if I want to continue to draw large numbers to the church I will have to work very hard."

"I don't think it ever troubled Mr. Barton," said Lily. "There are a few truly devout folk in the parish and that was enough for him. In this house it is only Aunt Hyacinth and my sister Violet who are among them."

At her last words the rector gave what could only be an anxious glance at the two ladies she had named. When he turned back to her he had a serious look on his face. "I thank you for this very valuable information, Miss Lily. I see I shall have my work cut out for me. Drunkards, indeed! And hardly anyone truly devout! You shock me. I have half a mind to institute a series of pastoral visits to these backsliders and get them to reform their ways. By Easter I will fill that church to overflowing, and not because of any vulgar curiosity."

Lily was stricken with astonishment. How wrong she had been about him! It had not been fully apparent until now just how serious about his duties the new rector was. She foresaw trouble. "I pray you will consider your pastoral visit to the Hall already made, then, sir, for aside from the two I have mentioned, I doubt anyone here would thank you for an extra sermon. You will see us in our pew on Sunday but I do not think you will find much success in converting backsliders here."

The rector's frown grew deeper. "I see. And I did wonder, you know, why the squire's family did not keep Lent as it should."

"Why, what do you mean?"

"I mean the eating of meat at dinner today. Naturally, I partook so as not to offend my hostess, but I cannot approve of completely ignoring the Lenten fast."

"I do hope you will enjoy your herring and pease porridge, then, sir," she said coolly, wondering at the hearty appetites of this hypocritical rector and his curate when the chickens and joint had been served.

She returned her attention to her needlework in a way that he could not interpret as anything but dismissal. To her relief she heard him begin talking to Olive, and though her opinion of him had fallen very low, she noticed that he was surprisingly patient with her sister's flutterings and gushing.

The curate, Mr. Hollister, she noticed, had fallen into a difficult spot between Aunt Hyacinth and Violet, and from the look on his face she guessed that the one was interrogating him and the other admonishing him. There was something very uncuratelike in the look he flashed her as she gazed at him sympathetically. It was almost as though he were sharing a joke with her. In fact, there was something decidedly odd about both him and Mr. Vernon, something she could not quite put her finger on.

As the days passed this impression became stronger, especially when, during her walks about the village, she several times encountered the new rector conducting his pastoral visits. She was bringing a basket of jellies and preserves to a poor woman who had just had her seventh lying-in when she heard the rector's voice emerging from the doorway of a laborer's cottage nearby.

"And do not forget, I shall expect to see you at church every Sunday, and I want to hear you singing the hymns very loudly, do you understand?"

The rector emerged and the inhabitant of the cottage followed him, touching his battered hat. "Ay, rector, sir," the man said, swaying a little. It was plain that he was a little worse for drink.

"And sober, if you please," added Mr. Vernon. Lily thought she saw him press something into the man's hand but she was not sure. What a fool he was if it were true, she thought. She had known for a long time that in this family's case, any but the most direct assistance in the form of food, clothes, and repairs to their cottage only ended up at the local tavern being spent on drink.

She hurried after the rector and caught up with him a few yards away. "Mr. Vernon, I could not help but overhear your conversation with Ned Cooper and I hope you won't take it amiss if I give you the benefit of my experience in dealing with him and others like him."

Mr. Vernon seemed caught by surprise, and at first he smiled at her, only to seem to remember himself and assume a stern expression. "Please go ahead and give me the benefit of your vast experience, Miss Lily."

She could not like his tone, but she persevered, explaining the habits of men like Cooper, and the best way to assist their families.

He listened impassively, and then said, "And I suppose you know best about their souls as well as their material welfare? My job is to get them to church, and that is what I am going to do." He bowed stiffly. "If you please, Miss Lily, I have another visit to make."

So saying he stalked away across the street to a dilapidated house where Lily knew that a large, pugnacious family who had recently defected to the dissenters' Chapel in a neighboring village lived. She stopped and waited for the inevitable.

The rector, after some delay, was admitted by a ragged little girl. It was only a few seconds later that raised voices emanated from the house, and Lily heard the deep, calm tones of the rector, followed by a resounding crash. Mr. Vernon exited hastily, as if propelled from the house, looking back at it in distaste. Lily could not help giggling. As the rector turned and glared at her, she hurried away to make her visit of comfort, knowing her presence in any of the cottages would be more welcome than Mr. Vernon's.

One day her errands took her to the rectory, to pick up a receipt Mrs. Philpott had promised Lady Flora, who was forever stinking up the stillroom with peculiar remedies and urging them upon her family. A little curious, Lily wondered whether she ought to call upon the rector himself. In spite of the fact that he obviously disapproved of her, she thought she owed it to her friends in the village to try to reason with him. She had heard reports of his urging church attendance on everyone, without troubling to first win the trust of the parishioners. Finally she decided to enter at the kitchen door first and find out from the housekeeper whether the rector was at home.

It was past ten, and Lily fully expected to find Mrs. Philpott resting from her morning's labors with a cup of tea, but instead that lady appeared to be in the midst of preparing a sumptuous breakfast.

"Oh, it's you, Miss Lily!" she cried, hurriedly plucking some slices of toast away from the fire and wrapping them in a linen napkin. "And how is poor Mr. Teague's cough? I'm sure her ladyship will be pleased with the receipt for that cough syrup — only give me a moment."

Lily watched in amazement as eggs, bacon, kidneys, sausages, and bowls of marmalade were piled onto a massive tray. Mrs. Philpott, after having arranged everything on the tray, plopped down in a chair for a moment, sighing. "I have never worked so hard in my life, Miss Lily — not that I'm complaining, mind you, for the rector and Mr. Hollister are very kind — it's only that they have such peculiar habits, not at all like dear old Mr. Barton!"

"I can well imagine," said Lily. "Eating such a breakfast at this hour! Whatever have they been doing all morning—hard manual labor?"

Mrs. Philpott looked up ashamedly. "Sleeping, I'm afraid, Miss Lily. They have never risen before nine, you know, but today was the worst. They were up very late last night—shut up in the study with piles of books writing this week's sermon, they claimed—but I really shouldn't say . . ." She hesitated, but by her expression she was obviously eager to relate more details.

Lily obliged her. "What is it, dear Mrs. Philpott? Do go on."

Thus encouraged, the housekeeper continued in a hushed tone, "I can hardly believe it, and I wouldn't wish to say anything disrespectful of a man of the cloth, though goodness knows Mr. Barton was fond of his wine, but I found four empty bottles in the study this morning, and the fire was only just dying away when I went in to clean at six."

"That means they must have been up half the night drinking! I suppose it could take that long to write a sermon, but that it requires so much stimulation I doubt."

Then fully aware that she was gossiping and that it was unbecoming in the squire's daughter, whatever her private doubts, Lily said firmly, "Well, I daresay it's nothing to worry about, Mrs. Philpott, only that it is rather inconsiderate of them to make so much extra work for you." She hefted the tray experimentally. "It is much too heavy for you," she decided. "I will take it in, if you will just open the door to the passage."

The housekeeper leaped to her feet in protest. "Oh, no Miss Lily! It wouldn't be right, it wouldn't!"

"Nonsense, I can see you are exhausted, and I'm sure this late breakfasting has been interfering with your duties. I shall simply explain to the rector—"

"Please, miss, don't say a word, else I'll lose my position." Anxious tears formed in the woman's eyes.

"Dear Mrs. Philpott, you must not think anything so foolish. I shall emphasize what a good and hard worker you have always been, and merely suggest to the rector that if he wants his rectory run properly he must be more accommodating."

Despite the housekeeper's begging her not to carry out her plan, Lily finally prevailed upon her to open the door, and she proceeded to the dining room bearing the tray full of coffee and viands. The door was fortunately open, and she paused a moment on the threshold, surveying the scene.

The rector and his curate, attired in elegant brocade dressing gowns and embroidered leather slippers, sat at their ease, legs crossed, perusing the newspapers. Neither of them looked up as she entered, a dangerous look in her eyes.

As she set down the tray with a thump, the rector merely said, "Thank you, Mrs. Philpott. That will be all for now."

"Not quite all, Mr. Vernon," she said in a deceptively calm voice.

The gentlemen practically leaped to their feet in astonishment. "Miss Lily! What are you—but where is Mrs. Philpott?" was the first thing the rector said.

Lily thought he looked suspiciously guilty, and wondered if he were quite as rigid in his ideas about propriety and piety as he had taken pains to appear. "She is in the kitchen, sir, trying to continue her duties, but much tired out, I fear, by your demanding this excessively large breakfast at this late hour of the day."

"Late?" The curate, Mr. Hollister, regarded her with a glance of almost imbecile amazement. "It's only just past ten, and we barely got to bed before five! Being a bit hard on us, aren't you, Miss Lily?"

"Indeed," the rector agreed, by this time having regained his appearance of poise and having led Lily politely to a chair. "Especially when our labors were concerned with the welfare of the parish."

"Of course." Mr. Hollister, who had been looking a bit anxious, brightened. "In addition to the sermon, we were discussing how to improve the health and well-being of the poor in our flock."

Lily smiled and said sweetly, "That is most admirable, but I doubt that staying up all night drinking to their health will measurably improve it." She pointedly eyed a half-empty bottle and pair of dirty glasses which the distracted Mrs. Philpott had apparently missed.

The curate flushed crimson, but the rector went very pale and for a moment Lily thought she saw anger flash across his face.

"Is there something in particular you wanted to speak to us about, Miss Sterling?" he asked icily. "Or did you merely come to accuse us of being drunkards?"

Suddenly Lily's confidence evaporated and she was a little ashamed. What business of hers was it if the rector and his curate had polished off almost five bottles of wine between them in one night? From what little she knew of the world, she was sure that such behavior was not uncommon among gentlemen, even clergymen, many of whom made little pretense of being devout, but regarding their calling as simply another occupation suitable for a gentleman, like the diplomatic corps or the Army.

In truth, she had had only a vague purpose in this call, but swiftly thought of a plausible reason. "I was simply wondering, Mr. Vernon, if you would care to let me know what you plan for the Easter celebration. My friends in the village have been asking me, since in years past I have helped organize the pageant."

"Easter celebration?" The rector looked at her blankly.

"Why, yes, the sword dance, the mummer's play, the procession, the games for the children—of course you will want to plan the special church service yourself, but I thought I might offer my help in planning the more secular part of the feast."

Lily watched with dawning amusement as the two exchanged inscrutable glances.

"Ah . . . yes, the Easter celebration. As you say, the service will be up to me . . ."

"Of course," chimed in Mr. Hollister, bobbing his head. "Candles, hymns, and such."

"But as for a mummer's play and a procession, well . . ." Mr. Vernon looked disapproving. "I do not know that I can countenance such frivolity on what is, albeit the most joyful, still a solemn holiday. The celebration should be in keeping with that and take place entirely in the church, I think."

"Oh," said Lily. Her heart sank a little, for she had always enjoyed working with the old rector to give the people of the village a lively celebration at Eastertime, and she knew that they would be dreadfully disappointed to have their harmless entertainment vetoed by a stern new pastor. She was on the point of warning him that his refusal to countenance a pageant would bring no great crowds into the church at Eastertime, but a thought came to her, and she smiled.

The people should not be deprived of their fun just because they had a haughty old stick for a rector. After all, she didn't need him or the church to put on the Easter pageant. But all she said was, "I see. Well, I shall explain to the villagers that the new rector has his own ideas about how Easter should be celebrated. I'm sure we will manage to enjoy the holiday without the usual church pageant." She simmered with suppressed excitement. She, Lily Sterling, would show this hypocritical newcomer just how much the villagers resented his unwarranted interference in their lives.

The curate gave her a sympathetic glance, but the rector was unbending. She rose from her chair. "I shall bid you good day, then," she said, and hurried from the room.

When she was gone, Sir George looked at Lord Vyse accusingly. "Did you have to do that, Quentin? The poor girl was disappointed, and it ain't exactly the way to endear yourself to the parish, taking away their holiday fun."

The rector calmly began his breakfast. "My aim is not to endear myself to the people of Mickleford, George, but to pass myself off as their rector and convince Thorpe that I have done it. Do you think my becoming involved with the entrancing Lily Sterling and her pageant will help me to achieve that aim?"

45

"Well, no," Sir George admitted, "but I think instead of avoiding trouble you have run full tilt into it."

Lord Vyse munched a piece of toast. "That's preposterous. Whatever do you mean?"

"I think that she's going to simply ignore you and go on with it herself. And where do you think the villagers will be on Easter morn? Not in church. Oh, Thorpe will be laughing up his sleeve at you and your lonely congregation of one."

Lord Vyse looked chagrined. "The little minx might just do it, confound her! I know she isn't very pleased with my efforts to do my duty here. In spite of the fact that she is an indifferent churchgoer, she seems to regard the welfare of the village as her own concern, and does not approve of my methods." He brooded, staring into his coffee.

"Well, if from what you've been telling me is true, the villagers don't either," replied his friend.

"That doesn't matter," said Lord Vyse. "I only pester them to make it clear in their minds that I am in charge, and bribe them to fill the church. This way when Thorpe comes spying about he'll hear about nothing but how concerned I am to get the people to church and how I rage fire and brimstone at them — at least beginning this Sunday."

The men grinned. "I don't doubt this sermon'll wake them up," said Sir George, tapping the sheets of paper they had spent much of the night filling with admonitions to the sinful.

"By Sunday everyone will know that I mean business, and by Easter even Thorpe will be thoroughly convinced that I've made everyone believe I'm the rector."

"Even Miss Lily Sterling?" said Sir George slyly.

"Yes, even the delightful Miss Lily. Although I think she is suspicious of me, I must convince her above all, for I find her too deucedly attractive for my own peace of mind, and I will have difficulty avoiding her, as she is so much a part of things in Mickleford."

"Do you think you will be able to resist her long enough to fool Thorpe?" asked Sir George as he attacked a sausage and a pile of eggs.

"I must," Quentin said simply. "And the easiest way for me to resist her is to give her a disgust of me."

"Which you are well on the way to doing, judging by this morning's encounter," his companion replied with a laugh.

Quentin continued his breakfast but remained thoughtful. "I must watch my step. I must not appear too interesting. I'm afraid we shall have to take up country hours, George, and drink no more of that fine claret we brought along."

"Of course you're right," Sir George said reluctantly, with a longing look at the half bottle remaining.

Lord Vyse gave a sad smile. It was essential for him to get a reputation for being strict and stern. Regretfully, he would have to make Miss Lily Sterling, who seemed not disposed to like him much anyway, thoroughly bored with him.

Chapter Three

"Forego license and pleasure, repent and prepare for Easter morn!"

By the end of Quentin's sermon the little church was buzzing. Never had the stolid parishioners of St. Peter's heard such exhortations as in the last half-hour. They had been called everything from miserable sinners to wicked hypocrites. "Shocking!" Violet was whispering to Olive. "Why, it's no better than the nonsense they're filling people with at the Chapel!"

Olive's gaze was still fixed on the pulpit, her eyes shining. "I don't know if it's nonsense or not," she whispered back, "but righteous anger is certainly becoming to Mr. Vernon."

Indeed, Quentin was flushed with the thrill of his first real bit of sermonizing. He supposed this was how actors must feel when they took their bows. Unfortunately, he could neither bow nor receive applause, but the whispered amazement of his congregation was a more than adequate substitute. To his satisfaction and amusement, all the sleepers had been startled awake at the first sound of his ringing tones, and now looked disgruntled, cheated of their Sabbath nap.

"If Thorpe could only see you now, eh?" muttered Sir George, as Quentin came down from the pulpit.

The viscount would have been astounded, Quentin reflected, and perhaps would even have conceded the bet then and there. Equally astonished would have been everyone else who had known Lord Vyse in London. Lily Sterling, however, was not at all surprised.

"Just what I might have expected!" she spluttered once the family was outside the church. Not even the faithful Ladies' Society waited to speak to the rector after the service. They were all, Lily reflected, probably too timid, while the rest of the congregation was too offended.

Mr. Vernon stood alone with his curate, looking very proud and satisfied with himself. He gave Lily a haughty nod, which she ignored, but the rector's smugness was unimpaired by this cut, and she felt unaccountably annoyed. He looked at her, said something to the curate, and they both smiled. Lily felt an angry warmth rush up her face.

Meanwhile she had missed what Arabella was saying to her, and her cousin had to nudge her to get a reply. "Whatever do you mean?" Arabella repeated. "How could you have expected it? His last sermon was nothing like it at all!"

Lily turned away from where the irritating rector stood. "I mean that, considering how he has been going about the village stirring people up, it is not at all surprising that he has now taken to berating us all in this disgraceful fashion. As though he were any better himself!" Then recalling that no one else but Mrs. Philpott had seen those empty wine bottles in the rector's study, she desisted, leaving Arabella still more curious. But Sir Richard was now organizing his large family into parties for the trip home.

"Why don't you take one of the girls up with you, my dear?" he said to his wife, who announced her intention of driving back in the gig, instead of the stuffy closed carriage in which she had arrived. "I'm just going to have a word with the rector and then I'll walk home."

Lily hoped her father was going to warn the rector that such sermons as the one he had preached would not be tolerated in Mickleford, but she had no time to ascertain his views for he was handing Lady Sterling up into the gig.

The baronet then bustled away to the rector and the curate, who still stood alone on the church steps.

"Oh, dear," said Lady Sterling, having shifted the burden of Baby to her eldest stepdaughter and settled herself in the gig. "I only hope the Ladies' Church Society will not be too upset with Mr. Vernon. They were accustomed to Mr. Barton's much gentler ways."

"And so was every one else," said Violet, shushing the whimpering Baby expertly and handing the struggling bundle up to Lady Sterling before settling herself in the gig. "I only wonder what he has in mind," she said thoughtfully, glancing at the rector and then down at Lily.

"He is determined to turn everything topsy-turvy in this village, that is quite obvious," Lily told her. The gig pulled away, Violet at the reins, and Lily, her cousin, and Olive began to walk home, the children trailing behind them, Lady Flora, the aunts, and Uncle John having piled into the closed carriage. Olive and Arabella talked excitedly about Mr. Vernon's new style of sermon, and wondered if the parish would rebel.

"Well, I for one won't stand for him ordering us about in that fashion," Lily said stoutly. She had told her family about the new rector's disapproval of the Easter pageant, and all the Sterlings from Lady Flora, who didn't hold with disrupting tradition, to the children, who wailed at losing what had been an annual treat, had been gratifyingly shocked. After all, the pageant was a hallowed village custom, centuries old. "No rank newcomer, rector or not, is going to call our villagers despicable hypocrites to their faces!" pronounced Lily.

The other girls looked at her curiously. Rarely had they seen her so aroused to ire. "One would think you owned the village," Olive remarked. "Or that the rector had snubbed you personally, and not just banded you together with the rest of us unworthy ones." She giggled. "I thought it was splendid. Like being at a play."

Lily was startled by a sudden realization. Olive was right, she did feel it as a personal affront. Was it only because of the misleading way the rector had behaved when she had met him on the road the day of his arrival? He certainly had not seemed stern them, and had most definitely admired her.

But his behavior ever since had been so carefully cool — yes, it was exactly like a play. It seemed as though Mr. Vernon were going out of his way to make it clear that he wanted to be taken in dead earnest, perhaps even exaggerating his position as a man of the cloth to achieve this end, and that he had no kind words to spare for Lily Sterling, whom he no doubt looked on as an obstacle to his authority.

"Well, he shall not have it all his own way," she declared as they reached the gates of Sterling Hall. "I shall certainly not let him ride roughshod over the villagers, and if he dares to take me to task for it I shall let him know I am not to be trifled with."

Olive and Arabella exchanged glances, but Lily did not notice, and swept into the house, determined to pick up the gauntlet the interfering new rector had thrown down. She hoped that her father had given the encroaching clergyman a strict talking-to, but at dinner she learned to her dismay that Sir Richard was only mildly amused at Mr. Vernon's new style, and had merely gone to speak to him on behalf of one of his tenants whose infant was due to be christened.

"Thought it odd, though," Sir Richard said, "that he put me off about the christening. I said I supposed he'd do it first Sunday of next month, as usual, but he looked at me as though he were the fox with the hounds at his heels, and finally said he was awaiting the arrival of a new silver baptismal font that a generous patron in London was going to present to us."

"Hmmph!" interjected Lady Flora. "Useless frippery. In my day we didn't hold with such Popish notions! Christened over a plain china bowl, myself."

Aunt Hyacinth frowned. "You could hardly accuse Mr. Vernon of inclining towards Rome after such a ranting sermon, Mama," she protested.

Long experience had taught Sir Richard not to let these incursions upon his speech continue too long. "Deuced odd. No matter what I said, Mr. Vernon insisted that he'd perform no christenings without the silver font, lest he insult his patron."

"Odd, certainly!" pronounced Aunt Hyacinth. "Mr. Vernon does not seem to me the sort of man who is dependent on the good opinion of a wealthy patron."

"Yes," added Olive, "he seems quite proud, even perhaps a trifle arrogant. I should tremble to see the likes of a patron that could put such fear into Mr. Vernon!"

Lily mulled over this unexpected new development. It seemed ludicrous, on the face of it. Yet it might explain the new rector's eagerness to impress everyone with his authority. As her aunt had said, he hadn't seemed the sort of man to bow to the powerful, but perhaps it was all pretense.

"Who do you think Mr. Vernon's patron could be, Aunt Poppy?" she inquired of the aunt whose mildness often induced people to confide in her. Aunt Poppy spent a good deal of time shopping and visiting in Mickleford, and could be depended upon to know, if anyone did.

Aunt Poppy's look of habitual vagueness cleared immediately. In her own quiet way she was as intimately connected with all circles of activity in the village as Lily was, and proud of it because she knew it irritated her sister Hyacinth.

With certainty, she said, "Why, to be sure, it must be Lord Vyse."

"Gossiping at the shops again?" Aunt Hyacinth sniffed. No one ever passed any interesting bits of news to *her*.

Lily wrinkled her brow. "Lord Vyse? I've never heard of him."

Lady Flora snorted. "No doubt, my child, because his high-in-the-instep, toplofty family considers Mickleford beneath its notice. The family seat is in Yorkshire, but even when their lands here passed into the family some fifty years ago, when I was but a girl, it was well known that they had no interest in local affairs, only in the

53

income the property generated."

Aunt Hyacinth frowned. "Of course Lord Vyse holds the gift of the living of St. Peter's, and since it was his father who presented it to poor Mr. Barton, this must be the first occasion the young Lord Vyse has had of bestowing such a favor."

"Indeed." Aunt Hyacinth shook her head. "I hope it does not prove to have been bestowed on one unworthy of it. I fear his sermon today—"

"Was excellent," proclaimed Lady Flora. "Just what the lazy folk of this neighborhood require. And entertaining, too," she continued with a chuckle. "A sight more lively than the pap old Barton used to give us. I didn't sleep a wink today!"

Pondering all of this, Lily came to the conclusion that it was, after all, this absent landlord, Lord Vyse, whom Mr. Vernon was trying to impress with his strictness, and said as much to her family, adding, "Then it can only mean that this Lord Vyse is at last going to favor Mickleford with a visit, for how else can Mr. Vernon prove to him how attentive and efficient a rector he is?"

"How else indeed!" cried Olive. "Oh, just think, we may soon be meeting this Lord Vyse. Do you think he will bring a party from London with him? I do hope so—I should love to see what the ladies are wearing."

"Pray do not run on in such a foolish fashion, Olive," Violet reproved her. "Even if Lily is right, and this Lord Vyse does plan to visit and observe Mr. Vernon's progress—"

"And bestow a silver baptismal font upon us," added Aunt Poppy.

Violet patiently went on, "We have no reason to believe that such an elevated personage will be interested

54

in meeting us. Oh, he might condescend to attend service, but pray do not plague our stepmama with visions of entertaining a lord to dinner, Olive. It would be too much of a disturbance to her nerves in her Condition."

Olive looked suitably chastened, while Aunts Hyacinth and Poppy looked shocked at the mention of such a delicate subject at table. Lady Sterling herself looked pointedly around at the groaning table and its many chattering occupants and said, "I do not doubt that my nerves would be adequate to the strain of having one more person to dinner, Violet dear, whoever he might be."

Lily, meanwhile, decided that her attack on the rector would be two-pronged. Firstly, she would begin to swiftly gather her forces to produce a rival Easter pageant. If she correctly gauged the sentiment in the village towards the new rector, she would have her pick of participants and Mr. Vernon would have to get by with whomever he could bully. Secondly, she would take every opportunity to study her foe, to discover what she could about his obvious eagerness to please this mysterious patron, and to uncover his real character, as it had been revealed so very decidedly to her that day in the lane. From now on, Mr. Vernon should have no peace from Lily Sterling.

Chapter Four

In spite of Lord Vyse's intentions, he found it a challenge to put his worst foot forward when it came to Miss Lily Sterling. It seemed he was forever tripping over her in the village, and it took some work before he acquired the habit of assuming a stern and disapproving expression when in her presence. He was far more inclined to simply admire her, or draw her into conversation for the delight it gave him to see the quick change of expression across her delicate features, or to raise a blush on her fair cheek.

But the thought of the wager and his own vulnerability where ladies were concerned muted his overwhelming desire to make Lily Sterling smile upon him. Instead, he took every precaution against charming her, maintaining his position as someone who was bent on disapproving of her and overturning her comfortable little parish, and soon she appeared rather disgusted with him. This did not, however, as he had hoped, keep him out of temptation. Indeed, he began to suspect that Lily saw herself as leading a crusade against him and all his works. Rather than avoid him, she seemed bent on confronting him.

One chilly, gray morning he was in the churchyard, which he had just realized was a very neglected bit of ground, directing the dull and taciturn sexton in the removal of some withered plants and shrubs, resetting some fallen headstones, and adjuring him to generally tidy up the place. Satisfied, he took a stroll around the church grounds and rectory garden, wondering how to relieve his intense boredom. He supposed he could accept Sir Richard's offer to mount him on one of his hunters, or the invitations of various families to dine, though, after his last sermon, he doubted whether they would renew them so cordially. The wry thought that he might have destroyed his own last respite from rural ennui made him grin.

Just then he rounded the church wall, and came upon a small female figure crouched near the largest monument in the churchyard. She was examining one of the shrubs he had just ordered to be torn out. It had been particularly large, and to his city-bred eyes, unsightly. Now Lily Sterling was busily engaged in undoing his work, or rather the sexton's, for, armed with a spade, she began to dig out the dirt filling the hole where the shrub had been.

Even the realization that it was his nemesis failed to restrain him. He strode over. "May I ask what you think you are doing, madam?"

She started, then jumped up with a grace he could not but admire, brushing a tangle of hair out of her eyes. It left a smudge across her nose but perversely, Quentin found her more beautiful than ever. She was dressed in a worn but serviceable cloak of a deep rose color, with a blue gown peeking out beneath. Her dark blue gros-

57

grain bonnet had slipped back, allowing the curls to dance about her piquant face.

"I am repairing the damage and the insult to my family monument, sir," she replied. There was the light of battle in her green eyes, and Quentin was somewhat taken aback both by her words and by the sight of her.

Belatedly, he read the inscription on the massive, elaborately carved block of stone. The letters said STERLING, with a biblical quote beneath and then the names of several people, presumably the affronted lady's ancestors. The shrub had been so large that he had not troubled to take note of whose marker this was. Not that it should have stopped him. Was he or wasn't he the rector here? Or at least supposed to be? He drew himself up and assumed his most dignified expression.

"I assure you, madam, no insult was intended to you or your family. It is merely that it is high time someone tended to this neglected churchyard. I have instructed the sexton to remove all these unsightly dead shrubs and vines." He pointed to a mound of vegetation that had been set aside for burning. "I fully intended to plant new ones."

Lily did not seem a bit mollified by this explanation. In fact, she grew very pink and appeared to be struggling between rage and laughter. Then she looked at the pile of plants and shook her head sadly. With more gentleness than he had expected, she said, "Then I wish you had consulted someone other than poor simple Tim Proper, sir. He doesn't know a daffodil from a dandelion, and is only able to follow orders. Anyone else would have been able to tell you that most of these are merely dormant. In a few weeks they would have turned green again, and eventually flowered."

She cast a rueful glance at the shrub. This close, Quentin could see, to his chagrin, the beginnings of a tinge of green along its withered stems, and here and there something that might have been a leaf bud.

"There is a chance this lilac might just survive such rough treatment. But I suppose there is no hope for the roses or that lovely vine that used to twine so prettily over the stones." Her voice turned hard again. "I hope, Mr. Vernon, that you will be able to think of something to tell the people whose families are buried here."

Quentin felt an unaccustomed flush rise to his face. Why had he to be such a damned arrogant fool, anyway? Had he come to believe that he was really in charge of this church? He should have asked George first; his friend would have told him not to be so cloth-headed as to imagine that he knew anything about plants, having been town-bred and leaving all matters to do with his country estates to others.

His mortification was extreme, and he would have liked to have been able to humble himself before the lady's superior knowledge and admit his wrong-doing, perhaps earning a softer look from her than the one with which she was now favoring him, but that would not be consistent with his character as the severe, autocratic rector of St. Peter's.

With a strong effort, he replied, "I assure you, madam, I had no intention of allowing such rampant, unchecked growth as this in my churchyard. I was going to replace it with something more suitable."

He could see that the lady was beginning to waver, faced with his assurance and firm stance. She looked at him with an expression of disbelief tinged with uncertainty. Probably she thought it was exactly what such an arrogant fellow *would* take it upon himself to do, right or wrong. Or maybe she believed that he just did not want to admit to his mistake.

How wrong she was! He longed to admit to it, to beg Lily to impart to him her knowledge of nature, to tease her laughingly about her passionate defense of growing things and to let her in turn tease him about his ignorance. He would have been enjoying just such a delightful dalliance as this, had it not been for the damned wager.

"However," he continued, before she could reply, "I do apologize for distressing you. If that shrub has a sentimental meaning for you, by all means let us nurse it and pray that my interference has not done it irreparable harm." To illustrate his good intentions he picked up the spade she had dropped, but she all but snatched it out of his hand. Her voice trembled a bit.

"No, thank you, sir. You have done quite enough. I shall attend to it. I only hope the others will accept your . . . explanation . . . as readily as I have."

So saying, she turned her back on him, bent, and began to dig again, enlarging the hole from which the shrub had been removed . He knew it had been difficult for Proper to dig in the hard soil to remove the shrub, roots and all, and now Lily's brow furrowed in the effort as she dug. He could not bear to see her labor thusly, nor to think of her small white hands, ungloved, being roughened with such dirty work.

Instinctively, he bent and removed the implement from her grasp, took her hand, and massaged her cold fingers. She drew a sharp breath but quickly stifled it. The sweet face so close to his turned away, but not before he saw a most gratifying expression in her eyes. Once

60

again he cursed the wager that had brought him to Mickleford in this tedious disguise, dropped her hand, and set about digging.

She leaped up and stood watching for a moment, then said, "That will be enough." She began to lift the shrub, heavy with its ball of roots and hard earth, but Quentin was too swift for her, and had it out of her grasp and settled into the hole before she could protest. She seemed to soften a bit, and even directed him to break up the large clods of earth with the spade before he piled it about the roots once more. Satisfied, she glanced up at the sky as Quentin stood and surreptitiously stretched, envying her lithe grace. "I believe it will rain quite soon, so we need not water it. It will likely die anyway." She shot him a sharp glance of reproof. "I must go. And next time you require something done about the grounds, Mr. Vernon, I beg you will consult with someone knowledgeable before you give your instructions to the sexton."

Quentin could only bow wordlessly. But he had only a few days' respite before their next battle.

Miss Lily Sterling, accustomed as she was to meddling in the villagers' concerns, had apparently been used to having the run of the rectory as well. She was there far too often for Quentin's comfort, although often she only came to see the housekeeper. But even then, Quentin could sense her presence in the house, like a fresh spring breeze blowing in through open windows on a fine day.

This irresistible message drew him out of his study one morning, and into the kitchen before he was aware of it. He had barely enough time to make up some excuse for invading his housekeeper's territory, but the sight of Lily Sterling, ever ready with one of her re-proachful glances, steadied him somewhat.

She gave him no time to feel secure, however, as once she had greeted him she said immediately, "I hope you are working on Sunday's sermon, Mr. Vernon. The neighborhood is all agog to know of which sin it will be accused next, and my own curiosity is almost as great." Her wide-eyed gaze was provoking.

Quentin could not resist the chance to return fire. "Guilty conscience, my dear?" He was gratified to see a slow flush creep up her face. "Rest assured that I shall leave the congregation in no doubt about the correct course of conduct, especially in this holy season. Speaking of the season . . ." He hesitated. Could George have been right about the girl planning her own Easter celebrations in spite of the rector's veto? He supposed he had better find out now.

"I hope that you and the other ladies of your family will volunteer their assistance in organizing the church celebration. You, I am sure, will know better than a rank newcomer like myself who in the parish is to be trusted with the candles, singing, and the church decorations. Oh, and of course, we will be reenacting the scene of the discovery of the empty tomb."

George had told him that this was often done in rural churches at Easter, and he decided to take over this activity himself, so that Lily Sterling could not make it part of her secular celebration. It belonged, properly, to the church, and evidence of such organization and the cooperation of the parish would impress upon Lord Thorpe most strongly that his fellow wagerer had truly been accepted as rector.

To his dismay, an arch look came over the girl's face.

"Oh, dear," she said, in a fair imitation of Lady Sterling, "I am so sorry, Mr. Vernon, but all of us find that our time between now and Easter will be quite full with . . . family matters. But you will have no trouble, I am sure, in finding enough people to help—some of the Ladies' Society members would be delighted, and I am sure you could use Tim Proper and some of those drinking men whose souls you have been endeavoring to save. Good day."

Too late Quentin perceived his error. Would she . . . could she? If the entire village were influenced against him he would have a damnable time trying to arrange an Easter celebration that would impress Thorpe with his mastery of the parish. But if he moved quickly perhaps he could recruit participants enough.

However he found that he had been too sanguine in this hope. Lily had not been far from wrong in suggesting that the Ladies' Society, the sexton, and several of the drinking men Quentin's money had attempted to reclaim would be the only people receptive to the idea of joining the church pageant. It seemed that the villagers had already heard about the new rector's denouncement of their usual Easter amusement, and most people did not approve.

"No sword dance?" A shake of the head and a tip of the hat was all Quentin could get from one village merchant, a man of influence and substance. "I and my father and grandfather before me have danced the swords at Easter, sir . . . I reckon this church affair won't be at all the same."

"Sorry, Father Vernon," said another Mickleford worthy, when Quentin tried to recruit him for his biblical scene, "I've already promised . . . er, I mean

63

I'm afraid I'll be too busy."

The answer was the same all over, and in the end it was Proper the sexton, two hard-drinking men, and two rather flinching and fluttery ladies from the church society who gathered round Quentin and Sir George in the rectory sitting room one morning for the first rehearsal of his Easter ceremonial.

"All right then," Quentin began with a disappointed sigh. "We shall have Miss Finch as Mary Magdalene . . ."

"Oh, my!" bleated the pale, thin spinster. The two village men exchanged sly winks, and George could be seen to hide a smile.

"Only to represent her at the opening of the tomb, you understand, Miss Finch," Quentin said with what he hoped was reassurance that Miss Finch's virtue was not in question.

"And Miss Hicks for Mary, mother of James . . ." He glanced over the Bible he held, open to the Easter story according to Luke. "We shall have to do without the other women. Now, let us see . . . hmm, two men in shining garments . . ." He glanced up dubiously at the dully clad, none too clean village men, Bert and Ned, who had finished the one glass of ale allotted to each of them and were now shifting uneasily on the rectory's fragile chairs.

"Aye, Mr. Vernon," muttered Bert. Ned nodded his agreement. "So long as we be given summat to say," he added. "The wife'll be right proud to see me give a speech in church yon Eastur."

"Of course, you have a fine speech—two lines," Quentin assured him, wondering if he and his pathetic band would end up the laughing stock of the village.

"Now for Peter . . . I suppose Tim can manage it . . . nothing to say, just act surprised when you view the empty sepulcher."

The sexton regarded him impassively, gulped and nodded.

By now Quentin could feel the perspiration beading on his forehead and an ache, as though a tight band were drawn around it, increasing its pressure. He would look a damned fool at Easter, he thought, and though it might not cost him the wager, Thorpe would dine out on the story of Lord Vyse's ridiculous Easter play for months afterwards. But there was no help for it.

"That's all then. Mr. Hollister here will copy out parts for each of you to study, and in a few days we'll meet in the church to practice them."

"But what about the apostles, and who will build the sepulcher?" Miss Hicks wanted to know.

"I'm afraid our little reenactment won't be quite that elaborate, my dear lady." Quentin put all the charm he could into his smile. He wanted cooperation, not questions, but he sensed that he would have to use a light rein on this team if he was not to lose them altogether. "This is, after all, a solemn occasion, and the important part of it is that Christ is risen, is it not?" He briefly assumed his stern rector face.

Thus subdued, his little band filed out, and George began to laugh heartily. "I'll vow the village will never have seen such a cow-handed production of an Easter play, but damme, you are thorough, my dear fellow. Thorpe himself, faced with a similar challenge, would have shied at it."

"Thorpe would never have been so easily gulled into accepting this ridiculous wager," Quentin muttered. If that sneering, arrogant peer had shown his face in Mickleford at that moment, he would have been in severe danger of having his cork drawn just for having the temerity to appear. Fortunately for him and for Quentin, Easter was still three weeks away.

Since the morning of her encounter with the rector, Lily had walked about in more of a daze than usual. But now her dreams of mysterious heroes had been replaced by the dilemma of a very real, but equally mysterious Mr. Vernon.

She had been at once amused and annoyed by his high-handed foolishness over the churchyard greenery. For a moment her attitude towards him had even softened, but as usual, his arrogance had carried away her impulse to like anything else about him but the way his hair waved back and the intense blue of his eyes. His hands on hers had, to her annoyance, made her horridly conscious of her vulnerability to masculine charms, a vulnerability which had rarely disturbed her before. Prior to meeting the maddeningly inconsistent Mr. Vernon, she had always been the one in control where flirtation and courtship were concerned. Suddenly to be overpowered by delicious and confusing feelings while in the presence of one she had every reason to distrust and dislike was a disturbing experience for her.

In any case, Lily was in no mood to be accosted by her Aunt Hyacinth the next day when, returning from a long, dreamy walk to view the tortuously slow return of spring to Mickleford, she entered Sterling Hall by way of the kitchens as was her habit. Aunt Hyacinth, though proud, was not too proud to make use of her knowledge

66

of her wayward niece's peculiar habits when she was determined to bend Lily to her will.

Now she appeared, slightly flushed and even a tiny bit disheveled, which forebode something very important indeed. "Here you are, my girl, skulking in the servants quarters again!" said the lady indignantly, taking her niece's arm in an uncomfortable grip before she could escape. "Come, upstairs with you to make yourself presentable. Mr. Smythe has called with dear Mr. Watson and is in the morning room."

Lily sighed, gently extracted her arm from her aunt's almost feral grip and rubbed it. "Not again!"

Aunt Hyacinth was bustling away, fully expecting to be followed. "No nonsense from you now, Lily. Your grandmama and I and your mama too have been entertaining him while he waited for you. Dear Watson is waiting to take Arabella for a drive — a concession I feel I can make now that they are properly betrothed, and this being the country . . ." She digressed, a rare smile of satisfaction crossing her taut face. It was brief, as her irritation with Lily soon returned.

"But Mr. Smythe declared he would wait for you, although we told him we had no idea when you would be home, as usual." Aunt Hyacinth pinched her mouth even tighter than usual and said, "I believe he is unwilling to take no for an answer this time, my dear."

Why her family, and her Aunt Hyacinth in particular, was so eager to marry her off was beyond Lily's comprehension, especially now that Arabella's betrothal was fixed. She had hoped that her cousin's impending marriage would remove pressure from her to accept one of the worthy but dull young men who had sued for her hand. But Aunt Hyacinth, who had always looked upon her niece's beauty as dangerous competition for her own fair offspring, was obviously taking no chances.

Dutifully, Lily followed her aunt upstairs, but protested, "Violet and Olive aren't married, so why must I be?"

"Hush, child! Was there ever anyone so ungrateful?" Aunt Hyacinth addressed an unseen sympathizer. "Violet and Olive are past the age where anyone expects them to make a match. Besides, all the single gentlemen here are far too young for them," she added practically. "Apart from my dear Arabella, you, Lily, are regarded as the beauty of the family, and it is only proper that you marry well if you can." The hem of her gown flounced over the landing and she swished away, no doubt to visit Arabella and hurry her along in her preparations for her drive with her betrothed.

Lily trudged up the last step, turned down the corridor, and headed toward her bedchamber. "One would think that the family fortunes depended upon my marriage," she grumbled. Of course she would not want to be a disappointment to her family, but she really could not see that it was incumbent upon her to marry someone just so her family would be happy. No, unless she could have her ideal, she would be quite content to enjoy dancing and flirting and all the little busy tasks of her life without calling herself someone's wife. Of course, in her heart she cherished a secret hope that one day *he* would arrive, the heroic figure who would overwhelm her with his passion and carry her off to some bright, fairy-tale future, but if she had said as much to her family, they would think she was mad.

She poured some water from her pitcher into the washbasin and briskly washed her hands and splashed her face, shivering at the chill. She put off her old gown, one of several that she wore to make her rounds in the village, and pulled on a long-sleeved round dress of grayish blue kerseymere, one of those she kept for entertaining morning callers. A quick glance in the mirror told her that her hair was in a disastrous state, so she spent an impatient extra minute pinning it back up and then dashed downstairs to the morning room, anxious to be rid of her unwanted suitor.

Mr. William Smythe, known since childhood to the Sterling family simply as Billy, had made it a regular practice for the past six months to offer for Lily's hand. On his first application, which, very properly, had been to the squire himself, Sir Richard had looked at him with pity, wished him good fortune, and given permission for his daughter to be addressed directly, knowing of course, that the girl would have none of it.

The ladies of the family, however, had not ceased to expect that in the end Mr. Smythe's persistence would win out. After all, he and Lily had been friends since childhood, always in and out of one another's houses, and were as equal as could be in status, Billy being the heir of an old county family of wealth and importance.

Brought up short before the sitting room door by the sound of gentle female voices, with her grandmother's more robust tones in counterpoint, and Billy's baritone underlying it all, Lily took a deep breath and wondered how long it would be before her mother, Aunt Poppy, and Grandmama would discover some excuse to leave her alone with Billy. Not that she was afraid—oh, no she had long since learned how to handle importunate suitors gracefully—but it was becoming increasingly painful to her to reject her old friend's offers, and she would just as soon not have to do it again.

Perhaps if she could prevent the others from leaving somehow . . . but she had not been in the room five minutes, blissfully greeted by Billy, given an admonishing look by Lady Flora, and a gently sad one from her mama, when all three ladies gradually faded away upon one excuse or another, and she found herself alone with Mr. Smythe.

Said gentleman, of some four and twenty summers, with curling brown hair, guileless brown eyes, and a slim but active-looking figure, turned to her with a smile upon the exit of Lady Flora, who had winked at him encouragingly.

"My, Lily, you do look pretty in that color," he ventured, when she had given him leave to seat himself next to her on the sofa.

He always began with a compliment. Lily wondered whether it were kinder to allow him to complete his entire speech or to cut him off before he could work himself into a frenzy of admiration. Before she could decide, he was continuing, "We missed seeing you at the assembly last month—I had hoped we could dance. I do love dancing with you, Lily. You are light as a fairy on my arm."

Lily had stayed away from that assembly because as much as she enjoyed dancing, she had been feeling particularly bored with the local swains and preferred to stay home and dream over a lurid romance, complaining of some vague indisposition so that her family would not suspect. She wondered if it would work at the next assembly?

But Billy was going on. "I suppose you know why I am here," he said with an air of diffidence which would have been engaging to a female of less lofty standards.

"Why, to call upon us, I supposed," said the heartless Lily. "I hope your mama is well?"

Billy looked resigned and replied in the affirmative, as he did to her subsequent inquiries about his horses, his hounds, and his father's farms. Finally even the patient Mr. Smythe could endure no more.

"Dash it all, Lily, can't you see that I won't give up— I'm here to ask you to marry me again." His cherubic features took on a mulish cast. "I shan't let you get away so easily this time." With that he actually took her in his arms.

Lily was a bit disconcerted, for except for a little girl and boy foolery in the way of childish hugs and kisses, since they had grown up Billy had not yet so lost control of himself as to actually touch her. For a moment she was still in his embrace, awaiting whatever feelings might arise from such a romantic situation. But she felt more discomfort and embarrassment than anything else, she decided, and was about to pull away when he suddenly kissed her.

It was a poorly aimed and not very skillful kiss, and Lily was more amused than outraged by his audacity, but she pulled away and stood up. Perhaps this would be a good excuse to rid herself of poor Billy's unwanted attentions once and for all. Then maybe he would find some sensible, worthy girl who would agree to be his wife. He would be a good match for someone, but not for Lily Sterling, whose head was in the clouds.

"I beg you will not subject me to a repetition of such behavior, Mr. Smythe," said Lily, drawing herself up very tall and affronted. "If you think that such a demonstration will have the effect of making me change my

71

mind about your offer, then you are sadly mistaken. I have said that I will not marry you, and nothing will make me change my mind."

Billy's red face and stammering apology were only what she expected, but the genuine regret in his eyes softened her heart. She took his hand and reverted to their usual informality. "Look, Billy, dear, if you thought about it at all you would realize that we should not suit. Why, we have known each other since we were babies and are practically like brother and sister. You know I am very fond of you—"

At last she could see dawn beginning to break. It was apparent that there was nothing more likely to discourage an ardent gentleman than to be told that the woman of his dreams was "very fond" of him.

"—But I simply do not feel for you what I would wish to feel for a husband. Also," she added, "in a very short while you would feel yourself to be under the cat's paw, for you know that I have bossed you and led you about our entire lives, and married or not, I doubt you would be able to change any of my distressing habits. Why, remember what a merry dance I led you when we were young—and all the dreadful fights we had."

Mr. Smythe, his fair skin returning to its natural shade, his tempestuous emotions now in check, sadly agreed that she was probably right. A smile even crept over his face at the memory of their childhood arguments. "You always did win, Lil," he admitted. "Perhaps us being married wouldn't make much difference."

"Of course not. We have known each other far too well and too long," Lily said briskly, pressing her advantage. "Husbands and wives should be more mysterious to one another."

Billy looked doubtful at that, but offered, "I suppose it might be hard for you to think of me as your husband when you remember having seen me with all my front teeth out, or having watched Nurse spank me for something I did when I was five."

"Exactly! And so you won't trouble me any more with this business, but will go and find yourself someone more suitable?" Lily demanded, seeing that she at last had him on the run. She laughed. "After all, an absurd pair we would make. Although Mr. and Mrs. Smythe sounds very well, there is something ridiculous about a husband and wife called Lily and Billy!"

The young man laughed despite the very real sadness in his eyes. "I suppose you are right again. Still . . . I couldn't help but think of you, Lil, for you must know, you're deucedly pretty!"

Strangely enough, Lily felt herself blushing over this. She had been told it often enough, and had evidence enough in the ways gentlemen reacted to her, but she never really *felt* it to be true. Now if Billy, who had known her when she was a skinny, freckled hoyden, thought her pretty, it must be so. As she parted from her old friend, she gave him an impulsive hug. Unfortunately, Aunt Poppy was just strolling by the very properly open door of the morning room and chanced to see this demonstration of affection.

"My dears! To think that today is the day. 'Faint heart never won fair lady', eh, Mr. Smythe? Oh, I must go and find your Grandmama, Lily. She will be overjoyed!"

Lily and her erstwhile suitor immediately sought to disabuse her of the faulty notion which she had taken into her head, but did not succeed before most of the family who were at leisure had been drawn by Aunt

Poppy's cries of joy into the vicinity of the morning room.

There ensued a scene the likes of which Lily hoped never to have to repeat in her life. Grandmama scolded, Aunt Hyacinth seethed, and Mama said "oh, dear" in various accents of distress, but the Sterlings were at last made to understand that there had been no betrothal made that day between Mr. Smythe and Lily, and that, on the contrary, the interview had at last put an end to the young man's pretensions to her hand. By the time Billy was allowed to depart, Lily was amused to see that he was more relieved at being permitted to escape the general lamentation than disappointed at the ultimate failure of his suit.

But for Lily there was no such relief. The family pounced upon her all during dinner.

"Ungrateful girl! To have turned down *two* such unexceptionable suitors! Thank goodness my Arabella had more sense," said Aunt Hyacinth.

"My dear Lily, are you quite sure? Such a fine young man, although a trifle thin . . . I shall make up a batch of my special biscuits to send him," said Aunt Poppy.

"Mark my words, young lady, you'll regret turning down a fine youngster like Smythe," warned Lady Flora. "Good breeding, good bloodlines, that one has. You won't find better in the county."

"So you've sent him to the rightabout at last, eh, my dear?" said Sir Richard, more jovially than Lily had expected. "Ah, well, I supposed that one day we'd see the last of him. Surprised he held out this long. Didn't think he was much of a stayer."

"Lily, my thoughtless niece," Uncle John scolded gently, "Smythe is just the sort of boy I would have liked

74

to welcome into the family. Plump in the pocket, generous to a fault, and so bad at cards — why, I won ten bob from him just last week. A pity you've turned him down."

Lady Sterling contented herself with, "Oh, dear, I only hope you have not hurt the poor young man's feelings. I should have liked the match, but perhaps one day you will meet the man who can make you happy."

And that made Lily feel worst of all, for she was beginning to have the distinct feeling that that day would never come.

The rector and Mr. Hollister dined again at Sterling hall that Sunday, and though the family had not yet forgiven Lily her final dismissal of Mr. Smythe, to Lily's relief not a word about it was mentioned during the noisy discussion that passed for table conversation in that household. Lily supposed she owed this to the presence of guests.

She was gratified, moreover, to see that when a dish of pease porridge she had specially ordered was placed before Mr. Vernon by a manservant in her confidence, the rector nearly choked on the mouthful of roast beef he was enjoying. So much for his Lenten fast! When he was recovered from his fit and Lady Sterling had wondered aloud about the surprising appearance of that poor dish upon her table, the rector looked squarely at Lily, who smiled innocently as she expressed a hope that his choking would not spoil his enjoyment of the next two courses.

Aside from this interlude, during the meal Mr. Vernon made the ladies variously bored, surprised, or pleased by holding forth upon a number of topics suitable for a Sunday, elaborating, albeit with a strangely conscious look, on that morning's sermon which had touched on the sins of gluttony and pride. He earned a guilty glance from his curate, who was allowing Aunt Poppy to stuff him with food, and a distinct look of derision from Lily, who thought she had never met a prouder man than the insufferable Mr. Vernon. If only she didn't have to wait till Easter to have her little victory over him, she thought.

Her own plans for the Easter pageant were coming along nicely. She had begun gathering the materials for her grandmother's special Easter egg dyes—logwood chips for purple, gorse blossom for yellow and anemones, or pasque flower, for green. The sword men were already practicing, the children were keyed up, and the villagers in general were especially looking forward to Easter this year, for most of them had conceived no great liking for the new rector who had sought to spoil their fun.

But Easter was weeks away, and the spring warmth that was steadily but slowly growing in the air, the emergence of the early flowers, tender buds, and wisps of greenery, and the agitation she always felt in Mr. Vernon's presence made Lily feel as if she wanted to jump out of her chair.

Mr. Vernon seemed, strangely, to be a major cause of her restlessness lately. So far, though she had continued her visits to the rectory, she had not been able to catch him out in any impropriety, even drinking. Mrs. Philpott, delicately questioned, had reported no more evening bacchanals or empty bottles in the morning, no more late breakfast banquets. Everything in the rectory appeared to be scrupulously normal.

Fortunately for Lily's impatience, she soon received

the opportunity she had been waiting for to discomfit the rector. When the gentlemen rejoined the ladies after dinner, Lady Flora, who had kept Lily next to her to sort some of her silks, took them out of her hands, gave her a pat, and said, "There, girl, I have told the rector you would show him the garden. This is the first fine day we have had. Run along, now." The words were casual but her tone brooked no argument.

Lily looked up and saw the rector standing over her, offering his arm, his features stern, as usual. It always annoyed her that this did nothing to conceal their charm. What on earth could Grandmama have in mind? Silently she acquiesced, putting her hand on Mr. Vernon's arm, surprised at the muscular firmness she felt underneath the smooth cloth, and took him downstairs and to the rear door of the hall which led to the garden.

The looks of curiosity on the faces of Arabella and Olive had told her nothing, but the sly satisfaction on Aunt Hyacinth's face, the determination on Lady Flora's, and the hopefulness of Aunt Poppy's pale blue eyes hinted at a plot.

Just as they approached the door, enlightenment came in the form of Lady Sterling herself, who had been summoned downstairs by some small domestic crisis, and was on her way back to the drawing room.

"Lily, dear," she said, "I hope you will listen very carefully to what Mr. Vernon is going to say. You know that Papa and I do not wish to force you into anything distasteful, but your grandmama feels that you have not thought this through properly. It is not only Billy, you know, but the other young men you have snubbed." She patted her daughter's head and smiled sweetly at the rector before drifting back upstairs.

Torn between annoyance and amusement at her mother's obvious relief at leaving the duty of the forthcoming lecture to someone else, Lily saw at last the opening she had awaited. She certainly would not accept the rector's interference in this private matter, be it Grandmama's idea or not. But this might be a good opportunity to bedevil Mr. Vernon.

The rector had listened with apparent dismay to Lady Sterling's speech, having obviously hoped for the advantage of surprise. Lily supposed that he had advised her grandmama not to let anyone trouble her about her refusal of Billy, so that his lecture should have an impact all the stronger.

Behaving as though she had not understood a word of her mother's speech, Lily merely smiled at her companion as they emerged into the weak March sun. "Shall we go down this path to the fountain?"

Mr. Vernon gave a nod. "As you wish." Some of his habitual assurance seemed to have left him.

"We must walk back along the shrubbery—I thought I saw some of those dead twigs beginning to bud," she added slyly, glancing sidewise at him.

She had hoped to annoy him, but instead his mouth turned up just a bit at the corners and a small sound escaped him. However, he quickly brought himself under control.

For a few moments they walked in total silence, anticipatory on Lily's part, seemingly thoughtful on Mr. Vernon's. Finally Lily could wait no longer.

"I hope you know, Mr. Vernon, that whatever lecture you are preparing is completely unnecessary," she said as she continued to stroll along beside him.

Instantly he assumed a patronizing air. "On the contrary, my dear young lady, it was, as your mama said, considered very necessary by your grandmother. She felt that as a clergyman I was the proper person to speak to you on the subject of your recent behavior. Now, while I am not well acquainted with the gentleman in question, I am sure that he was painfully surprised at you disregarding his offer in such a decided, and I hear, unflattering fashion. I hear that Mr. Smythe would have been an unexceptionable match for you. A well thought of, amiable young man . . ."

Pooh, what did he know of it? This Johnny-come-lately must be put in his place. "Fiddle," she said calmly. "He's a dull farmer's son with nothing but straw between his ears."

For a moment Lily thought she had succeeded in angering the rector, as his shoulders seemed to shake, but in a moment he replied in a voice only a little choked, "Regardless of your opinion of Mr. Smythe's mental assets, he is considered by your family to be a desirable match. It was thought that there was some understanding between you."

"For you information, Mr. Vernon, Billy Smythe has been offering me for the last six months, and I have been refusing his offer for as long. He knows that I haven't the slightest interest in becoming his wife. Although he isn't, like most of the young men in this neighborhood, merely ambitious to marry one of the squire's daughters, he simply fixed on me, who he has known all his life, rather than exert himself to find some other, more suitable lady. He is certainly not in love with me."

Lily stared defiantly back at the rector, whose disapproving expression began to change. She thought she caught a flash of surprise, and the impression was confirmed when he said, "I cannot imagine that the silly young—I mean, Mr. Smythe would be so persistent if you had not somehow engaged his affections."

"Affection, yes. We have known one another forever. But do not fear that I have broken his heart, Mr. Vernon." She smiled archly at him. "I wonder at a serious clergyman like yourself even thinking in those terms. I had supposed you would merely counsel me to obey my family's wishes."

The rector drew his features into an expression of patriarchal concern. "If at times it seems, Miss Lily, that I am oversevere with you, it is because I know only too well, from personal experience, the dangers of heedless behavior," he said in his most solemn tone.

Impossible for such a stuffy fellow to have had any such experience, was Lily's first reaction. Yet she remembered their first meeting and his undeniable flirtation. Now his insufferable smugness was nearly driving her mad, but Lily restrained herself by stopping to remove a non-existent stone from her shoe.

"Indeed?" she managed to say. Had any of her family heard the note in her voice they would have been forewarned.

Mr. Vernon, however, merely paused while she completed the imaginary operation, then took her arm and placed it upon his once more. Lily thought she would draw it away, but the contact offered her some warmth, for the capricious spring sun had drawn in and a stiff March breeze had blown up. Besides, if she could induce him to return to his previous unclergymanlike behavior with her, she would have the advantage over him. Just what she would do with the advantage she would have been hard put to say. Perhaps complain of him to his wealthy patron, Lord Vyse, when he arrived? She mused on it but was interrupted by the rector's continuing his tale.

He seemed not at all put out by her apparent lack of interest, nor disconcerted by the way she strengthened her hold on his arm. "It is a sad, and oft-told tale, I suppose, that of a young man gone wrong. You see I was much indulged as a youth, and though not yet thoroughly sunk in dissipation, I became rather notorious for my scrapes — primarily unkind dealings with the fair sex."

Lily's mouth had fallen open in sheer amazement, and for a moment she thought he was going to laugh at her extreme reaction, but he merely cleared his throat and continued even more pompously, "It was three years ago when I broke the heart of an innocent young lady who, when she saw that my intentions were not serious, went into a decline and subsequently married unwisely indeed. To my shame, I realized I was trembling on the verge of becoming a hardened rake."

Lily finally allowed herself to speak. "*You*, sir?" But indeed, why was she so surprised? More and more, she reflected, the rector's stern behavior seemed like make-believe. Although he seemed entirely respectable, even dull at times, there was a hint of devilment in those speaking eyes and that sinewy body. But would a man of spirit become a pompous prig merely because of a brush with impending rakehood? Perhaps he was not really the strict upholder of virtue that he liked to seem.

He stopped and turned towards her, but kept his fine blue eyes cast up to heaven, sighing, "To my great sorrow, Miss Lily, it is true. Luckily, I had a rather easy escape from that sort of life. My family had already destined me for the church, and so I studied to take my place as minister to this flock."

Lily was conscious of at the same time a heavy disappointment that she had missed by a matter of a paltry three years the chance to know a real rake, and a resurgence of interest in the rector. With memories of such deeds, he surely could not be as dull as he was trying to be. Hadn't she once or twice seen a sparkle of fun in his eye? Wasn't he just now looking at her as if she were something good to eat, and supposing that because she had lowered her lashes she couldn't detect it?

Perhaps she could seduce him from the path of righteousness just a bit. It would be wicked, but Lily was tired of always being good. Cautiously she drew closer until their sides were pressed together, entwining her arm more firmly about his. She smiled up at him, and felt the muscles under his sleeve tense, his breathing quicken. This was beginning to be interesting.

"How very fortunate for us, then, Mr. Vernon. It has long been my opinion that clergymen who are too good themselves and unacquainted with temptation are unsuited to deal with the common run of humanity. But you, my dear Mr. Vernon," she squeezed his arm, "you with your tumultuous personal history can surely understand the failings of the ordinary man . . . and woman."

"I—" The rector now seemed totally nonplussed. Finally he cleared his throat and replied, "I am gratified by your appreciation of the matter, Miss Lily, and I hope that you will allow yourself to sometimes be guided by me, and not to let your impulses rule you so thoroughly as they seem to. You have once or twice spoken to me quite rudely, you know, and as the local representative of the church . . ." but his voice was becoming a little labored. He was trying for pomposity but was not quite succeeding.

Lily made one last effort. Sighing, she lightly leaned her head against his shoulder for the tiniest moment. "I am so sorry. I shall try to remember my manners. It is so irritating to be lectured — but so delightful to be understood," she said vaguely. This time she definitely heard him gasp. As they were approaching the house again, she disengaged herself quickly and moved on alone.

As she was about to enter the house she looked back, and was completely gratified by the expression on Mr. Vernon's face. He was flushed, his eyes glittered, and he swallowed several times. At last she had discovered how to bring back what she was sure was the *real* Mr. Vernon. But to her dismay, in the process of teasing him, she had discovered that such a flirtation was too dangerously exciting. She doubted she would attempt it again.

Chapter Five

Damn the little vixen, thought Quentin. The fragrance of her lingered, and when he touched the shoulder of his coat, he found it still warm from the brief pressure of her head. It seemed he could do no right. Pretending to be a stern moralist only made her behave like a minx, tantalizing him all the more. His imaginative tale of a misspent youth, instead of adding credence to his identity as the rector, had only piqued her into teasing him. With difficulty he composed himself to face the Sterling family once more, and reported to the eager Lady Flora on his attempt to bring young Lily to see her error in refusing Billy Smythe's offer.

"I am afraid, ma' am, I was not quite persuasive enough. Miss Lily, it seems, is inclined to be a trifle . . ." He thought of how many ways he could end this sentence and wondered which would be most diplomatic, but Lady Flora, throwing down her embroidery, finished it for him.

"Stubborn. The gel is stubborn, and a foolish dreamer to boot. I don't know what will become of her." The old lady sighed and gave him her hand. "Ah, well, I am sure you did your best."

It had been impossible to refuse the matriarch's request that he speak to her willful granddaughter, and Quentin hoped that he would not again be put in such a position. Being alone with Lily and having to pretend disapproval when all he wanted to do was kiss her tempting lips had almost proved his undoing. He did not know if his disguise could survive another such ordeal.

Besides, Easter was coming and there was more playacting ahead for him as rector. He could not endanger his masquerade by giving in to his impulses where Lily was concerned. He would lose whatever ground he had gained, and when Thorpe arrived his careful deception would be in a shambles if he did not take care.

Although Quentin was ready to send Thorpe and the stupid wager to the devil, he felt it had become a personal test of his self-control, one that he must not fail. His modest success in Mickleford encouraged him to believe that if he would but make the effort, he could stay out of trouble where beautiful women were concerned.

Of late Quentin had found irate husbands, tearful mistresses, and demanding high-flyers increasingly tiresome. His newfound freedom from London intrigues and entanglements was refreshing, and he had even begun to wonder if his life would not be more comfortable if he gave up his footloose existence and married. Dozens of eligible girls had been all but thrown at his head ever since he had come on the town, but he had been too busy tasting the less respectable joys that had so easily come his way to bother with finding a wife.

Popular though he still was, Quentin knew he must take care that his adventures did not harm his reputation. After all, despite his title, he was not as great a catch as some others, his enemy Thorpe included. His properties were small, his income fluctuating in these difficult times. He knew he could not rely on a handsome face and engaging manner forever. And the tale of this wager, he now realized, although it might amuse his friends, would shock many upright members of the ton, whether he or Thorpe emerged the winner.

Quentin gave voice to some of these thoughts over a late luncheon with his "curate."

"When all this is over, I believe I shall stay away from town for a while, perhaps even retire to the country. This foolish wager has taught me a lesson — I'm safer away from society and all its temptations for now."

George stopped chewing and stared at him in dismay. "What the devil has gotten into you, Quentin? Keep away from society, indeed! It's being isolated in the country that has made you so liverish." He began to munch again, mulling over his friend's strange mood. Then he brightened. "I know! Why don't we run off to Town for a few days, say we've church business, must be off to see the bishop or some such thing? A few nights of gaming, good wine, and a flirtation or two will set you right up," he said eagerly.

Quentin actually thought about it for a moment,

daring to hope that escape from his self-imposed task would be so easy. Finally, with regret, he shook his head. "I cannot. For one thing, Thorpe is likely to be still in Town and I don't care to let him know that I've taken on more than I bargained for. For another, all our acquaintance knows of this wager by now, and I'm in no mood to hear myself gossiped about." He picked at his food, and finally set down his fork. "And it isn't only our friends in London that worry me. I hate to think of the reaction of Mickleford when it finds it has been hoaxed!"

George shrugged and took another slice of ham. "It would be a three day's wonder and then the village would go back about its business." He grinned. "But I do pity the poor fellow on whom you eventually bestow this living. How could he compete with the memory of the amazing Mr. Vernon, aristocrat and man of fashion disguised as clergyman?"

Quentin groaned. However was he going to explain this nonsense to a *real* clergyman, and expect him to take the reins after the fun was over? "I wouldn't be surprised if the villagers become angry when they discover that a gross deception has been practiced upon them. And by a man who, as a local landowner, should have their welfare, and not his own amusement, at heart."

George brooded over a slice of pickle. "I can see your point. Shouldn't like to be there when, for instance, the ladies up at the Hall come to hear of it, should we? I mean, Lady Flora, and Miss Sterling . . ."

For a second Quentin thought that he observed a

hint of self-consciousness in his companion's broad, bluff face. A most unusual phenomenon, he mused.

"Indeed, each is a formidable lady in her own way. And yes, I shouldn't like to be there when they find out about my little sporting deception. I hope to be long gone by then." But it seemed a cowardly thing to do. Upon accepting the wager Quentin had not considered its effect on other people. Now that he knew the village, he began to feel remorse, and not only for hoaxing the villagers. Just as George did not relish the thought of Violet Sterling knowing of his deception, he himself would not wish to appear, even in absentia, such a shallow fool in Lily Sterling's eyes.

George, meanwhile, appeared to have recovered from his brief qualms. "Have some more of this pie," he advised. "Quite excellent."

Quentin did not hear him, imagining instead what that sensitive and insightful young lady would have to say about him when she found out that "Mr. Vernon" was really Lord Vyse. He closed his eyes and shuddered.

"No, really," urged his friend. "Beef and kidney, none of this wretched Lenten fare. Just the thing to put some heart into you."

"No pie," Quentin said with determination, and pushing away his practically untouched luncheon, rang for Mrs. Philpott to clear away the remains. "Have you copied out the parts, such as they are, for our Easter revels?"

George stuffed a last bite in his mouth, nodding.

"I've told our cast of players to be ready to rehearse this afternoon in the church."

Quentin stared gloomily into his wineglass. "Do you think we've any chance of making something presentable out of them, something that won't make Thorpe burst the seams of his coat with laughing?"

"Oh, I suppose after fifty or so repetitions they should have it down well enough," said George without much hope.

Mrs. Philpott's entrance put an end to this discouraging conversation, and the two gentlemen retired to the church to meet with their players.

Lily was on her way to the rectory kitchen to see how Mrs. Philpott was getting on, when she decided she had better check on the condition of the churchyard, lest the overeager rector had continued his depredations upon the foliage there. Everything seemed well, and by some miracle even the poor torn-out lilac was beginning to come back to life again. There were primroses and violets coming out in odd corners, as they were all over Mickleford, and everything looked most promising for a blossom-filled spring. She was about to proceed on her errand when she heard the noise of footsteps and voices inside the church. Curious, Lily walked around to the side entrance and peered in. What she saw inside made her pause.

Before the altar, two village men who were more likely to be found in the tavern than the church stood shifting uneasily, while her aunts' friends Miss Finch and Miss Hicks seemed fairly twittering with excitement. Tim Proper was merely passive, a simple smile on his face.

She was about to go in to ask what they were about there, when Mr. Hollister and the rector himself came into view. Mr. Vernon looked unusually harried, his thick fair hair standing on end as if he had been running nervous fingers through it. The curate was cheerfully passing out pieces of paper to the rector and the ladies, the only ones able to read, and verbally instructing the others. "Now, for a start, Tim, stand here, and look surprised when I give the sign. Then Ned and Bert will say their lines," he told the sexton.

The rector was going over parts with the others, repeating the simple lines to Ned and Bert, and having them say them over and over. Lily fairly giggled as she heard the two fellows mumbling in a monotone, "Why seek yer the livin' amoun' the dead?" and "E's not ere, but is rizzen," as if they were incantations.

The rector gave them a strained smile. "Er, very good. As you see, it is a fairly simple reenactment of a brief scene from Scripture, and we should be able to do it very easily."

Lily smothered another giggle. Obviously she had interrupted a rehearsal of the rector's church pageant. She settled herself in the shadowy doorway, secure in the knowledge that the others could not see her, and prepared to be entertained.

She was not to be disappointed. The spinsters bleated their lines with alternating pride and nervousness, the men shuffled and mumbled, and poor Tim could not even manage to look surprised when so instructed, but only grinned foolishly. After a very few minutes Lily's chest ached with suppressed laughter, and when a gasp finally escaped her she stood up and began to back out of the doorway. But the rector was too quick for her.

"Miss Lily Sterling, please do come in. Your advice would be invaluable." There was no resisting that firm voice or indeed the firm hand that had hold of her arm, drawing her inside the church. Lily sobered at once, especially when she saw the anxious, anticipatory expressions of the Misses Finch and Hicks, and Tim's shy grin. Amusing as it was, and triumphant as she felt over what was sure to be the rector's downfall, she could not be unkind to them.

"Indeed, sir, I am not qualified to give an opinion, but I am sure that it will be a most inspiring Easter play," she said hastily, and began to leave.

But the rector's stern eye was upon her. "I am happy to hear you say so, Miss Lily. It is important that someone in the parish remembers what is due to the solemnity of the occasion, and not fill the day with pagan foolery, like sword dances, mumming, and colored eggs."

Lily stiffened. Of course, she had been wrong to spy upon him, but she was not to be upbraided in such a fashion by this upstart. "The 'foolery' you refer to, sir, is a hallowed tradition of this and many other villages, and is no more pagan than—than I am!"

The rector gave her a curious look, as though he doubted that she was not somewhere deep down, a primitive creature in flimsy drapery, worshiping nature. A brief light in his blue eyes seemed to indicate that he found the idea entrancing.

At this Lily faltered and looked away from his disturbing gaze. "And I do not . . . that is, the villagers deserve a bit of amusement on a holiday, and as long as you see them in church for services, they need no permission from you to spend the day as they like!"

She flounced out, her heart beating very quickly, ashamed at having lost her composure before the shocked little audience. She heard footsteps behind her and in the churchyard the rector caught up with her. His voice was amused, which infuriated her the more.

"So you have been caught spying, my dear. You ought to own up to it more gracefully."

Lily shrugged off his hand from her shoulder. "I was not spying. I heard voices in the church and went to see who was there."

"And stayed to watch our rehearsal, well rewarded for your curiosity," he persisted.

Lily looked up at him, and disarmed by his warm smile, her anger melted. Thinking of the ludicrous performance she had witnessed; she smiled too. "Well, you must admit it *was* just too funny."

"Oh? And I suppose that your little band of revelers presents a show of professional quality?"

Piqued, Lily said, "Why don't you come and watch us tomorrow, Mr. Vernon? We practice at ten on the green, if it is fine. Then you will see for yourself some of the traditions of Mickleford which you are so anxious to eradicate."

Without hesitation, to Lily's surprise, he said, "Very well. I will." Mr. Vernon released her arm, bowed slightly, and went back into the church. Lily stood there a moment, her face very warm, her heartbeat still agitated. What was there about this peculiarly unclerical cleric that disturbed her so? She regretted now having invited him to watch the rehearsal, but there was no help for it. Perhaps it would rain and be called off, she thought hopefully.

But perversely the next day was as fine a March day as there had ever been in the history of the village. The sun shone, the grass on the green looked as though it were coming to life, buds swelled, and violets scented the almost-warm air.

Around the green the village itself, small black and white timbered houses, the church and rectory, a few shops and taverns, huddled. A road ran past the church and led away to the little hedged fields, out past the meadows, skirted the wood and the mere where small boys liked to bathe in summer, and where even now Lily knew her favorite ducks were returning, up into the gray hills, where she loved to walk, looking back on the view of the little village snugly ensconced amidst its fertile fields.

But with the arrival of the Easter pageant players, Lily's attention was diverted from the fineness of the day to the business at hand, and for a few minutes she even managed to forget that she was expecting a visit from the rector.

The sword men lined up and showed Lily the results of their practice — although it was hardly needed, since most of the men had been playing their parts in this ancient dance for a good many years, taking over from their fathers before them.

The men, not yet in their curious costumes of King, fool, and besom betty, the man-woman, but still impressive in their handling of the swords, wove about

forming intricate patterns with the swords, clashing
and thrusting, forming a chain and a lock, which they
danced about. The fool knelt while the others rested
the locked swords on his shoulders, and at a shouted
command each man withdrew his sword. The
fool fell, and they shouted for the "doctor" who came
in and restored the life of the supposedly decapitated
fool. The sword dancers went through it without a
single stake, obviously more than ready for the pageant.

"Most impressive. Quite pagan, but most impressive indeed, my dear Miss Lily," came a voice, together with the sound of a single pair of hands
clapping.

Lily, still rapt in the performance, started and
stared as Mr. Vernon emerged from behind the Jack
o'Lent — a tattered straw figure, meant to represent
Judas, who was put up on the green for the amusement of the children and others who enjoyed throwing
sticks and stones at him and burning him once Easter
had come.

The Jack was one of the village traditions Mr.
Vernon had tried to eradicate, but his suggestion that
it be taken down had been so stonily ignored that he
had desisted. Now, it seemed the figure had provided
a convenient place behind which the rector could observe the pageant without being noticed.

The sword dancers, taking no offense at their art
being termed pagan, smiled and bowed, thanking the
rector. Lily stood unsmiling, her arms folded across
her chest. "I see nothing wrong with it, nevertheless,
sir. And with its very obvious theme of resurrection

after death, even you should concede that it is a very appropriate dance for Easter."

To her surprise, the rector dropped his haughty demeanor and smiled. "Why, so it is, I suppose. In any case. Please do not let me interfere with your practice. Do go on."

Somewhat anxiously, Lily organized the next group of players and heard them run through their play. St. George entered with his sword, announced that he had slain the dragon and asked for a challenger. Bold Slasher, the Turkish knight, entered, fought, and fell defeated. Again the doctor was called for and cured the wounded man. Then Devil Doubt with his broom entered and threatened to sweep out the spectators.

With a few stops for clarification and repetition, it went very well, and once more Lily forgot the rector's presence. "And then Devil will collect money from the audience, to be donated to the workhouse," she directed. "And the landlord of the Hare and Hound will give cider and ale along with the cakes we will be sending down from the Hall."

There was a respectful murmur of thanks at this announcement, and nods at the landlord, who was one of the swords. He received this tribute proudly, with thumbs tucked in pockets, beaming.

This warm moment was broken by a traveling peddler, one of several people who had gathered along with the rector to watch the rehearsal, suggesting that two of the characters in the play be replaced by Napoleon and Lord Nelson. "Being as that's how it's done lately, in other places."

However no one was much impressed with the

peddler's news from afar. "No," they all said, "we don't hold with such modern folderols. St. George and Bold Slasher stay."

Lily instinctively glanced over at the rector, and found to her surprise that he was as amused as she was at the little exchange. What the outside world did, the villagers had made plain, meant nothing to Mickleford, which would stick to its own ways. If only he would not just laugh, but learn a lesson from it, she thought.

"Now," Lily continued, "I've asked everyone to send their eggs to the hall on Saturday. Lady Flora has made batches of her special dye."

"An don't her la'ship make the prettiest dyes in the county!" noted one village worthy, the others agreeing.

Lily stopped and smiled, for her grandmother's dye recipes were a secret long coveted by certain village housewives, which not even Mrs. Philpott, who traded recipes for a good many concoctions with her ladyship, had ever been permitted to know.

For the first time Lily began to feel excited at the holiday preparations. Dying the eggs so that the villagers could bear them in baskets to be blessed at church was an annual event that all the Sterling women enjoyed. Abruptly her spirits plummeted, and she looked over at the watching rector with a frown. No doubt that part of the proceedings would have to be done without. But they would have their egg rolling, rector or no rector.

Lily then gathered her participants together and discussed the procession, which usually had begun at church and circled the green, returning to the church, before which the plays were performed. But this year, she told them, unable to resist a sidelong glance at the rector, it was being done differently. They would not have an egg blessing nor would they proceed from the church.

"But why?" interrupted Mr. Vernon, abandoning his station behind the Jack and planting himself in the midst of the players. "I have no objection to your conducting a seemly procession after services."

Lily did not know whether she wanted to thank him or box his ears. The others looked at her uncertainly, and finally she turned to the rector and said, "If you feel it will not interfere with your church pageant, Mr. Vernon, it would be most convenient."

"Besides," said the local shopkeeper, "that's the way we always done it. Stands to reason . . ." The others began to murmur, some asserting that that was indeed the way it was done, and others muttering that if their pageant weren't good enough for the church, then they didn't have to go near the church at all.

To Lily's gratification, the rector began to look perturbed at this mutinous outburst, but to forestall a riot, she quelled it with a few words. "I think it is a fine offer and we ought to accept it. After all, everyone in the village and in from the farms will be expecting to see the procession from church as usual, and there really is no more suitable place to begin."

One wag suggested beginning at the Hare and Hound, but was quickly shushed by his companions. Even so Lily detected an incipient grin on the rector's face, quickly stifled. He turned towards her and bowed. "I only ask that the actual site of your performance be well across the green from the rectory. I am expecting very important visitors from London on Easter, to, er, . . . observe our service and to dine later, and would not wish them to be disturbed by the noise."

Lily had to bite back the words, "You mean you don't want them comparing my pageant with yours," but managed to assure him that they would perform well out of hearing of the rectory. She could not resist adding, however, "Will your visitor be the generous patron I have heard about, the one who is to present St. Peter's with a silver baptismal font? I assure you, Lady Flora thinks it a very popish idea, but the parish will be grateful."

To her surprise he looked like a startled hare at the mention of his patron, and again she was amazed that a man like Mr. Vernon could find himself beholden to some wealthy sponsor. But she supposed that was how most clergymen must obtain preferment, no matter how proud they were.

He bowed again. "Indeed. It is little enough to do for the parish," he said inscrutably, and went away.

"Oh, do call the rector back!" Olive Sterling, puffing from running the last few yards across the green, reached her sister's side, her round face sagging in disappointment. "I wanted to remind him about the willow gathering."

Lily, having almost forgotten herself that the Saturday before Palm Sunday was fast approaching, now was relieved that no one had mentioned it. "I wish you will not say anything to the rector, Olive," she said. "I don't think he would approve at all, and would only spoil our fun."

"But miss," said the landlord of the Hare and Hound, "Mr. Vernon behaved like a proper gentlemen about our mumming. Maybe he wouldn't mind going along to bring in the willow."

"But Mr. Barton never did so," Lily told him. "And why should we give Mr. Vernon the opportunity to disapprove? It's best left as it is."

The innkeeper thought a moment, then sighed and touched his hat. "I suppose you're right, Miss Lily."

"But Lily," Olive protested after the crowd had begun to disperse, "Mr. Barton was an old man, and its only the young people who go out to the wood to bring in the willow for Palm Sunday. Mr. Vernon might—"

"Oh, please do not go on about Mr. Vernon, Olive," Lily snapped in spite of herself. "He has made it quite plain that he cares nothing for our customs, and that he takes great joy in interfering with them. We shall *not* invite him to go to the wood with us on Saturday. Besides, he stays abed so late that we shall be back before he is awake, and when we carry the willow in to church on Sunday, he will have no recourse but to accept it."

Olive giggled at this. "Oh, to think of the look on his face! Lily, I believe you are a very wicked girl," she said in a perfect imitation of Aunt Hyacinth that set them both laughing.

On the way home, Lily thought of yet another bedevilment for the rector. "I'd almost forgotten about Maundy Thursday," she said.

"Why, that is nothing but alms-giving," said Olive.

"It is now, but it wasn't always so. I believe I will talk to the warden of the workhouse about reviving an ancient custom," said Lily with a wicked grin.

"Oh my!" cried Olive, looking at her anxiously. "You wouldn't dare—"

"Oh, would I not?" Lily grinned, thinking of the look on haughty Mr. Vernon's face when confronted with the poorest of the parish's poor, appearing at church for the ritual foot-washing and distribution of the Maundy purses.

Lily continued with satisfaction, "I heard someone ask him about the time of morning service on Maundy Thursday and he looked surprised, as if he had never heard of it. I daresay the fashionable people he has lived among never trouble themselves with the poor."

"Why, how do you know he has lived among fashionable people?" Olive asked. "We only suppose that Lord Vyse is his patron, but not that Mr. Vernon is anyone of importance outside the parish."

Lily was not quite sure why she felt this way, but there was certainly something very different about Mr. Vernon. "Perhaps it is his clothes—you know his coats simply cry out London tailoring—like the gentlemen we saw last year at Harrogate," she reminded her sister.

"That's true." Olive nodded. "He does dress better than any of the other gentlemen of the neighborhood, and so, strangely enough, does Mr. Hollister. Our last curate was almost ragged by comparison."

"And is there not," Lily asked, "something in the way he speaks, and in his manner, that proclaim him

100

someone accustomed to ordering his life very much as he pleases?"

"Why yes, but most men, you know," said Olive, "are quite accustomed to having things their own way. Anyway, it seems absurd. If he were someone of consequence, he would hardly be here in Mickleford, would he?"

Lily thought much about this in the next few days, and even the increasingly exciting preparations for the holiday, which was now only a fortnight away, did not distract her from the mystery of Mr. Vernon. She was determined, at Easter, to see this wealthy patron for herself and judge the rector's behavior in his presence. That it was the mysterious Lord Vyse who was Mr. Vernon's benefactor she had little doubt. She even felt a bit of excitement at the thought of meeting this important personage.

A solid two days of rain and one of weak sun and mud sufficed to make tempers rather short at the Hall, and Lily was glad when the next day proved fine and dry once more. Although she had finished gathering for the egg dyes, she felt the need to take one of her rambling walks. When she had managed to finish all her household chores, seen that the children were safe in the care of their nursemaid, and that her mother, whose confinement was drawing near, was resting, she put on her comfortable old dress and boots and started out eagerly.

Once past the walls of their own park, she trudged along a lane that petered out into the merest track, leading up and away from the village. Her spirits rose the farther she went, and she looked about her with

101

interest at the ever-changing country scene. The spring corn—the "Lenten corn"—had been sown, the daffodils were shooting up their green leaves and would soon be nodding yellow heads over the countryside.

In a small wood she paused, listening to the bustle of birds nesting and sniffing the fresh green fragrance of returning life. It was so quiet, aside from the birds, that she imagined could hear her own heartbeat. She walked on but as she was emerging from beneath the trees and preparing to climb as the track sloped up toward the hills, there also came a distant rustling which sounded like clumsy footsteps, or hands pushing branches aside. She had rarely met anyone on her walks, and she turned curiously to see who was also out enjoying the day, but the sound stopped and she could see no one.

Lily walked on, climbing till she was tired and then she sat, bundling her skirts beneath her, on a chilly but convenient outcropping of reddish sandstone. The steps she had heard behind her had never returned, and now she faced out over the countryside, squinting into the distance, trying to see the steeple of the church of the next village, just making out white blobs that were grazing sheep.

Could the sound have been just the noise of some animal, or a bird scratching in the dirt behind her? She told herself it was not important and closed her eyes, rejoicing in the peace. This was her favorite daydreaming time, free from village and family duties, free from being nagged about her unseemly behavior or her duty to marry.

But the usual pleasurable dream of the handsome, mysterious stranger who was to arrive and bear her off to some unspecified bliss did not come today, no matter how hard she tried to conjure it up. Instead she saw the stern face of Quentin Vernon, breaking into a smile that melted her heart. Angrily she sat up straight and shook herself, as if to rid herself of this troubling dream. Was the fellow even intruding on her own secret meditations?

Peace destroyed, she got up and descended once again into the wood. The sun had gone in and she shivered, drawing her cloak close about her. Once under the trees she was even colder. But the day was still cheerful enough with birdsong and the unmistakable feel of spring and she soon shook off her troubled thoughts.

Suddenly, there came definite sound of a human being's approach, and Lily saw coming towards her a tall male figure. It drew closer, and she stifled a gasp. It was the rector himself.

To his credit, she thought, he looked almost as startled as she did. At first the wild thought had crossed her mind that he had been following her, but how could he have known that she was walking this way? Now it was obvious, from the deepening color in his cheeks and his quickly shuttered expression, that he, too, had been hoping to be alone.

Even as his surprise was quickly smoothed over with a smile that would not have been out of place in a drawing room, Lily controlled her own quick reaction and tried to pretend that this sudden meeting in the wood was a mere commonplace, and that she was indifferent to the fact that they were completely alone.

Lily was about to say something—anything—just to break the awkward silence, but he spoke first. "What have we here? Mickleford's own pagan priestess communing with nature?"

His grin was infuriating, and Lily decided that she would render a sharp retort and pass Mr. Vernon by. Lifting her skirts as though afraid that they might be contaminated by contact with him, she brushed past, saying, "Nature, at least, is honest, Mr. Vernon. Unlike some people."

She almost got past him but suddenly stepped across her path. "Knowing your opinion of me, Miss Sterling, I suppose it was myself that you meant. And what exactly is it that I am not honest about?"

Somehow he had placed her hand cosily in the crook of his elbow and they were now strolling, as if along a tame and regular garden path, and not the wild, undisciplined wood. Taken aback by his quick response, Lily for a moment was sorry she had ventured on her mild insult. But very well, she thought, here in the wood with no one to hear, she would finally say what she thought of Mr. Vernon.

"You are right, sir. With all due respect to your cloth," she said with a pointed glance at his richly made, unclergymanlike coat, "I find that your lips say one thing in church, but from the first moment we met—you do recall that meeting that you never mentioned to anyone—your eyes have ever been saying something else."

The rector stopped and turned to face her, putting his hands on her shoulders. Lily felt alarmed for a moment, but the expression on his face was all amusement. "And just what have these treacherous orbs of mine been saying to you, Lily?"

Lily swallowed, her mouth suddenly dry. At the same time the amusement left his face, to be replaced by a very different expression. Striving for coolness, she said, "Why, sir, the very thing they are saying now."

He pulled her a little closer, and smiled in a way that made her heart's regular rhythm feel uneven. "That I find you distractingly lovely? That I would like above all things to show you how much? But eyes alone are not so eloquent."

Suddenly she was wrapped in his arms, and their faces were so close she could see the tiny flecks of green in the blue of his eyes, an imperfection she had never noticed before, but which suddenly seemed vastly interesting. Her capacity to think was rapidly leaving her. All Lily knew was a feeling, the feeling that the warmth and pressure of his body and the look in his eyes had lifted her out of her dull existence and into that fairytale realm where her daydreams had so often taken her.

It took no more than an instant for his lips to close the tiny gap between them, and Lily felt herself soaring ever higher as their mouths joined. She had never guessed, from the boys like Billy who had courted her, that this simple act could be filled with such incredible sweetness. His arms tightened around her, and she shyly put her hands up on his shoulders, enjoying the feel of them under her fingers.

It was a long moment before the danger of her

situation was brought home to her. In fact, it took no less than Mr. Vernon's hands beginning a slow, caressing journey down her body to awaken her to the fact that she was being compromised, and with her own complicity.

She was pressed with such indecent tightness against his form, that she could feel the tension in his muscles and the heat of his body all along her own. Thought and reason returned slowly, but she realized that she had let it go on too long. With difficulty she made herself break away from his embrace. As soon as her intentions were thus made clear, Mr. Vernon let her go without an undignified struggle. But her relief at being free was overwhelmed by her sudden fear, and anger at his having shown her just how abandoned she could be. Why, she was just as bad as he, first avowing herself his enemy, and succumbing at a touch to his wiles.

In desperation she turned on him, her voice trembling at first, then growing stronger as she saw the devastating effect her words were having on him. "So this is how the strict, uncompromising Mr. Vernon conducts himself away from the eyes of his parishioners! You shall not be allowed to get away with such an imposture."

Here the rector noticeably flinched, and encouraged, Lily went on with renewed venom. "You have been pretending to be so righteous and good, denying others their innocent pleasures, and a moment's temptation finds you no better, nay far worse, than any other gentleman of the parish. We have been harboring a—a fraud! I wonder what your patron, Lord

Vyse, would have to say if he heard of your behavior?"

Mr. Vernon whitened, and there was a flash of anxiety across his face. But all was quickly smoothed over in a way with which Lily was becoming all too familiar. In a moment, the old self-confident, assured Mr. Vernon was facing her, as though their passionate interlude had never taken place. He gave her a sardonic smile, and bowed deeply.

"Indeed, ma'am, as a gentleman of the world, and not a hypocritical prude like myself, Lord Vyse would no doubt understand, though of course he would not condone, my falling into such an error under the temptation that unfortunately crossed my path." With that he tramped on past her, and Lily heard him crunching clumsily in his townsman's way out of the wood and up the hill path.

Was this Lord Vyse of his just such another who would wink at the masculine failings of his appointed rector? For after one moment's anxiety, it had become clear that Quentin Vernon was quite ready to dismiss his disgraceful action as a mere peccadillo. After letting him get well away, Lily forged on through the wood angrily. Was that all it was to him, that moment of magic?

Mr. Vernon's hypocrisy was right now the least painful aspect of the whole affair to her. It was becoming all too clear to Lily Sterling that she had derived far too much enjoyment from the interlude. If she were to be fair, she must admit that she had offered no opposition to being expertly kissed by the most attractive man she had ever met. But though she had told herself she would confound the new rector at every turn, her falling victim to his undoubted charm did not make her as much of a hypocrite as he, she reassured herself.

All the way home Lily pondered over what she should do. The rector's brief but fearful reaction to her impulsive threat to inform Lord Vyse had proved interesting. She must make certain that she was introduced to Lord Vyse at Easter and perhaps contrive a moment alone with him. With such an opportunity, she might cause the odious Mr. Vernon some trouble. But she knew in her heart that she did not wish to deprive him of his patron's trust, or perhaps, even the living itself.

And although at that moment Lily was ashamed of having kissed Quentin Vernon with such enjoyment, she was more ashamed at knowing that she could not bear to do anything that might cause him to have to leave Mickleford. It was a lowering reflection.

Chapter Six

Returning to the rectory chilled and in a mood that could only be described as foul, Quentin found himself being greeted at the door by an irritatingly jovial Sir George.

"Look at this!" he cried, holding up an oversized armful of wriggling dog. The canine burst into a frenzy of barking upon seeing Quentin, and George's explanation of its presence was drowned out. It was only after Quentin had put on his sternest rector face and sharply ordered the animal to desist, that he discovered that the rectory was now the proud owner of the lively mongrel.

"Isn't it famous?" said George. "One of the farmers gave him to me — says he's a good hunter and watchdog."

He put the wriggling bundle down, at which it frantically ran around in circles and snapped at the air. A sharp, "Down!" from Quentin quelled it temporarily.

"What on earth possessed you to accept it?" he demanded. "We don't hunt anything and we have no need of a watchdog. Don't we have enough to contend with?"

Seeing the thundercloud look on his friend's face, George moderated his transports of delight. "I—I suppose I didn't think about it really. Thing is, always wanted a dog—Mama wouldn't allow it. And now we're in the country, it's just the thing. Take it for walks, and such." Seeing that his companion did not look any less displeased, he ventured with a wink, "Make it look more convincing, you know, us keeping a dog . . ."

The animal crouched on his haunches and looked from one to the other, seeming to follow their conversation. Quentin, observing it, felt himself break into a reluctant smile, as it was a most ridiculous-looking creature, with legs far too long for its little, stubby-tailed body. It had big, sharply alert ears at odds with its sunken little eyes and flattened snout. Its fine, long coat was a motley assortment of colors, with tan predominating, and it had a black patch over one eye, that made it look as though it had recently been engaging in a mill.

Quentin sighed. He looked from the dog's tongue-lolling grin to George's eager face and gave in. "Very well. But *you* shall take care of him, and I don't want him having the run of the house. In fact, I never want to see or hear the sorry beast."

But this wish was not to be granted. It proved impossible to keep the dog out of the house, for it howled fit to wake the entire village when put in the empty stable. For the sake of peace they allowed it to crouch at their feet while they ate dinner. For some reason the creature had conceived an affection for Quentin, totally ignoring its putative owner, and although it would condescend to take food from George, it was when the meat came from Quentin's hand that it looked up with absurd gratitude in its bright little eyes. The dog almost followed him upstairs, but was at length persuaded, with Mrs. Philpott's reluctant agreement, to bed down before the kitchen fire.

When Quentin at last found himself alone and at leisure to think over the mess he had made of this day's work, (for he had no intention of confessing his foolishness to George) it was very late, but sleep eluded him. He wrestled with his conscience, wondering what had possessed him to give in to his impulse out in the wood. Was he so weak where women were concerned that he could not resist any chance for dalliance, even when it meant ruining a precarious wager and breaking his own vow to himself? But his conscience also told him that if it had been any other woman than Lily Sterling who had crossed his path that afternoon, the episode would never have happened.

Quentin felt as if the very foundations of his world were caving in. Was he the same man who had played at love with less intensity than he played at cards or hazard? Was this the Quentin who had always been impervious to the powerful entrapment of a pair of speaking eyes or soft lips, except for his own amusement? The thought crossed his mind that he would probably lose the wager to a gloating Lord Thorpe, but suddenly he realized what really troubled him; he had very likely spoiled whatever chance he had of winning Miss Lily Sterling's regard. He had not known that it was at all necessary to his happiness until now, and he was not altogether sure he was pleased with the knowledge.

After tossing uneasily all night, he cursed himself for a fool and got up just after dawn. Dressing hurriedly in the chill, with no appetite, a sour taste in his mouth, and a fog in his head, he decided to go out for a walk. He had just descended the stairs when a loud bark and the sound of frantically scratching paws almost made him jump out of his skin. It was undoubtedly the rectory's new pet announcing his desire to go out. Sighing, Quentin went to the kitchen passage door and opened it, releasing a bounding bundle of noise into the hall.

"Silence, Dionysus, you miserable mongrel!" He commanded. It was with such an unsuitable appellation that George had dignified the creature he had brought to the rectory yesterday, chiefly because of the dog's happy grin while lapping up some spilled wine last night at dinner. The animal followed him out, and it soon became plain that Dionysus would not permit his new master to take a solitary walk. "Damn you, if you must . . ." muttered Quentin, after trying to send the dog back to the rectory, and continued with the now thankfully quiet animal trotting happily at his side.

Mickleford was hung with tendrils of mist, and the newly risen sun was barely visible in a gray sky that promised rain, but the morning silence was pleasant, thought Quentin. He crossed the green and headed for the lane that led between the fields. The walk cleared his head, and soon he was able to turn his mind to constructing some plan of action to compensate for his mistake of the day before, especially as he could not totally avoid Lily and all the Sterlings for the next fortnight. The thought of this period, stretching before him, along with Thorpe's visit and Easter itself to be got through almost made him groan, but he manfully returned his thoughts to the problem at hand.

Obviously, boldness was the only thing that would see him through. He must behave as though nothing had happened. He doubted that Lily would run to Sir Richard and proclaim that the rector had abused her innocence. No, she was much more likely to do as she had threatened and try tell his supposed patron, Lord Vyse. And of course upon discovering that this paragon she expected did not precisely exist and would continue to be unknown to the inhabitants of Mickleford, she would kick up even more of a dust.

Quentin knew he could never, after this episode, reveal himself as the true Lord Vyse. Lily's frustration at not having the opportunity to complain of the rector to his "patron" could not be helped. The best thing to do, he thought, would be to let the squire and his family see that the rector was the same upright character as before, and not at all ashamed to face any of them.

Before he could sort out exactly what was to be his plan of action, Dionysus stopped, ears erect, flattened nose twitching, his stub of a tail pointing. Obviously, some interesting aroma had come to his attention. They were in the lane, all but surrounded by the budding hawthorne hedges that edged the fields on either side, and there was not a sound that Quentin could hear except an occasional bird and some farm laborers calling to one another in the distance.

But he stopped and looked in the direction where Dionysus was directing his interest. At first he could see nothing, but he did hear a minute rustling under a hedge a couple of yards away. He began to approach, but Dionysus was quicker and shot out on his long legs to the spot, where his furious barking came just in time to warn some frightened creature of the approach of an enemy.

The creature, which first looked like a handful of dirty white fur, turned out to be a rabbit. It was only because it couldn't move fast enough to outdistance the dog that Quentin was able to see it clearly at all. There was apparently something wrong with one of its legs, as its hop looked more like a hobble and it could barely run. Dionysus was in a frenzy of excitement, and upon catching up with the poor creature he almost grabbed it in his jaws, apparently intent on bringing it to his master, if not killing it himself, but Quentin had a sudden idea, and called the dog off. Miraculously, the animal obeyed.

Now he approached the rabbit, which must have been frightened indeed, for it could not run at all now. Its plump white sides were moving rapidly in and out, its nose was twitching and its pale eyes seemed to look at him in supplication. A plan, hazy in detail, was momentarily growing clearer in his mind. Of course, country people like the Sterlings no doubt thought of rabbits and hares as vermin to be exterminated, but

114

he supposed that children might be fond of the little creatures, and there were certainly, to the best of his memory, children at Sterling Hall. What more natural excuse for a visit than to beg Lady Flora, whose healing skill was well known, to help the poor lame creature, and ask the children if they would like to make it a pet?

He grinned as he pictured the scene. Would a man who had saved a poor wounded rabbit from the ravening jaws of a ferocious dog be the sort of fellow who would compromise the squire's daughter alone in the woods? Certainly not! Even though Lily probably wouldn't complain of him, it could not hurt to secure his good reputation with the Sterling family. And she was known to be fond of wild creatures herself. Perhaps, just perhaps, she would see him differently now.

He gathered up the rabbit carefully, trying not to cause any more pain to its poor afflicted limb. Followed by the disappointed but obedient Dionysus, he made his way back to the rectory, deposited the creature in a nest of rags in the kitchen and instructed the astounded and disapproving Mrs. Philpott to put out water and food for it. After he had quickly breakfasted and dressed in his best clerical-looking garb, he set off for the Hall with his wounded offering.

His reception was not at first everything he had hoped it would be.

"Oh, dear!" cried Lady Sterling, startled. "A rabbit. It looks hurt, and rather . . . dirty." She stared doubtfully at it.

Quentin did not allow this to discourage him. He turned the rabbit over to a stolid-faced manservant,

115

who accepted it with as much aplomb, as if he were being handed a hat. "I do hope that I haven't been presumptuous," he said. "But I wondered if Lady Flora's skill with healing could save the poor mite, and if the children might like to make a pet of it."

His hostess's face brightened. "Oh, of course, it would be the very thing. Do come into the sitting room." As she led him in, she said, "You see, they had been keeping a horrid little field mouse that dear Lily had found, and of course as soon as it was better it ran off to be with the other field mice, leaving the poor children quite cast down."

Lady Flora, to whom he made his bow next, ensconced in the sitting room's best chair like a queen on her throne, begrudgingly agreed to examine the wounded animal. "Hmmph!" she said, looking Quentin up and down with surprise. "I wouldn't have thought you one of those sloppy fellows who dote upon wild creatures, like my granddaughter Lily does. Forever bringing home strays for me to nurse, ever since she was able to walk." But when the servant, who had followed them bearing the rabbit, showed her the animal, she softened. "Bring it to my stillroom," she ordered, "and have my salves and a hot kettle made ready, and some bandaging. Help me up, rector."

Quentin did so with alacrity, sure that when Lily discovered his act of charity towards the rabbit she would look at him more kindly, and thanked her. "It is really most obliging of you, my lady. I am sure it will recover soon with the benefit of your famous skills, and it will make the boys an excellent pet."

Mrs. Hyacinth Forbush came in just then, with a

pouty-looking Arabella trailing behind her, and Aunt Poppy following, murmuring, "There, there, now. Mr. Watson *could* have simply forgotten. There's no need to be in such a taking, my love."

Arabella gave a haughty sniff, while her mama, seating herself with an imperious flourish next to the rector, acknowledged his presence graciously. Then she turned to her sister with a warning glance. "I do not really care to discuss the matter, now, Poppy." Quentin thought she looked furious. He wondered what had occurred to disturb the three ladies and in spite of Mrs. Forbush's ban on discussion of the matter, he was soon enlightened.

"Now, young lady, what is the reason for that sulky face?" demanded Lady Flora, postponing her ministrations to the rabbit in the face of this interesting development.

"Oh, Grandmama," Arabella wailed, "it's Mr. Watson. He's behaving horridly to me, as though he has forgotten that we are betrothed. It would serve him right if I cried off!"

"Not in front of visitors, Arabella," her mother warned.

The girl ignored her and poured out her troubles to Lady Flora. "It began at the dance, you know, when he only stood up with me once, though twice or even *three* times would have been perfectly proper. Then he simply forgot me, fussing over those bold Lewis girls."

Poppy bleated with sympathy. "It is quite true, Mama," she told Lady Flora. "The young man does seem to be neglecting poor Arabella. Why, this is the second engagement he has missed. He never called for

117

her last week to take her driving, sending some paltry excuse about the estate —"

"— and today he was supposed to call, and now I have a note that I should not expect him till Easter week, as he has some business to attend to for his father," Arabella sniffed. Quentin thought, however, that she looked more insulted than hurt. Obviously her pride and not her heart had been injured. He almost pitied Mr. Watson.

"Could it not be," he said, hesitant to interfere but mindful of his role as clergyman, "that the young man is being kept busy with duties about his father's estate?"

The women all looked at him with scornful pity. Lady Flora, ignoring his foolish remark, made her way to the door. "Going to attend to that poor rabbit now, Mr Vernon." She smiled at him a bit slyly. "I shall see that Lily knows of your good deed. And as for you, my girl," she turned to Arabella, "it shouldn't be beyond a clever child like yourself to find a way to keep your betrothed attentive. Put your mind to it."

After her departure, Mrs. Forbush and Poppy made embarrassed noises, begging the rector to take no notice of an elderly lady's plain speaking. Knowing they meant her advice to Arabella, he assured them that he had taken none, but he was more concerned with what she had said of her other granddaughter. Did the matriarch suspect him of hankering after Lily, and was she, for matchmaking or purely mischief's sake, determined to add her mite to the contest? He left soon after, assuring the ladies that he would call again to inquire after the health of the rabbit and receive the thanks of the children.

This he did the next day, but though there was good news that the rabbit's leg was going to heal, and the boys told him they were delighted and grateful to have a new pet, he thought only of Lily.

She behaved to him with chilly propriety under the curious and watchful eye of Lady Flora, who obviously could sense some tension between her granddaughter and the rector. Quentin was not surprised when she sent them together into the drawing room to fetch something for her, a pointed command that could not be ignored despite the curious glances it evoked from the rest of the family. John Sterling winked at them in a way that made Quentin want to call him out, and Aunt Poppy smiled on them benevolently, which was equally irritating.

Lily, however, lost no time in laying the blame for their situation where it was due. "How dare you?" she demanded, when they were alone and Quentin had closed the door, ignoring propriety. To calm his own nerves, he pretended to be looking for the bit of embroidery Lady Flora had supposedly left. "It's not here—perhaps under this cushion? And how dare I what?" he asked as he made his futile search.

He snatched a glance at her now and then, and what he saw only made him want to repeat his hasty and ill-judged action in the wood. She was in a delightful, springlike gown of primrose sprigged muslin. Her eyes looked bigger than ever and her hair curled in soft tendrils about her cheeks. She was, in short, absolutely enchanting, and temper only gave her a more pleasing color.

"You know exactly what I mean, Mr. Vernon. I shall not be so undignified as to refer to it more plainly." She lifted her chin, her eyes gleaming with emotion. "And now you have the audacity to come here and bring a *rabbit*," she said scathingly.

Quentin smiled in spite of the tension. "I'm sorry it offends you, but it was all because of this dreadful dog my curate insisted on bringing home to the rectory." He was determined to admit to no wrongdoing. Poor Lily, it would enrage her, but he had no choice.

She ignored him. "You pretend to be so concerned about one of nature's creatures, when all you wanted was to come and torment me! You are daring me to tell Papa, aren't you? Well, I shan't—not that you don't deserve it."

Quentin stopped the fruitless searching that had kept him safely occupied and looked at her. By now she seemed more confused than angry. Was it possible that she was trying to sustain the anger in order to forestall other, more troublesome feelings? His moment of hope dissolved in sudden pity for her, and disgust for himself.

Could he not have left well enough alone? He had brought enough trouble to this peaceful village, and would bring more before Easter was over. Must he hanker after a charming, beautiful, but shockingly innocent creature, who if he had not disturbed her placid world, would have been happy eventually with some local boy?

But Lily had such a hold on him that he knew it to be impossible. For her own sake he wished he was able to leave her in peace. But the memory of her in his arms would not leave him.

Slowly he approached her, and the look he saw in her eyes was compounded equally of fear and eagerness. He slid his hands up her arms to her shoulders, tempted to kiss her again, and show her that this anger between them was unnecessary, but to do that here in her father's house would brand him irretrievably in her mind as a libertine. He must give her time — time to know her own mind and heart, as he had just begun to know his.

"Lily, my dear, I . . ." But he had no idea what to say that would not simply land him in more trouble.

He felt her tremble slightly beneath his hands. Her lips looked full and inviting, but her head was up proudly and it was almost as if she dared him to take the liberty he ached to enjoy.

With more difficulty than he would have believed possible, he gently, regretfully, removed his hands and stepped back. "I'm afraid we must tell Lady Flora that we have failed to find her embroidery. And I thank you for your forbearance. It would indeed be distressing to me if your father, who has been so kind, should know of my moment of . . . weakness."

It was the nearest to an apology he could come. A look of surprise crossed her face. Was it tinged with disappointment, as he imagined? Quickly it was gone as if it had never been, and she was composed and expressionless. She nodded stiffly and preceded him out of the room, addressing not a word to him for the rest of the visit. Though he found his gaze inadvertently drawn to her again and again, she never looked at him.

He returned to the rectory, knowing he must look as stricken as he felt, shrugging off George's anxious questions. Next time he and Lily Sterling met, he swore to himself, he would try once more to explain his behavior, a difficult thing to do if he were not to give himself away. But next time he would not lose courage, and she would not escape him He was determined that she would at least look into his eyes, for if she only did that for a moment, what she saw there might soften her heart.

As it fell out he did accomplish this aim, even though afterwards Miss Lily Sterling's adamantine heart appeared no more receptive than before. It was early on Saturday, while the rector and curate were breakfasting, that raucous sounds of merriment penetrated through to the rectory, which faced the green. At the sudden noise, both men looked up from their meal.

"What on earth—" Sir George shoved back his chair and stood up, his head cocked, listening. They both heard the music of pipes and drums and cymbals, playing a little march, and the laughter of children. A yelp and a bark told them that Dionysus had managed to worm his way out of the kitchen to join the fun.

Quentin wondered if this were yet another pagan remnant that as rector he should attempt to quash, but suddenly he was tired of all that posturing. He decided instead simply to indulge his curiosity and see what Mickleford was up to.

When Mr. Vernon and his curate appeared, the villagers were so engrossed in their procession that no one took any notice, and thus Quentin was able to

122

watch and enjoy the spectacle. It looked as though all the young people of the neighborhood, from the land-owning classes down to the lowliest laborer were marching from house to house, arms linked. At each house more young people would join the line, led by musicians. The men and boys wore their workaday breeches but sported bright coats and waistcoats, and the girls and women were beribboned and flower-decked. They sang a song Quentin did not recognize, and there appeared to be no particular purpose to the procession.

George shared his bewilderment, for he said, "I wonder what it's about? Surely it can't be anything to do with the holiday, for they would have spoken to you of it—" He stopped, his face red, and looked apologetic.

"Don't worry," said Quentin with a short laugh. "The fact that the rector of the parish has been left out makes no odds to me. It only means that I succeeded too well in my role as a strictly no-nonsense clergyman."

They watched as Dionysus, tired of capering about the edges of the procession with the other dogs and running among the children who followed the line clapping and shouting, began to roam among the marchers, tangling in the women's skirts and generally causing mayhem. The middle of the snaking line was just then passing the rectory on its way out of the village, and Quentin saw that the not only were four young ladies from the Hall marching along with the others, smiling and singing, but that Dionysus was just now menacing the steps of Lily Sterling, who was

123

burdened, as were many of the others, by a long shallow basket.

She almost tripped as Dionysus, not requiring a formal introduction to recognize her as a sympathetic soul, wound himself about her ankles and gazed up at her worshipfully. Without allowing himself to think, Quentin stepped to her side. "Dionysus! Down!"

To his amazement the formerly obedient dog merely wagged his tail and barked, and then resumed admiring Lily. She did not look at Quentin, but merely put a hand through the dog's collar and bent to whisper something to him, at which he sat beside her quite placidly.

Quentin did not know whether he should be more amused or annoyed, but he took the opportunity to engage Lily in conversation. "I was going to apologize for the pup's bad manners, Miss Lily. But I can see you have Dionysus well in hand."

Her expression told him that he was the last person she had expected, or indeed wanted to see on that cheerful morning, but she met his eyes gravely and replied, "Oh, he is no bother. But Dionysus? Why, what a very pagan name, to be sure, Mr. Vernon." This barbed comment was delivered in a tone of perfect innocence.

Delighted that she was not too angry with him to forget to fence, Quentin was about to reply, but by now the people behind them, frustrated at being stopped, began to shout, urging them forward.

"Move on, we're losing t'others!"

"Aye, Mr. Vernon, come along of us to the wood!" cried a burly young man. Instead of a basket,

124

he carried a leather bottle and sipped from it.

"Yes, do come and help us gather the willow in, Mr. Vernon sir," begged one comely village maiden.

Quentin almost laughed, for Lily Sterling's look at these celebrants said very plainly "Traitors!" but he allowed himself to accept graciously and the line moved on. He marched along at Lily's side, picking up the singing while putting a hand on Dionysus's collar. In this he happened to touch Lily's hand and she jerked away as if from a hot coal. Quentin looked down at her, willing her to meet his gaze, but she stared straight ahead. Nevertheless he was heartened to see a blush spread beneath the shadow of her yellow bonnet. He let go of the dog's collar, and Dionysus ambled peaceably along between them, blissfully unaware of the tension hovering over his motley furred back.

Meanwhile George Hollister had lost not a moment in discovering that Violet Sterling was also of the party, and had slipped to her side, even convincing her to let him carry her basket. The long line of revelers made its way out of the village and to the wood, where, to the accompaniment of more music and singing, the celebrants gathered willow branches. These, George told Quentin, were meant to represent the palm and were to be carried to church on Palm Sunday. George slipped one into his buttonhole, smiling.

"And how do you know that, my clever curate?" Quentin asked when they were momentarily separated from the ladies.

"Why Vi—I mean, Miss Sterling told me. She is

ever so knowledgeable," he said. He followed this lady with his eyes, and indeed, even Quentin noticed that she was looking younger and prettier today than before, with a ribboned bonnet and gay color in her cheeks.

Quentin laughed. "I wonder what other quaint customs they have been keeping from us. But of course, it is my own fault for not having studied my subject more thoroughly. Run along and enjoy yourself."

His friend having deserted him again for Miss Sterling, Quentin sought out Lily, and stuck fast to her, helping her fill her basket and chatting cheerfully about pleasantries, despite her lack of encouragement.

"You are most kind, but your attendance on me is not necessary, Mr. Vernon," she said, sweeping him a cold glance. "And I would not willingly subject you to yet another remnant of our heathen past, for of course though we do this to prepare for Palm Sunday, it must once have been an activity dedicated to some god of the wood."

"I am not at all offended," he said blithely, determined not to be shaken off. "In fact I find it a charming custom, whatever its origin. And since I have been remiss in not bringing my own basket," he replied, "I may as well help you with yours. But first you must decorate me as befits the season."

He handed her a little willow slip. Frowning, she fixed it in his buttonhole. He put his fingers over hers, but she slipped them away and went back to their gathering. As there seemed to be no way she could stop him, she simply ignored his contributions but the basket became filled much sooner than those of the other ladies, Violet's included, for she and George, Quentin saw out of the corner of his eye, were doing more talking than gathering. The other young people also seemed to have paired off, some disappearing deeper into the wood, where the morning sun did not penetrate and where there were cozy little spots of dimness.

Lily looked up from depositing a willow branch and found that she and the rector were alone. She felt a moment of panic, for she knew that her brave show of distaste for him was simply that, a show. And now not Violet or Arabella or even silly Olive was nearby to defend her. Slowly she looked up at Quentin Vernon. He was not, to her relief, looking at her in that particular way that made her knees go weak, nor was he coming any closer. His face was full of an unfamiliar concern. There were lines of worry across his brow. She felt a sudden tenderness overwhelm her, and had a strong impulse to put up a hand and smooth the lines away, but she hardened her will.

Ever since his arrival the rector had been playing false with her. She knew now that the first man she had met, the one who had flirted with her in the lane, must be the true Quentin Vernon, and the stern rector who had tried to bend the parish, and her, to his will was but a role he acted for who knew what reason. But was the flirt a man to be trusted? She did not think so.

He put his hand on her arm. "Lily, I know that you and I made a bad start, and that my subsequent behavior must seem puzzling to you."

"Indeed, Mr. Vernon," she replied, moving away.

His hand slid off her arm. She was rather surprised when he did not attempt to touch her again. "I am not at all sure that I know what sort of man you really are."

What he said next surprised her. "I'm not sure I know myself, although once I thought I did."

She looked up at him, searching his eyes. What she saw there softened her momentarily, but she could not forget the trouble this man had caused her, and the unsupported hopes that had sprung in her breast when he had first cast that seductive gaze upon her. "I think that before a man is given charge of the welfare of people's souls he ought to be more cognizant of what resides in his own," she said in a didactic tone reminiscent, even to her ears, of Violet or Aunt Hyacinth.

It did not appear to deter her companion. "But you are an idealist, that much I know, my dear Lily," he said with a sudden smile. It lifted years from his face, and the sight of it caused Lily's heartbeat to quicken. "I hope that you did not look to me to exemplify any of your ideals," he continued, his tone teasing.

She shook off the urge to smile back. "If I did, I would be extremely foolish, and also disappointed," she replied. "For it has become obvious that you are no more and no less than other men."

"Poor child. Was that discovery so disappointing for you?"

Lily turned away and pretended to shake some dirt and leaves form her skirts. "I expected nothing from you, although Mickleford probably did. But you must admit that if you had been honest with us all from the beginning, and not pretended to be so strictly moral, everything would have been much more pleasant. The parish would have welcomed you, and you could have—" she stopped, a bit embarrassed.

"You mean I could have courted you openly, if I had wished?" She heard a bitter laugh. "Ah, but Lily, the real truth is the one thing that is impossible for me to tell you. Believe me, you would not wish to hear it, for then you would despise me even more than you already do." There was a strained silence.

Suddenly she heard the undergrowth crunch as he stepped nearer, took her shoulders and gently turned her to face him. Captivated by the intensity of his gaze, she did not attempt to pull away. She looked up at him expectantly, feeling as though her heart and body had both betrayed her mind, which was urging her to be sensible. But the pulse that pounded through her would not be quieted.

He pressed his lips against hers, fiercely, as if afraid that she would escape. His arms encircled her, and she gave herself up to the feeling of sheer joy, joining her body to his, lost in the long, warm kiss. Slowly he released her, and by then they were both gasping for breath.

Then he choked out the words that made her newly risen spirits plummet. "I am sorry. I swear to you I will not make this mistake again." Before she could protest, he had turned and gone, plunging through the woods, leaves and branches crackling under his feet.

She listened until the sound died away, and she could hear the far-off laughter of the other revelers.

Again, Lily thought dully, raising a hand to her throbbing lips. Once more seduced and abandoned in a wood. She blinked back tears. Was he so cruel as to toy with her, or was he really so afraid as he seemed to tell her the truth, whatever that might be? She sat down, her skirts huddled around her, suddenly cold, gazing sightlessly into the basket he had filled for her.

Gradually, her natural sense of humor reasserted herself and she wanted to laugh at her own absurdity and melodrama. She had spent far too long reading fairy tales and romances, and would soon be dramatizing every moment of her life, she scolded herself, even the mending and the jam making. Slowly she rose, chilled, and began walking to warm herself.

She now knew even less than before, she thought, about Quentin Vernon. He had obscured his image even farther with these layers of mystery. She wished she could discover what secret hung over him. But he had told her himself; she would despise him all the more for it. Oh, why had she not told him that she did not despise him, never had? But the alternative was too frightening. To pin her love and hopes on such a will-o'-the-wisp as Quentin Vernon seemed to be would be foolish beyond measure. On one thing she was determined; he should not so toy with her feelings again.

She must put a guard on her behavior; for no one, she cautioned herself, must suspect what had been happening between herself and the rector. And him she must keep at arms length, quite literally. As her anger grew, she became almost eager to expose him, especially to his patron, but in so doing she was in danger of exposing herself. She would have to tread carefully.

At Palm Sunday service, she tried as hard as possible to behave as she usually did, evidencing no more interest than usual in the sermon, and indeed trying not to look up at Quentin Vernon at all. Fortunately, she held Baby on her lap as she usually did, and thus had something to occupy her, though the placid child fussed not at all.

The willow branches decorating altar, pulpit, and pews should, she thought, have counted as a sort of victory for the village over Mr. Vernon's determined opposition to its customs, but for Lily there was no joy in seeing them. Her fleeting feeling of satisfaction came during the sermon, during which not once did Mr. Vernon berate or chide his congregation for its sinfulness, but only read a popular sermon to them from one of the late Mr. Barton's books.

Lily could hear the old folks sigh gratefully as they settled into their naps or dreams, and the younger ones with disappointment as their Sunday entertainment eluded them, but she was glad to be spared an emotional harangue by the very rector who was already causing so much turmoil in her heart. Finally giving in to an urging, she glanced up at him and was shocked to see how drawn and tired he looked. Obviously he was in no fit condition to browbeat anyone today. Indeed, Lily thought with a new surge of resentment, he had no right to condemn anyone else, after his own actions.

She looked longer than she intended to, and thus was caught when he looked up from his book, closed it, and at once searched for her in the congregation. As his gaze met hers she felt a sudden jolt, whether of excitement or of guilt she could not tell. The corners of his mouth seemed to turn up in a little, knowing smile of complicity meant just for her, and she looked away, her face flaming. How dare he, before the entire parish? But when she looked up again, the prayers were continuing and no one seemed to have noticed the exchange.

Lily hardened her heart. Whatever his real feelings, obviously the stolen kisses could lead to nothing farther—at least nothing that was not completely unthinkable—and she must simply become accustomed to shutting Quentin Vernon and his mysteries out of her life.

"It's the post, miss," said the manservant as Lily passed through the hall on her way to the sitting room to join her half sisters the next morning. He handed her a tray with a bundle of letters.

As she rarely received any post, she only looked through it absently before leaving it on the table to be brought to her father. Consequently, she was amazed to see in the pile a much-stained, crumpled, and badly addressed missive bearing her own name. She opened and read it on her way to the sitting room. "Oh, dear," were her first words as she stepped into the room.

"You sound just like Stepmama," said Olive, who sat netting a purse but keeping a wary eye on two-year-old Blossom, jumping up to rescue the child whenever she appeared near to toppling over or menacing any of several small tables and delicate chairs. "Is that a letter? Who is it from?"

"You may well ask!" Lily waved the letter in despair. "I had totally forgotten Signor Marco. However shall I explain it to Papa?"

Violet looked up from her work. "Do you mean that funny little Italian man we met at Harrogate last year?"

"Yes, the very one. Do you recall me having invited him to visit us?" She crinkled her brow. "I confess I do not remember the occasion very well. I *might* have mentioned something about his calling on us if he were ever in the neighborhood. Well, apparently he has taken a fancy to see how we celebrate an English Easter and will be arriving very soon."

"Gracious!" observed Violet. "He certainly took you very literally." She frowned. "Though you do have a tendency to become too intimate with strangers of the most unsuitable kind whenever we go to a watering place, Lily."

Lily only smiled, remembering their acquaintance. "I could not help it in Signor Marco's case, Vi. He was so amusing, and so generous—treating us to tea and cream cakes. Although I believe it was partly because it gave him an excuse to eat what he shouldn't. He was supposed to be taking a cure."

Olive had been conspicuously silent at this news, but now she looked up, her face composed, but betraying hidden excitement. "There is nothing at all wrong with inviting such an unexceptionable young gentleman to visit the family," she offered, setting a whimpering Blossom upright after a fall, "especially as

133

he is a visitor to our land. And do you not recall him speaking of his uncle the count? It is obvious that he is of an old important family. I for one should be delighted to show him about the neighborhood." She turned to her half sister. "Do not worry, Lily. Your mama will hardly notice if another person should suddenly appear at the dinner table, and Papa will be so flattered by Signor Marco's admiration of Sterling Hall—for I feel sure he will admire it and our fine farms very much—that it will all pass off very pleasantly."

"But what about Grandmama?" Lily reminded her.

There was silence and consternation for a moment. Violet sighed. "Well, I suppose we must only hope that despite her dislike of foreigners she will be diverted enough by Signor Marco not to make things difficult."

With this hope all had to be content.

As it happened there was not much time to debate the matter, for as the condition of the letter indicated, it had been long delayed and the signor was already upon his journey. He arrived at the Hall that afternoon.

The rector and his curate had just arrived, the latter calling to have a quiet conference with Violet, ostensibly about the Ladies Society's plans to provide new Easter clothes for certain poor children of the village. The rector himself seemed to have no other aim in this visit than to indulge Baby's whim of chewing on his watch fob and to stare Lily out of countenance, which she affected to ignore while nearly pricking herself with her needle in the agitation it caused. She was still confused over her own response to him despite trying to put him out of her mind.

However, she was scrupulously polite to the rector, unwilling to expose herself before her family. It appeared that despite what had happened between them, he intended to outwardly carry on as usual, and thus so must she.

It was an unexpectedly fine day, so everyone was out in the garden, where the visitors duly admired the first blooms and listened to Olive prophesy a fine year for the dogwood and cherry trees. Having tired of the watch fob, Baby took a few staggering steps, fell down, and wailed, while Blossom ran about chasing birds and butterflies.

William, with difficulty restrained by Steven, was energetically feeding and petting the rabbit, still limping but looking much more bright-eyed and happy than the dirty scrap that had almost fallen victim to Dionysus's hunting ardor. Teague was sitting on a swing, fiercely scribbling in a little book, while Arabella, decked in a fetching bonnet and apron, was working daintily and ineffectually in the garden, and occasionally consulting with her cousins on how to bring about a return of Mr. Watson's attentions.

Uncle John, having exercised his wit on this subject in a very improper fashion, had tired of his nieces' disapproving looks and now sat in a comfortable slouch, booted legs stretched out before him, a newspaper resting upon his face. To Lily's relief, as she did not much relish being under their scrutiny in the presence of the rector, Lady Flora and Lady Sterling remained upstairs resting upon their beds.

Mr. Vernon had strolled about, duly admiring the garden and then taken a new seat beside Lily, who was determined not to say anything until he did, when a bemused-looking footman stepped out into the garden. He was followed immediately by a small, jolly-faced man with dark hair, a little moustache, bright brown eyes, and a hideous green brocade waistcoat.

Olive flushed with suspicious pleasure, and the other ladies merely opened their mouths in surprise.

"At last, the home of the gracious Misses Sterling! And the English garden in spring! Such a refreshing sight to the heart of the weary traveler," he said with a deep, affecting sigh.

Olive beamed and rose to greet him, while Quentin, some imp prompting him, whispered behind his hand to Lily, "I did not know that particular organ had been blessed with the gift of sight. He may not know how to dress but I daresay he has many such unsuspected talents."

She suppressed a smile, gave him what she hoped was a stern look and went to greet her guest. "Signor Marco, welcome to Sterling Hall. I vow we hardly expected to see you so soon."

"Ah, but Signorina Lily, your English roads so well laid and maintained, and the coach, she goes like the wind." This heavily accented speech was accompanied by many illustrative gestures, and he ended by bringing Lily's hand to his lips. The rest of the family watched, fascinated.

When the visitor turned to greet Olive, who had bustled up to him, unable to wait a moment longer, Quentin murmured almost in Lily's ear, "Now your true continental gentleman will not kiss the hand of an unmarried lady. I wonder where your signor learned his company manners?"

Lily raised her eyebrows and eloquently turned her back to him.

Meanwhile Olive was in raptures. "Oh, Signor Marco, how lovely that you have come! Why, I never dreamed you really would!"

"Ah, *la bella* Signorina Olivia!" He signed deeply and expressively, and saluted Olive's plump hand as well, which brought a rise of color to her cheeks and a giggle to her throat. "But of course I come, as your sister was good enough to invite me. I come to meet the squire," he announced with an absurd little bow, and the boys began to chortle.

But the visitor laughed with them good-naturedly. "And of course," he added, "I come for the English *Pascqua* — Easter, you say. For, signorina, as you know, I am a great traveler and am composing a book about my journeys. I wish to know everything about your country."

"And what have you learned so far, Signor Marco?" Violet asked dryly. George had been looking anxiously at her, as if to ascertain whether she was as impressed with the intriguing foreigner as it seemed her sister was, but Violet's expression was unreadable.

"I have learned, dear signorina, that her ladies are the most charming in the world," replied the Italian, approaching her and the rest and renewing his acquaintance, while being introduced to the children, who goggled at him unabashedly.

"Good lord," Quentin could not help but whisper,

although knowing his aside was unlikely to be appreciated by Lily, "the fellow is an endless fount of compliments! Soon I shall begin to quake lest he tell me that he finds English clergymen charming too."

Lily replied to this sally with a glance of disdain, although she was tempted to smile. How absurd the signor was, but so much more agreeable, she told herself, than the rector, who pretended to be what he was not. She left the garden to inform her mother and grandmother of the arrival of their guest.

Thankfully, the immediate worry of how her grandmother would receive him could distract her from Quentin Vernon's persistent and disturbing presence. Lady Flora, upon being informed of the signor's imminent arrival, had grumbled and made disparaging remarks about foreigners, while Sir Richard had sighed and said, "Since you have already invited him, my dear, I fear there is little we can do but welcome the fellow."

Lady Sterling had resorted, of course, to her usual exclamation and had rung for the housekeeper with one hand while putting the other to her head in distraction. But Olive's delight with their guest's arrival might make up for the lack of enthusiasm of the rest of the family, Lily thought shrewdly. She was glad that the results were no worse than they were, for she had not precisely invited the signor, she recalled, and this certainly was a difficult time for the family to have a houseguest.

Less than a week till Easter, and Lily knew she would be quite busy till then with the holiday preparations and Signor Marco's entertainment to see to, along with her other duties. No time to mourn the fact that she had enjoyed far too much the dalliance with Quentin Vernon, and that he now appeared unwilling to let her forget the matter in peace. What could he be about, inflicting his presence on her with such a lack of sensibility? But she would get her revenge, she told herself at moments like this, when Lord Vyse arrived.

She had almost forgotten the imminent arrival of the clergyman's patron, for of course, she told herself, it must be Lord Vyse he was expecting. He could certainly be counted on to shed some light on the mystery of Quentin Vernon.

When she returned to the garden, it was in the midst of commotion. William was crying, Steven was clutching the poor rabbit tightly to him, and Blossom was jumping up and down, pointing at the signor and shouting, "Bad! Bad!"

"What on earth has come over all of you?" Lily demanded, hurrying over to the scene of confusion. Olive looked embarrassed, while Violet, Lily could tell, was endeavoring not to laugh, and the signor was red-faced and apologetic.

"But have I done wrong? I merely congratulated Signorina Violet on having fattened a fine rabbit for the Easter meal."

At this, renewed outrage broke out among the children, and Lily, while trying to restrain her own amusement, happened to catch Quentin's eye. His merry look almost undid her, but she managed to sort out the tangle, explaining gently to the signor that the rabbit was a pet and that they always had roast lamb for Easter. He was profuse in his apologies, and while

139

all this was happening a servant had come out to the garden and was vainly trying to attract the attention of the rector.

Violet brought this to the attention of Quentin, who turned. "Yes?"

"I have a message from your housekeeper, sir," said the man, bustling with self-importance at being the bearer of this important message. "She said to tell you that Lord Vyse has arrived."

George, who had been at Violet's side through the entire visit, reluctantly pulled himself away to attend the rector, whose face for a split second reflected a high degree of amazement and consternation.

"Is anything wrong, Mr. Vernon?" asked Violet. Everyone's eyes were now fixed on the rector's suddenly white face.

"No, not at all. Quite the contrary," he said in a tone that betrayed some effort. He looked at Lily and his smile was almost harsh. "My patron, Lord Vyse, has arrived a bit earlier than I expected. I beg you will excuse me. I must attend him there. Come, George." With that the two men, one looking icily furious, the other simply shocked and confused, were escorted back into the house by the servant, leaving wild speculation behind them.

Lily's heart sped. The mysterious Lord Vyse had at last arrived! It was decidedly odd, however, for Mr. Vernon to be so angry and Mr. Hollister to be so surprised. After all, he was no doubt expected. But of course Mr. Vernon was a very odd clergyman. Most important to Lily, however, was that now she would very likely have a chance to talk to his lordship and perhaps just mention that his chosen rector was not all he pretended to be.

The others chatted excitedly about the possibility of at long last meeting the neighborhood's principal land-owner.

"I don't think that rector of ours would object to a friendly game of cards, do you Violet?" asked John Sterling lazily. "I'm sure Lord Vyse will want some amusement. I shall ask that curate fellow if he wouldn't see to arranging a table for us all."

"An English lord! Why, this is a circumstance of the most fortunate!" cried Signor Marco. "If your good Papa the squire might present me, it shall be an honor to be remembered forever, and would form a most interesting chapter for my book."

The children seemed to be the only ones unaffected by the news, except for Teague, who put down his book and ventured to hope that Lord Vyse might be prevailed upon to talk some sense into his mama. "His lordship must know that a boy of my age should be at school with other boys." He struggled manfully to cover up a cough.

Meanwhile Olive wondered aloud about the possibility of persuading Papa to hold a ball after Easter, while Arabella, still scheming to bring on a renewal of Mr. Watson's attentions, concurred that one would be very agreeable.

"I'm sure Papa would have no objection," said Violet. "It will be an occasion to wear our new spring gowns."

Lily looked at her in surprise. She had never known Vi to hanker after parties and balls and dresses. But lately, she realized, her stern sister had been looking softer, and was smiling more often. It mystified her. But in the next instant she realized that her older sister had not changed so very much after all.

"Then again," said Violet, calmly taking up her needlework once more, "I sincerely hope his lordship has brought that promised silver font that the rector mentioned. Mr. Vernon will christen no babies without it, and if he does not do it soon all of the candidates for baptism will have grown to a most unwieldy size!"

Chapter Seven

A harried-looking Mrs. Philpott greeted Quentin and George at the rectory. "I've put the gentlemen in the library, sir," she said. "And their rooms will be ready soon. I only wish I'd had more notice!" She was about to bustle away, but Quentin stopped her.

"Gentlemen?" he inquired. George was looking at him anxiously, but Quentin remained calm, despite the apprehension that was beginning to creep up his spine.

"Yes, Lord Vyse and the clergyman who came with him. He said he was an old friend from London," the housekeeper informed him. Hands bunched up in her apron, she asked, "Did I do right, sir?"

"Why of course, Mrs. Philpott," Quentin reassured her, forcing himself to smile when he would much prefer to scowl at Thorpe's iniquity. What the devil does the man think he's doing, he thought, pretending to be me — and bringing along a real parson as well? To the housekeeper he said, "I own I did not expect my old friend to arrive with his lordship,

143

but it is a pleasant surprise."

After Mrs. Philpott had been dismissed, George stared at his friend in frank admiration. "Well done! I daresay she has no idea what a shock this is. Damn the fellow, anyway. What does he mean by turning up here, proclaiming himself Lord Vyse? And who the devil has he brought with him?"

"Exactly what I ask myself." Quentin paused a moment to think before they made their way to the library. "The only clergyman a fellow like Thorpe could possibly be on speaking terms with," he pondered aloud, "is his younger brother Lewis. As I recall, he went into the church because he had no fancy for the Army, and as the youngest had no fortune of his own."

George nodded. "I remember him when he first came on the town, always tagging after Thorpe. But what the devil has he brought the fellow here for?"

"I think our friend intends to outmaneuver us. No doubt the viscount thought it a good trick to persuade a real man of the cloth to come to Mickleford and help discomfit me. But I have an idea that young Lewis might be of more use than harm, if we handle him right."

"I think I begin to see where you are leading. Parson Lewis might not approve at all of this wager," George speculated with a grin.

Quentin gave a short laugh. "That, my friend, is what I am counting on. Although I recall that he was never very pious—"

"But just as dull as if he had been!" George interjected.

"Quite so. But since taking orders he has received preferment from some of his excellent connections, and is now pastor to a fashionable flock near Mayfair. I have heard that he takes himself rather seriously these days. Thorpe, I'm sure, has underestimated his brother's malleability, which may be to our advantage."

"But supposing Lewis takes it into his head to climb into your pulpit and proclaim the truth to all of Mickleford?" George worried.

"It is a remote possibility," Quentin admitted, "but I doubt Lord Thorpe would permit it, or that Lewis has gained that much audacity since last I knew him."

"Lewis always did toady to his brother, and he ain't as clever as the viscount," said George hopefully.

They entered the library to find the two visitors standing with their backs to the door, glasses in hand, having apparently helped themselves to the rector's brandy. Lord Thorpe was tall and extremely thin. He was dressed with fashionable carelessness in buckskins, topboots, and a casually fitted black coat, and tied round his neck was a spotted handkerchief. Above this his dark hair was rumpled. An uneducated observer might think him a superior sort of groom, but the fashionable knew otherwise. Then he turned and Quentin beheld once more, with respect and distaste, his challenger's bold countenance.

It seemed all nose and eyes, with a thin, sardonic mouth. His brother the clergyman was a good deal shorter and plumper than his lordship, though they shared the same brown, slightly protuberant eyes, and he was impeccably dressed and coiffed.

"Ah, Vyse," the younger man said, coming forward. "How do you do? And Sir George." His bow acknowledged both men. "And now I see that what Geoffrey told me is alas true. How could you allow yourself to be talked into such a sacrilegious, scandalous—"

"There'll be no scandal if you will but keep your mouth shut, Lewis," drawled the viscount. His sour expression told Quentin that he was already regretting bringing his brother to Mickleford. He eyed Quentin and George, and smiled crookedly as he made a show of inspecting the comfortable library. "It seems you have landed in the cream pot, Vyse. But don't start making plans for that curricle of mine yet," he warned. "I thought things were too dull, so I spiced up the broth a bit."

"Yes—by announcing yourself as Lord Vyse," cried George, turning an irate face upon the viscount. "A dashed rum thing to do, and unsporting!"

Thorpe regarded him briefly, as one would a fly that had landed upon one's sleeve, and brushed him off just as casually. "Not at all. Vyse understands, don't you? Forgive me, I should become accustomed to calling you Mr. Vernon, or Rector, I suppose. By taking your real identity for myself, I have given myself an interesting handicap, you see, otherwise I could bankrupt your game at once by simply revealing who you are. But that I *would* find unsporting." An unpleasant grin stretched his mouth.

Quentin put on his most confident smile, although he was still far from sure what the best course of action would be. "I quite understand. And at this point my flock would be quite confused if you addressed me as Lord Vyse, since they accept me completely as Mr. Vernon. Why, I doubt anyone would believe such a tale! Lord Vyse is to them a distant, mysterious figure — or was till now. I regret the necessity of having them all think, even temporarily, that *you* are a local landowner. But I must also warn you that the village will not be totally surprised at hearing that Lord Vyse has at last deigned to visit Mickleford."

"What the devil are you talking about, Quentin?" asked Thorpe irritably. It was plain that his failure to disconcert his enemy had annoyed him.

"Why, only that you, *Lord Vyse,* have become, in absentia, suspected of being the friend and patron of the rector. I do hope," he continued, turning to George, "that Lord Vyse has brought us that silver baptismal font I was foolish enough to tell people my illustrious patron had promised us."

Quentin enjoyed the look on his enemy's face as he absorbed this news. He explained. "And so you see," he ended, "the village decided that my patron would soon arrive bearing this gift. I believe there are several children waiting to be christened by now."

The Reverend Mr. Thorpe looked shocked. "But I cannot believe that you would contemplate administering that sacrament to innocent babes. You, a mere . . ."

"Libertine?" Quentin assisted him politely. While the younger man spluttered, he said, "No I have only preached a few sermons. Though I doubt not I could

147

bless a babe as well as anyone." He went to a small side table where the brandy decanter resided and poured himself and George each a glass. "I see we shall have to put it about that the font is still at the silversmiths and will arrive later. The unnamed infants will simply have to wait." He sipped, and regarded the Thorpe brothers over the rim of his glass.

In truth, the idea of perpetrating fraudulent sacraments upon the innocent populace of Mickleford had troubled him, and Quentin knew himself to be fortunate in that no weddings were performed during Lent, and that so far none of the parishioners had required a burial service. Now it seemed he would shortly be relieved of at least one duty.

Thus he was not at all surprised to hear Lewis's protests at all the children left unchristened and in a few minutes the clergyman was making arrangements with George to have a silver font sent by wagon from Chester.

"At my brother's expense, of course," said the Reverend Mr. Thorpe, enduring a glare from his sibling.

"And with Lord Vyse's coat of arms engraved upon it, of course," Sir George suggested with a face innocent of any provocation. Quentin suppressed a smile at having so satisfactorily, if temporarily, routed his opponent.

"And *I* shall perform the christening," said the real clergyman.

"Nonsense," Quentin replied, enjoying his success in inducing Father Thorpe to do exactly as he had intended. "I won't hear of it. For it is one thing, we know, for a viscount's younger son to minister to the fashionable world," he said, "but quite another for you to lower yourself to dousing village-born brats, the children of no one of importance."

He was pleased to note that the younger Thorpe reddened. He had hoped that Lewis's loyalty to his profession would overcome his loyalty to his brother, and it seemed he was not to be disappointed.

"Nevertheless, Lord Vyse, I shall do so. And if the villagers ask why I am taking your place, you shall tell them that your . . . 'patron,' wishes it. We must make a point of seeing that these poor people are not too much inconvenienced by this game of yours and my brother's."

Thorpe scowled at him. "What you say in your prattling box is your own concern, but you have no call to queer my lay."

The reverend shuddered. "I had hoped, Geoffrey, that you would cease to use that dreadful slang by now. But no, I shall not, as a gentleman, interfere in a wager, nor need you fear any sermon from me. I know my duty to the head of the family," he said, a sanctimonious expression coming over his face.

Feeling that he had gotten the better of the episode and nothing more could be gained from encouraging discord between the brothers, Quentin rang for Mrs. Philpott to show the visitors to their rooms, and he and George retired to make plans. By nightfall they had decided that, with a bit of luck, Thorpe's posing as Lord Vyse would not be nearly as troublesome as the viscount had intended it to be.

149

The next morning Quentin took "Lord Vyse" and the Reverend Mr. Lewis Thorpe to call upon the village's principal family. He deliberately omitted all but the briefest description of the Sterlings, knowing that it was to his benefit to have his opponent kept continually off balance. That, he thought with glee, the spurious Lord Vyse would certainly be upon meeting that eccentric family unprepared.

To Quentin's delight, the squire's household seemed in fine form that day. After they had knocked for a long time, a distracted housemaid, laden with dirty dusters, let them in and promptly ran off in answer to a shout from the housekeeper. Upon entering, they spied two little boys noisily chasing a dog through the hall, with a toddling little girl stumbling and crying after them. A manservant hurried by, and from the morning room issued sounds of Miss Arabella Forbush's voice raised in not too skillful song, while from the breakfast parlor came the scolding tones of her mother, berating the maids.

While the stunned visitors were taking all this in, John Sterling crept into the hall from the door to the kitchen quarters, his dirty shirt wrinkled, his breeches stained with what looked like wine, obviously having been up all night and only just coming home. Still bleary-eyed, upon seeing the rector, Sir George, and the two strangers, he merely lifted a finger to his lips. "Shhh!" he said, and crept upstairs.

Lady Flora emerged a moment later from the squire's library, wrapped in shawls. "That demmed draft again! Where's my son John? He promised he would see to it." Not regarding them at all, she disappeared into the door from which her delinquent son had just entered. A moment later from the same door came Lady Sterling. Despite her discreetly draped gown she was obviously heavy with child. She murmured softly, "Oh, dear" and stopping short at the sight of the unannounced visitors.

The Reverend Mr. Thorpe looked puzzled, the viscount thunderstruck. He opened his mouth, but Quentin gave him a sharp warning look. He was not at all sure that Thorpe would remember his manners in the presence of a lady.

"Mr. Vernon! How do you come to be standing about here? Oh, I suppose the footman was not here to show you in. Lady Flora has him chasing about after a draft. I do beg your pardon, and yours too, Mr. Hollister," she said distractedly.

"May I present my friend and patron, Lord Vyse?" he asked with a smoothness that surprised him, considering how absurd he felt.

"Oh! Why, to be sure," she replied vaguely, looking up at the strangers with an unconsciously disarming wide-eyed gaze, reminiscent of Lily's.

Lily! Quentin's self-possession was briefly disrupted at the thought, but he gathered his wits about him and mechanically made introductions, while his mind worked at the seemingly insoluble problem of that disturbing young lady. He doubted that his actions at the willow-gathering would prevent her from complaining to Thorpe about him. What was so different about this girl, that at the first sign of trouble he could

151

not simply put her out of his mind, like all the others? Instead he had dug himself deeper into the intrigue, by giving into that irresistible impulse to hold her once more.

And now he must pay the price, for any suspicion that he was not behaving as a respectable bachelor clergyman might lead to forfeiting the wager, and worse, to revealing his identity to Lily before she was prepared to hear it. She was, he thought, no light-hearted London miss capable of enjoying a flirtation. And now she would be delighted that "Lord Vyse" had finally arrived.

Lady Sterling meanwhile appeared to accept these two strangers at face value, unperturbed, just as she was by most of the disorder that perpetually reigned in Sterling Hall.

The two unwanted visitors did Quentin credit in their polite greeting to the squire's lady, but he knew it was too early to feel relieved. Thorpe was out not only to make him lose, but probably to embarrass him in front of a village from which a good part of his income derived, and very likely the viscount had more tricks up his sleeve. Still, he felt as if he had the upper hand so far, as he was accepted by the family and knew their quirks, while Thorpe and Lewis did not.

Lady Sterling led them into the morning room, where Arabella, the two elder Sterling sisters, and Signore Marco were enjoying a musical interlude. Arabella had just finished playing and singing, and Signore Marco was voluble in his praise. *"Brava, bravissima,* Signorina Arabella! You English young ladies are so very accomplished." Olive was regarding her cousin sourly, and Arabella was beaming.

But at the entrance of the visitors, all attention turned away from the pianoforte. Quentin felt like wincing at the eagerness on all their faces when they saw that he was accompanied by two strangers. He only thanked his luck that Lily wasn't there as well. But no sooner had all the introductions been performed, than the door opened and in she came.

"Mama, I finally managed to get the children to go up to their lessons, and Nurse is taking Blossom out for an airing. I do wish that—" Seeing the visitors, she stopped. Quentin was interested to note, however, that after she had glanced briefly at them, her gaze seemed drawn to him. Before she could look away, he caught her eye.

He acknowledged her with a bow. "Miss Lily," he said, knowing that he might as well put a brave face on things and be the first to speak. If he pretended that he wasn't concerned by what she might say to "Lord Vyse," then perhaps she would lose confidence in the efficacy of that threat. "I would like to present to you my patron Lord Vyse, and the Reverend Mr. Thorpe."

Her eyes widened, but she greeted them demurely enough. Quentin, however, was not gulled. He knew too well the expression that was slowly replacing the polite smile on her face. She was calculating how she might discomfit him.

"Oh, do sit down, Lord Vyse, and tell me all about London," Olive said, breaking a slight, uncomfortable

153

silence. "We never hear any interesting news — even the papers are days old when we get them." Thorpe threw a swift, inscrutable glance at Quentin, and obligingly sat down next to Olive. But before he could speak, Signore Marco took the chair at his other side.

"I cannot believe this honor, my lord, to be introduced to a true English lord. It is more than I had hoped!"

Only Violet appeared relatively unmoved by the excitement of Lord Vyse's arrival. "Signore Marco," she explained to the puzzled Thorpe, "is a great traveler. He hopes to write a book of his adventures one day." George had immediately gone to her side and now shared a small sofa with her. To Quentin's amusement, he was looking rather protective, and glared whenever the signore or Thorpe attempted converse with Miss Sterling.

"I don't know what the signore will put in his chapter about Mickleford," Arabella said with a sigh. "Nothing of importance ever happens here."

Thorpe's attention was at once drawn to her, and evidently perceiving that she was one of the prettier females in the room, he at once abandoned the others and engaged her in light banter so successfully that soon she was laughing and flirting in quite a carefree fashion, as was apparent from the reproving glances directed at her by her cousins and her aunt.

Quentin knew that Thorpe, though ordinarily a brusque, heedless fellow, could make himself as agreeable as the most attentive cavalier when he wished. Soon Arabella's cheeks were very pink and she had apparently forgotten her recent distress at the inattentiveness of her betrothed. Would Lily, too, succumb to Thorpe's dedicated attentions? He must prevent any private conversation between them, not only because of what she might say to him, but because Thorpe had excellent instincts where the fairer sex was concerned, and he had probably already picked up the slight tension between Quentin and the younger Sterling daughter.

Indeed, pausing in his flirtation with Arabella, the supposed Lord Vyse gave Lily a discreet but searching inspection, then transferred his gaze thoughtfully to Quentin, who was chilled upon observing his enemy's ensuing satisfied smile. It would be just like the fellow to stir up a hornet's nest by trying to charm Lily himself. But there was little he could do about it now. It would only draw Thorpe's attention to the situation prematurely.

When Mrs. Forbush came in, had been introduced to the visitors, and had administered a disguised but firm rebuke to her errant daughter, the others took advantage of the pause to capture the attention of the man they thought was Lord Vyse.

Soon Olive and the signore, and even John who had heard the news and hurriedly made himself presentable, were engaged in a general and amusing conversation with his lordship, who had quickly overcome his surprise at the eccentric household and put himself out to conquer them.

Quentin was distressed at his enemy's success, but his hands were tied. All he could do was continue to

155

be the grateful clergyman proudly showing off his powerful patron. He noted with interest, however, that Lily was not part of the charmed circle around Thorpe. Instead she sat quietly sewing near her mother. When Lady Sterling was summoned by a servant to intervene in some argument between the cook and the dairy maid, Quentin casually took her vacated seat. Lily paid no attention, but kept her eyes on her sewing.

"Well, Miss Lily," he ventured, "you have your wish. Lord Vyse is here. I wonder that you do not immediately go to him and have me removed from my position."

"Oh, no," she replied, casting her eyes up just long enough for him to catch a glint of mischief in them, "I shall not do that. At least, not until the time is right."

One point to you, madam, thought Quentin. So she would keep him wondering. That might be all to the good. Perhaps he could prepare Thorpe in the meantime, tell him the girl had set her cap at him and was angry at being rebuffed. Immediately he was ashamed of the thought, though it would not have troubled him a couple of months ago, in the Town atmosphere of romantic intrigue and deception. And it was not so much because of any improvement in his moral standards, but because of Lily.

While the rector was thus preoccupied, he failed to notice that Violet and Aunt Hyacinth had taken the Reverend Mr. Thorpe aside and were subjecting him to a delicate interrogation about his connection with Mr. Vernon. Quentin, though only a few feet away, sat out of hearing and soon was distracted by Signore Marco, who to his obvious delight, had managed to corner both the rector and his illustrious patron. The bogus Lord Vyse and the spurious clergyman were attempting to satisfy his inquiries, each man watching the other's responses carefully, and endeavoring to trip one another up.

Lily, seated between the two groups and her attention claimed by no one in particular, soon realized that she was in an excellent position to hear both conversations, and very illuminating indeed did she find them.

Her aunt and her sister Violet seemed to be making Mr. Thorpe rather anxious with their very innocent questions. When Aunt Hyacinth said, "I suppose you and our dear Mr. Vernon were at school together," he took out a handkerchief and wiped his face. "Now where might that have been?" she continued.

Mr. Thorpe, who was some years junior to the real Lord Vyse and had not become acquainted with him until he came on the town, gulped. "Ah . . . Oxford, yes."

"Cambridge," Quentin was saying meanwhile with assurance to the Italian visitor, who had inquired about his education. He exchanged a glance with Thorpe, who was looking on in amusement. Quentin was delighted with himself and with how perfect he had become in the role of the well connected rector. "Kings College, in fact," he elaborated freely.

"Balliol," a nervous Mr. Thorpe was telling Violet and her aunt. "I, er . . . knew his brother . . .

157

introduced us."

Lily tried not to turn her head from side to side to follow these interesting and opposite revelations, lest she resemble someone following a game of battledore and shuttlecock, but strained her ears to hear both speakers.

"Mr. Thorpe is also an old friend of Lord Vyse. I met him at a dinner in our tutor's rooms, I believe," Mr. Vernon was meanwhile telling the signore.

Lily began to realize that there was something extremely odd going on, other than the contradictory responses. The Reverend Mr. Thorpe's nervousness communicated itself to her, and the inscrutable glances that were continually passing between Mr. Vernon and his patron drew her attention. Upon digesting the glaring inconsistencies revealed by the two conversations, her first impulse was to confront the rector, but instead she kept her counsel and listened. It was proving most interesting, if not altogether clear.

"Oh, yes." The Reverend Mr. Thorpe, relieved to find his lies taken as gospel, had allowed himself to expand upon his theme, undaunted by the increasingly skeptical scrutiny of Miss Sterling, and the surreptitious interest of Miss Lily Sterling. "Indeed, Mr. Vernon felt a calling from a very early age," he told the interested ladies.

"And were you marked for the church as quite a young man?" the signore was asking Quentin, who of course had not heard his youthful vocation already described.

"Good heavens, no," he felt no compunction in replying. "I was in need of a career, like most young men of no fortune, and my friend Mr. Thorpe recommended me to his friend Lord Vyse, who has very kindly, er . . . guided my rise to the pulpit." There was mischief in his blue eyes as he glanced at his patron.

The pretend Lord Vyse shot bowed slightly, acknowledging a hit. No one noticed, however, except Lily. So much, she thought wryly, for his tale of youthful excesses and his family's plans for him to take orders. What other things had he told her that were untrue?

Signore Marco was fascinated. "It is of great interest, your English system. Of course, in my country, the religious life is quite different for a man." The visitor smiled. "A priest may not have a wife and family. But you English clergy are like other men in that respect."

"Indeed," Lord Thorpe interjected with such energy that Quentin knew he had found a potential source of irritation and meant to use it. "I should like above all things to see Mr. Vernon well married. It would be a very good thing for the parish, you know," he said, assuming an expression of patriarchal concern.

Meanwhile, Hyacinth and Violet had got beyond the Reverend Mr. Thorpe's imaginative version of Quentin Vernon's early days, and were speculating on his future. Mr. Thorpe squirmed a bit under Mrs. Forbush's gimlet eye.

"The neighborhood has been wondering if the rectory will ever have a proper mistress," Aunt Hyacinth told him. "Do you think Mr. Vernon has any intention of marrying soon?" She shot an arch glance at Lily, who was trying to listen and avoid her aunt's observation at the same time.

"Oh, no . . . I mean," said poor Mr. Thorpe, perplexed as to what might be the safest reply. "I doubt it. You see, Mr. Vernon is . . . has, I mean he has suffered a heartbreak from which I doubt he will ever recover," he said deciding that he ought not to encourage a belief that the false rector might be looking for a bride.

"Indeed?" said Aunt Hyacinth, raising her brows. "Then that would explain it."

"Explain it?" asked a breathless Mr. Thorpe, wondering what he had said.

Nearby, Lily was nearly convulsed in amusement, but managed to contain herself and look down at her sewing.

"At first, you see," Violet explained to the sweating clergyman, "we found him a bit high-handed and cold, with a tendency to disrupt our little settled ways. Is that not so, Lily?"

Lily, fascinated but rather tired from listening to two conversations at once, gladly turned to her sister. If she knew Violet and her aunt, no stone would be left unturned to discover whatever they wanted to know about the rector. In fact, she was rather surprised that her sister had not taken advantage of Mr. Hollister's obvious interest in her to pry all the details of the rector's life out of him. It seemed she had managed to shake the curate off for a while, and he was politely attending Aunt Poppy, unaware that his

4 FREE BOOKS

TO GET YOUR 4 FREE BOOKS WORTH $18.00 — MAIL IN THE FREE BOOK CERTIFICATE T O D A Y

Fill in the Free Book Certificate below, and we'll send your FREE BOOKS to you as soon as we receive it.

If the certificate is missing below, write to: Zebra Home Subscription Service, Inc., P.O. Box 5214, 120 Brighton Road, Clifton, New Jersey 07015-5214.

FREE BOOK CERTIFICATE

4 FREE BOOKS

ZEBRA HOME SUBSCRIPTION SERVICE, INC.

YES! Please start my subscription to Zebra Historical Romances and send me my first 4 books absolutely FREE. I understand that each month I may preview four new Zebra Historical Romances free for 10 days. If I'm not satisfied with them, I may return the four books within 10 days and owe nothing. Otherwise, I will pay the low preferred subscriber's price of just $3.75 each; a total of $15.00, *a savings off the publisher's price of $3.00*. I may return any shipment and I may cancel this subscription at any time. There is no obligation to buy any shipment and there are no shipping, handling or other hidden charges. Regardless of what I decide, the four free books are mine to keep.

NAME

ADDRESS _____ APT

CITY _____ STATE ___ ZIP

TELEPHONE
(   )

SIGNATURE _____
(if under 18, parent or guardian must sign)

GET
FOUR
FREE
BOOKS
(AN $18.00 VALUE)

ZEBRA HOME SUBSCRIPTION
SERVICE, INC.
P.O. Box 5214
120 BRIGHTON ROAD
CLIFTON, NEW JERSEY 07015-5214

rector's life was being minutely examined behind his back.

"Indeed," Lily told the astonished Mr. Thorpe. "I am afraid we did not quite see eye to eye on a number of issues."

"But they seem to have reached a compromise," said Violet with a tiny smile.

"Not so much a compromise as a stalemate," Lily said.

Just then she heard the tag end of the conversation between the rector, his patron, and the signore.

"I had hoped," Lord Vyse was saying, "that your choice of a bride would soon fall upon one of the local young ladies. In fact, I had almost expected that you would announce a betrothal upon my arrival."

The signore seemed eager to hear Quentin's reply, but just then the other conversation was renewed and everyone could hear Mr. Thorpe, no doubt carried away with his success at confabulation, asserting loudly, "No, never. I fear Mr. Vernon has no intentions of ever marrying, and his patron, I know, prefers that he does not."

Lily saw Mr. Vernon's face grow red. She had never seen him acutely embarrassed before, and enjoyed the novelty for a moment. Of course she would get to the bottom of the mystery soon. For it had become apparent that the strangeness she had sensed about the rector was entangled with the arrival of his two guests. Was it that they did knew some truth about Quentin Vernon which they dared not reveal, or had he lied to them too?

Mr. Vernon quickly stood. "I—I thank you for your kind reception of us, ladies, but I fear we must no longer impose upon your time. And Mr. Hollister and I have preparations to make for the holy day."

The rector obviously felt that the call had gone on long enough. Lily noted that Lord Vyse looked just as disconcerted as Mr. Vernon did, and jumped up with an eagerness to leave that would have been rude if it had not been so funny. Only poor Mr. Thorpe still sat, looking confused at all the sudden activity, until Mr. Vernon took him by the elbow and hauled him up firmly. Lily glanced up at him, and he met her eyes briefly. His gaze was a bit rueful but it still held his usual innate confidence. Lily found that it lessened the satisfaction she had hoped to derive from his discomfiture.

Violet, though obviously as interested as the rest in the contradictory revelations regarding the rector, did not protest at the guests' sudden departure. When Mrs. Forbush seemed unwilling to let them go, obviously having more questions on the tip of her tongue, she shot her aunt a speaking glance that caused her to subside.

Lily, though for the moment satisfied to see them depart without attempting to clear up the contradictions that had come to light, could not resist taunting Mr. Vernon. When he took his leave of her, she whispered, "I wonder then, if I am to wish you joy, or to hope that your bachelorhood remains unbesieged, Mr. Vernon. I do hope your patron will make it clear in due time."

He smiled, to her surprise, and said, "I shall await his decision with anticipation, and be in haste to impart it to you, should you wish to be the first candidate in line."

She glared at his impeccably tailored back. Impudence! But just wait, Quentin Vernon, she vowed. You will not smirk so when I have had a little talk with your patron.

This, to her surprise, she found herself doing the very next day. She was in the stillroom, where she had been helping her grandmother to prepare the dyes for the eggs that the Sterling ladies would color for Easter. Already people were bringing eggs to be dyed, and there were baskets full of them in the cool rooms of the kitchen. Since Lady Sterling was busy about her own duties, and Poppy and Hyacinth were delivering new Easter clothes to the poor of the village, Lily, Violet, and Lady Flora were the chief workers in this operation. Olive, professing an extreme disinclination to having even her oldest gowns daubed with dye and her fingers stained, instead maintained a vigil in the drawing room. She wanted, she told her sisters, to keep an eye on Arabella, who had taken to driving out with the signore, and seemed intent on holding a monopoly on his company. "Of course the signore is too much of a gentleman to realize he is being used," said Olive with a sniff, "but the silly child is doing it merely to show Mr. Watson that she is not pining for his company."

Miss Forbush's delinquent betrothed had, in fact, come to call and been ignored in favor of the foreign

163

visitor. As for the signore, Lily thought him innocent of any deeper intent. It was simply natural, she thought as she stirred a kettle of deep red dye, that their Italian guest should flirt with a pretty young lady who seemed eager to do so.

"Hmmph!" Lady Flora said as she watched over her granddaughter's work and measured out dyes. "I told the fool girl to think of a way to get the fellow back, but never thought she'd stoop to setting her cap at a foreigner! Silly fellow in his ugly waistcoats; makes me queasy to look at him sometimes."

"Unfortunately," said Violet with a sigh, scooping up a pale yellow egg with a slotted ladle, and settling it in the bath of dye once more, "Olive also receives a good deal of attention from Signore Marco, and she is a lot more serious about it than is Arabella."

"Idiot girl," her grandmother said, "I won't have any foreigners in this house—not that he would be fool enough to offer for her."

"Perhaps he will, Grandmama," said Lily with a smile, "and carry her off to his estate in Italy. He once told us his uncle the count, whose heir he is, wishes him to marry."

"Pish!" replied that lady. "Don't know anything about that, and I don't hold with these foreign aristocrats. Counts as are common as dandelions on the Continent. Now mind you don't let that pot of green go to a boil, miss."

"Still, Olive is right about keeping watch over Arabella," said Violet as they worked, "even if it is mainly because she is jealous of the attention the signore pays

164

to her. The child is being too ridiculous over poor Mr. Watson's momentary lapse. She needn't say she is not at home to him, or refuse to reply to his notes."

"And I think she was much too forward with Lord Vyse," Lily said.

"Damme! To think that I missed Lord Vyse's call," said Lady Flora querulously. "I believe I saw him once, as a baby. Ugly, like all of them. Daresay he's improved now."

Violet and Lily exchanged amused glances over the steaming pots of dye. "Arabella seemed to think so," said the elder sister, "though I did not find him very handsome."

"Nor I," said Lily, "though he is very imposing, and I suppose that is just as good, for a man." In fact, comparing him to his protege, the rector, Lily had felt a sharp disappointment. She had expected his lordship to be something above the common run, not this thin, mean-mouthed man with a practiced but patently insincere charm. She had expected him to look more like . . . well, she admitted to herself, more like Mr. Vernon. The picture this thought called up, of his lean, graceful body and compelling blue eyes, suddenly disturbed her so that she stirred the pot of red dye too fast.

"Watch what you're about, Lily," scolded Lady Flora. "You are spilling it, and cochineal is expensive. Now as to this Vyse, I reckon he's not a proper landowner at all, never once setting foot on his property."

"But Grandmama, everyone knows that the Vyses have their principal seat elsewhere," said Violet pa-

165

tiently. "And their agent has always treated the tenants very fairly."

"And I have never heard you complain about him before," said Lily. "Why, I think you are simply annoyed because you haven't met him!" The swirling steam from the boiling kettles hovered in the open door of the stillroom, which led to the kitchen garden. Lily jumped when she heard a voice emerge from the cloud.

"I think we can remedy that situation immediately," it said, and in stepped Lord Vyse himself.

Lily felt a bit flustered, and she could see that even cool, calm Violet was also startled by this sudden entrance. Who could tell how long his lordship had been there, listening, perhaps?

But Lady Flora, true to her breeding, was unperturbed. "Is that you, my Lord Vyse? Well, do come in then. I'm sure you don't remember me — only a baby when we met."

"Ah, but madam, you underestimate the power of a charming glance like yours. Even as an infant I'm sure it made an impression on me," he said smoothly, bowing over her hand.

"Well! Very nice indeed, sir, but I'm an old woman, and such nonsense is beyond me." Nevertheless, she looked pleased, and inspected the unannounced caller minutely before asking, "What in heaven's name has brought you round to this entrance, my Lord Vyse? Is no one answering your knock at the front door? I suppose these lazy servants of ours —"

He held up a hand. "Please, Lady Flora, you are

unjust. I was greeted very promptly at the door by your footman, and when I asked to see the ladies he informed me that everyone but yourself and two of your granddaughters were unavailable. I'm afraid I insisted that I would prefer you not to interrupt your important occupation, and that I would simply make my own way here, to pay my respects."

"Hmmph! Very prettily said. I suppose you can stay if you like. As you see, we are dyeing the Easter eggs. I suppose you came to check on young Mr. Vernon's progress?"

Lily almost gasped at this blunt turn in the conversation, but Lord Vyse seemed more amused than surprised. "Indeed, ma'am. I was not sure when I presented him with the living if he would do for the parish, and of course it is my responsibility to see that he is carrying out his duties."

Lady Flora got up from the stool where she had been sitting and walked over to stir a kettle of blue dye. "Odd," she said casually, "you have not before this time seemed very concerned with your duty here in Mickleford. In fact, no one here even knew what you looked like."

Again, her directness did not seem to trouble him. "A fact of which I was more aware than you would think, ma'am," he replied with a smile. Lily was not at all sure she liked his smiles. They seemed to have nothing behind them, to be only a facade for a very different emotion.

"But I beg your indulgence and forgiveness. I intend to be more attentive in the future. I understand," he said, smoothly changing the subject, "that Miss Lily Sterling has had some dealings with Mr. Vernon on parish matters. If you could spare her for a few moments, ma'am, I would be most grateful."

Now was her chance, Lily thought, to tell him about Mr. Vernon's misbehavior. She glanced questioningly at her grandmother, who nodded. "Very well. Take off that stained apron, child, and show Lord Vyse the garden, while the weather holds. We shall carry on without you for a few minutes."

Lily obeyed, and led Lord Vyse outside and along the narrow paths of the kitchen garden to the shrubbery at the rear, where the privet was in leaf and the grass already lined the paths.

"I must confess to a little deception, my dear," said Lord Vyse, taking her hand and placing it upon his arm. "Of course, I am interested in Mr. Vernon's progress as rector, but since yesterday I find I have been regretting that you and I did not have the opportunity to become better acquainted."

Lily was rather startled by this confession, and was not sure she liked the feeling of being supported by his wiry, tense arm, or of having him smile so knowingly into her eyes when she glanced up at him. Then too, his professed regret at not having had the opportunity to speak to her the day before seemed blatantly false. It had been obvious that he was mainly interested in amusing himself with Arabella and in the flattering attention of the others to spare a thought for her.

But she remembered that this man could be very useful to her, and forced herself to respond pleasantly.

"How kind of you to say so, sir. Indeed, I was hoping to find an opportunity to have private speech with you. As you know, Mr. Vernon and I—"

But he interrupted, "Oh, but I daresay we shall have many opportunities to discuss Mr. Vernon. But right now a more pressing question concerns me. Has anyone ever told you that you have the most enchanting green eyes? Like a pixie—so sparkling, so mischievous, and yet so innocent." His smile told her that the mischief he was imagining was not particularly innocent.

Lily felt suddenly chilled, and her skin prickled. Obviously his lordship was more interested in beginning a flirtation with her than in hearing Mr. Vernon's sins. Judging by his current behavior, she had a very good idea that he might regard those sins as nothing of consequence. Still, she had to make the attempt.

"Again, you are most kind," she replied, putting as much firm detachment into her voice as she dared, "but I think you should know that for a long time the parish has been rather disturbed by Mr. Vernon's arrogant, high-handed disregard of our customs."

"Oh?" There was note of interest she did not expect in his voice, considering that he had been foiled in his flirtation. "How so?"

"Why, since he arrived he has been preaching hellfire at us, and has been determined to deprive us of our traditional celebrations. Why, I had to stoop to setting up a rival Easter pageant because he would not have it at the church, saying it was too secular."

"Did he indeed?" Lord Vyse seemed unaccountably

amused. "Do tell me more of this strict churchman. I confess I had no idea of his severity when I offered him the living."

Lily gladly launched into a litany of complaint against Mr. Vernon, including his having paid some of the village inebriates to fill the church pews, and his disregard for the sanctities of village life and tradition.

"What you tell me, my dear girl, is most distressing, of course," said Lord Vyse. He stopped and tipped up her chin so she was looking directly into his eyes. "Yet I sense that there is something else, something that perhaps you are a bit hesitant to tell me?"

Lily had a tight, breathless feeling in her chest, somewhat akin to the feeling that her recent interlude with Mr. Vernon had given her, but with an unpleasant edge of anxiety to it. Lord Vyse's brown eyes held no warmth.

She thought of Mr. Vernon's blue ones. Could blue eyes be said to be warmer than brown? She had never thought so till now. And there was again that superficial quality to his lordship's smile. Mr. Vernon's expressions, though sometimes infuriating, had never seemed anything but genuine to her. Could she trust this man? Would he take her confession—for after all, she had for a time willingly participated in the shameful act—as a hint that she was ripe for dalliance? She made a sudden decision.

She removed herself from his grasp and replied, "No, Lord Vyse, I do not think there is. I simply wish you would have a word with Mr. Vernon, perhaps persuade him to go more gently in imposing his will on the people here, and to respect our traditions." She tried to will herself to believe that indeed, there had been nothing else troubling her about Mr. Vernon, pretending that the episode had been imaginary.

Apparently Lord Vyse took her direct glance for proof of honesty, for he shrugged. "I will have a word with him. For you, my dear." Again that insincere smile, but now that she had determined that she would not put her trust in him, it bothered Lily not a whit.

"Thank you, sir." Knowing that she should be grateful to have escaped his attentions, she still dared to question him, for her curiosity would not be denied. "I wonder, Lord Vyse, if you will able to explain something that puzzles me? How is it that yesterday I heard such very different tales of Mr. Vernon? Of course, I have no right to interrogate you, but—"

"Correct, my dear, no right at all," he said, his cordiality unimpaired. "But do not trouble yourself. It was all a little joke, my dear, among gentlemen."

Disconcerted and not at all pleased at this dismissal, Lily knew the wise course would be to desist. But there were other ways to find out, one of them to confront Mr. Vernon himself, and though she was loath to put herself in that dangerous situation of being tête-à tête with him again, she had an idea that he would give her a more honest answer than would Lord Vyse. "I must return," she said. "Lady Flora will be very displeased with me if I am away much longer."

He did not attempt further intimacies, but to Lily his expression appeared to say that he was willing

171

to bide his time.

The conversation had confused her more than enlightened her. As hypocritical and wicked as she had sometimes thought Mr. Vernon, she had never felt the kind of distaste in his company that Lord Vyse inspired. In fact, the two men seemed unlikely friends. As she led him back to the house, she tried to induce him to discuss his connection with Mr. Vernon, and so to clear up indirectly the mysteries revealed by those simultaneous conversations of the day before, but Lord Vyse was evasive and markedly reticent on this point. Before she knew it they were back at the stillroom, where she took leave of him with more relief than she would have expected.

It was odd that her report on Mr. Vernon's conduct as rector had not seemed to interest him to the degree it should. It was but one more beam of light in a seemingly impenetrable fog.

Lily felt at a complete standstill, and was glad when Lady Flora recognized her growing distraction, after she had splashed red dye on herself by dropping two eggs carelessly into the pot, and told her, "You're of no use here, girl. Best go out for a walk. I don't know what that Lord Vyse said to you, but you needn't let it turn your head as if he's the prince you've been waiting for. He'll look higher than you when it comes time to take a bride, mark my words."

"Oh, but I could never think of Lord Vyse that way, Grandmama!" Lily said immediately.

The matriarch vouchsafed a thoughtful look at her abstracted, dye-stained granddaughter. "I won't say

I'm not happy to hear it, child. His sort's not for you. And no matter what his excuse, these absentee landlords do the country no good. Mind, young lady, if you would stop daydreaming you might notice that there is someone else about who has been discreetly making calf eyes at you for some time. Now, off with you!"

And Lily went, wondering. Was her grandmother merely pointing out yet another local admirer whom she had held at arms length? Or could she possibly mean . . . No, Lily decided. It was too absurd. Mr. Vernon, despite the warmth of his illicit embraces, the memory of which made her hug herself, trembling, was incapable of making calf eyes at anyone. Let alone, she told herself, the girl who had caused him nothing but trouble since his arrival.

Her walk brought her little refreshment and no clearness of thought. Suddenly her elaborate plan to inform on the rector had all crumbled to nothing. Nothing, it seemed, was as she had imagined it to be. Not Quentin Vernon, not Lord Vyse, and not her own feelings, which seemed to have run away on a course of their own, pulling her along only half-unwillingly.

Chapter Eight

At breakfast Lily found her Aunt Hyacinth and Cousin Arabella quarrelling bitterly over their toast and jam. It seemed that yet another missive from the neglectful Mr. Watson had arrived, this one containing an invitation to the ladies of the family and their houseguest to join an expedition of pleasure on the morrow. They would explore the nearby ruins of an ancient abbey, with refreshments and transport provided by Mr. Watson.

"I have taken the liberty of replying that *all* of the young ladies would be delighted to attend," Mrs. Forbush announced, fixing a stern gaze upon her daughter.

"How could you have accepted without consulting me!" cried Arabella, reddening. "I do not care to spend the day in Mr. Watson's company after the way he has neglected me."

But Mrs. Forbush seemed to feel that she and her daughter had indulged their offended feelings long enough and that salvaged pride would not make up for an opportunity lost. She folded her arms in a deter-

174

mined fashion. "You are still betrothed to Mr. Watson and I will not hear of you continuing to treat him so shabbily. It is only your silly fancies that cause you to carry on this way. Besides," she added, ignoring her daughter's continuing protests, "I will not have you spoiling the best match you are likely to make! Lord Vyse may flirt, but he will look higher than you for a bride."

All of Arabella's weeping and accusations of unnatural cruelty could not move her adamant parent. Lily, perceiving that she would not enjoy a peaceful breakfast until she had done what she could to reconcile the two, asked to see the note. Her eyebrows rose when she read that the party from the rectory had also been invited to join them. Although she had seen the ruins many times, she owned that it would not displease her to make one of the company and perhaps learn more about the intriguing Mr. Vernon and his guests.

"Come now, dear Belle," she consoled her cousin, "Mr. Watson writes very prettily about wishing to make up for his neglect by providing you with a day of pleasure. And the countryside is so lovely just now." To this Arabella's only reply was a sniff, so she leaned closer and whispered, "You know how many secluded little corners there are in those ruins. I imagine he means to spirit you away so he can have you all to himself for a bit, to show you that his feelings have not changed. Do give him a chance to apologize," she urged.

Aware that her mother had not heard this last bit of

advice, Arabella mopped her tears, somewhat mollified. She whispered back, "And he does say he has invited the signore, as well as Lord Vyse. I suppose you may be right."

While Lily hoped that her cousin did not harbor any ideas of conducting a triple flirtation in the romantic crannies of the ruin, Arabella informed her mama that she would attend the outing. "But this is his last chance to prove his affection," she said with a dramatic air. "I shall not be taken for granted!" With that she swept out of the breakfast parlor.

"Well! I don't know what you said to the foolish girl, but I am grateful to you, my dear."

Lily brushed aside her aunt's thanks. "Oh, she would have gone in the end. I think she simply enjoys a scene now and then."

"Still, I will not have her jeopardize her betrothal," Mrs. Forbush said anxiously. "Mr. Watson was neglectful, to be sure, but I believe he meant no offense."

"Don't worry, Aunt Hyacinth, I shall watch over Arabella tomorrow. I won't let her become carried away with herself. And I'm sure Mr. Watson will be very attentive."

That settled, Lily was left to a quiet breakfast. As she ate she wondered if Lord Vyse would accept Mr. Watson's invitation, and if he would try to continue his flirtation with her, as well as with her cousin. How would Mr. Vernon react to it? Not, she assured herself, that there was any reason he could object, especially when he was beholden to his lordship for his living. But she remembered the uncomfortable feel-

176

ings engendered by Lord Vyse's attentions, and on the whole decided that even to pique Mr. Vernon, she could not be party to such a distasteful flirtation.

They set out early the next morning in carriages provided by Mr. Watson. He and Arabella, the signore and Olive were to ride in the first, a large open carriage with vis-à-vis seating, gaily painted in bright blue with red wheels. Mr. Watson, who had bought it to impress his recalcitrant betrothed, invited Lily to join them, and she was torn for a moment. She had rather hoped to ride to the abbey with Mr. Vernon, Mr. Hollister, Mr. Thorpe, and Violet in another large open carriage that their host had hired, but as she turned her head to decline the invitation, she saw Arabella bend toward the signore, giggling, after Lord Vyse had gallantly handed her up. It seemed he had hired a horse and was intending to ride alongside the carriage.

This decided her. Arabella was a little fool who needed looking after, and Lily temporarily relinquished the opportunity to plague Mr. Vernon in order to do her duty to her cousin.

Behind Mr. Watson's carriage and the one that held the rector were two other carriages filled with some young neighbors, and a few gentlemen mounted on horseback prepared to accompany them, making a large, lively party. As Lord Vyse handed Lily up into her seat, his heavy-lidded gaze lingering on her uncomfortably, she glanced across the drive at the rector. To her great interest, he was staring intently at the little tableau they all made. It appeared he did not

177

notice her looking at him, for his eyes were mainly fixed on his patron, and Lily was amazed at the hostility she saw in his expression. Suddenly his gaze shifted and their eyes met. Lily merely nodded, but the rector gave her a quizzical smile and bowed in his seat. She vowed that once at the abbey he would not escape her questions.

The merrymakers were in high spirits, their excited talk and occasional shouts of laughter drifting by as they jogged along the road to the abbey ruins. Lily enjoyed the scene as they passed through the deep woods that began on the outskirts of the village and ended some miles later, skirting a sparkling little mere, where ducks flapped at their passage. Their carriage was quieter than the others, but Arabella was very gay, and divided her attention neatly between the signore and Lord Vyse, who stayed alongside the carriage whenever the road permitted, to Mr. Watson's patent dismay.

Lily tried to circumvent her cousin's determined flirting whenever she could, but Arabella would not be prevented from having her revenge on Mr. Watson, so all Lily could do was engage the glowering host and her indignant sister Olive in distracting conversation.

"You could not have chosen a more perfect day for this outing, Mr. Watson," she said, as Arabella tittered at one of Lord Vyse's sallies.

Mr. Watson acknowledged her with a rather forced smile, his mind still obviously on the misbehavior of his betrothed. "Indeed, but I fear that when it is so unseasonably warm it may lead to rain. I hope I did not judge ill in using open carriages." A frown of concern creased his brow as he gazed aloft.

It was still mid-morning, but already the day promised to be as warm as June. The sun had had sole possession of the sky when they started out, but by the time they neared the road that led to the abbey ruins, it was skirmishing with some large, grayish clouds.

Lily reassured him. "Oh, I do not think it will rain so soon. We shall have plenty of time to see the ruins and be on our way back before a drop falls, and if we should get caught, I promise you we are not so tender as to cry at the thought of a little wetting!"

Her host frowned and put a protective hand on his fiancée's arm. "I should not wish you to take cold, my dear," he said in an intimate tone designed to reestablish his proprietary rights to Arabella. "I would never forgive myself if you were to become ill."

Arabella tossed her head. "I never take cold. And I wouldn't mind at all if it were to rain. Why, perhaps we would be stranded at the ruins. Would it not be exciting?"

The signore, his dark eyes flashing, was full of delight. "I daresay, Signorina Forbush, that it would be a great adventure."

Olive saw an opportunity and joined in. "Oh, indeed! Why, what if some of us were to become lost in the old cellars?"

Lily watched with wry amusement as Arabella slowly drew her lashes down in a languishing but impartial glance at Lord Vyse and the signore. "Why, I should hope that I would be trapped with a strong and clever gentleman who would be able to take care of me."

Olive, obviously disgusted at her young cousin's unfair tactics, folded her arms across her chest and said bluntly, "Yes, and a sight you should look, Belle, with bats in your hair and spiders crawling up your gown and dirt all over."

At this Arabella squealed charmingly and all three gentlemen hastened to assure her that neither bats nor spiders should prevent them from rescuing her. Finally becoming aware of Olive's chilliness, the signore added, "And of course, my dear Signorina Olivia, I should hope that you would rely on me to protect you from such hazards."

Olive merely sniffed, but Lily gave the signore an encouraging smile and he spent the remainder of the ride engaged in trying to regain Olive's favor. Mr. Watson, meanwhile, had brightened because they had turned off onto a narrow lane leading to the ruin and Lord Vyse had perforce to ride behind. He, too, put the time to good use, and by the time they had pulled up near the old abbey everyone but Lily was in a tolerably cheerful frame of mind. The last thing she wanted to do was to remain with the estranged lovers but she felt it her duty to do so, especially as Lord Vyse wasted no time in seeking out Arabella as she descended, while her betrothed was busy conferring with his coachmen.

Olive had the signore firmly in hand and bore him away to a cluster of tumbledown stones which she declared to be excessively romantic. His lordship had just offered his arm to Arabella and was about to whisk her off, but Lily managed by some artful observations on the scene, and advice as to the most picturesque views to keep them from going until poor Mr. Watson had had a chance to reclaim his beloved. He did this with such alacrity that Arabella had time only for a rueful smile at Lord Vyse before she was carried off on her triumphant lover's arm.

To Lily's dismay, this left her at his lordship's mercy, and the thought of having to fend off his advances in the shade of the ruins appealed to her no more than being trapped in a cellar with bats and spiders. As she had feared he would, his lordship drew her hand through his arm and began to walk her away from the others.

"Well, my dear," he said, his satisfied smile increasing her discomfort, "I trust that you and I will find ample ways to amuse ourselves here. I would ask you to take pity on the ignorant visitor and point out the beauties of the spot, but I think I might prefer reflecting on some beauty of more recent vintage, and nearer at hand," he went on, pressing her hand and staring at her in a way that made her face feel hot.

Lily was momentarily unable to reply. No one had ever flirted quite so directly with her—except perhaps Mr. Vernon. As if the thought had summoned him, he appeared at her side. His expression and posture were deferential, as befitted a man in the presence of his patron, but his eyes seemed wary.

"Ah, I see you have forgotten your promise to instruct me in the history of this ruin, Miss Sterling," he said with a hint of warning.

Lily was confused. Did he mean by his lie to caution her against Lord Vyse, or did he simply want to spoil what he thought was a much-desired encounter? For a moment she was tempted to refute him and say plainly that they she had made no such promise, but the feel of Lord Vyse's suddenly increased pressure on her hand and what she told herself was her need to question Mr. Vernon more closely won out over her impulse to flout his wishes.

She gave Lord Vyse an apologetic smile. "Mr. Vernon has shamed me. I confess I had forgotten our previous engagement. I beg your indulgence, sir. I daresay the long ride shook the memory clear out of my head."

She could almost swear that it was relief that briefly crossed his features. "I do hope that you will not allow Mr. Watson to hear that. It would not do to let him think his carriages are not well sprung, rough though these country roads can be."

So smoothly that Lily could not have told anyone how it was done, she found herself transferred from Lord Vyse's arm to Mr. Vernon's. Could it be that in spite of all the trouble she had tried to make for the rector, he would risk displeasing his patron simply to keep her from being troubled by an unwanted flirtation? Perhaps, she reminded herself, he simply wanted to prevent her from complaining about him.

For a moment Lord Vyse's brow looked like a thundercloud. Then he suddenly smiled again, and nodded significantly at Mr. Vernon, as if acknowledging temporary defeat. Lily could not interpret the look that passed between them.

"I see that I have unwittingly trespassed. Do forgive me." He glanced about, and suddenly his gaze fastened on something that appeared to interest him very much. "Ah, I see that Miss Forbush has been abandoned for the moment." He waved.

Lily's heart fell as she saw Arabella wave back. She was momentarily alone while Mr. Watson was busy answering the questions of some of his other guests.

"I shall rescue her from her ennui," said Lord Vyse. "No doubt we can find an interesting cranny in which to lose ourselves until Mr. Watson is at leisure to escort her." And with that he strode off, leaving Lily sorry that she had decided to play along with Mr. Vernon's deception.

She was even more so when he said, "I apologize for interrupting your tête-à-tête with Lord Vyse, Miss Sterling, but in spite of your charms and your undoubted local celebrity as one of squire's daughters, that really would be looking too high. Besides, he only means to amuse himself."

"Oh!" Lily cried, infuriated. "And to think I believed you might be interrupting out of concern for me! It is my own fault for being so stupid." Sudden tears sprang to her eyes and she turned to walk away, but he put an unexpectedly gentle hand on her shoulder, and it stopped her where a more violent restraint would merely have induced her to struggle. She turned, but would not look at him.

"I am sorry," he said softly. "That was unworthy of

me. But I thought that you were enjoying my . . . patron's attentions, and knew that it could not lead to anything."

"Hmmph!" was her only reply, but she did look up, her eyes more eloquent than anything she could have said.

"Either that or you were planning to tell him all about my dreadful performance as rector, and how much trouble I have brought to the parish." His grin was like that of a mischievous schoolboy, begging her to share the joke.

Lily hesitated. When he looked at her in that way, she could not stay angry. Besides, she thought, it would be wise to stay on civil terms, so that she could gently interrogate him about the inconsistencies in the stories she had overheard. If she was careful, he might not even know what she was doing until it was too late.

"Strangely enough, though that had been my intention once, I soon saw that he was not much interested in most of what I had to say about you," Lily replied candidly, not objecting to the offer of the rector's arm.

They strolled by mutual agreement to the main part of the ruined structure, the shell of a bell tower. It was possible to go inside the arched doorway and stare up at the sky, for the stairs had long since fallen, the bell had long since been melted down, and the works rotted away. Their voices echoed against the cool stone.

"I must own that I was surprised to see you join the party today, Mr. Vernon."

"Indeed? I hope you are not one who believes that

184

my calling exiles me from all frivolity, Miss Lily." His mouth was very serious, but his eyes betrayed his amusement.

"Certainly not, sir. Indeed, the parish likes to see its rector joining in the ordinary amusements of other people."

"Is this another attempt to criticize my plans for the Easter celebration?"

"Not at all," Lily hurried to say. She wanted to keep him in this easy, jocular mood. "You are of course entitled to your own opinions."

He looked at her a trifle suspiciously, she thought. She hastened to press past the awkward moment so that she could get to what she really wanted to ask him. "In fact, I think I might have been too hasty in condemning your actions."

"Oh, you do, do you?"

"Why, yes. After all, you were no doubt only doing what you thought best for the parish."

By the incredulous look on his face she saw that in her eagerness she had gone too far. He led her out of the tower. The sky was cloudier than it had been, and a cool breeze had picked up. "Now to what do I owe this sudden excess of courtesy?" he demanded. "The last I heard you were about to denounce me to my patron, and now your attitude verges on the border of flattery!"

Feeling a bit foolish, Lily gave up the pretense. "Well, I thought I would try a different tactic. You must admit, it was refreshing not to be at daggers drawn for a change."

185

He laughed and she could see he wasn't really annoyed with her. Perhaps it was best that she simply be direct. "I want to know why you told me such a ridiculous story about yourself that day, when Grandmama asked you to speak to me about Mr. Smythe's proposal."

By his blank look she knew he had already forgotten it. Another mark against him. "And why," she went on, pressing her advantage, "you told the signore such a different tale of your history from the one your friend the Reverend Mr. Thorpe told my sister and aunt."

He had been leading her away from some of the other merrymakers over to where a sheltered nook was formed by the corner of an old stone outbuilding. A tree grown up since the destruction of the abbey now shaded it. He paused and frowned. "Why don't you ask my respected patron?"

Lily laughed. "That was the first thing I did. He said it was all in fun, a joke between gentlemen. But anyone who is not a fool could see that it was no such thing."

"And anyone can see that you are no fool," he replied, in such a way that Lily could not tell whether or not he were serious. "Why not sit down?" he suggested, indicating a flat, smooth stone that made an attractive seat. Lily sat, hoping that she would at last receive the answer to her question. But all he said as he sat beside her was, "As I am a first-time visitor, you must first give me leave to properly admire the view."

From their position they could see the entire site of

186

the ruin. It was most picturesque, with wildflowers and vines twining about the ruined walls, and the gaily dressed young ladies and their escorts wandering about, some sitting, as Lily and the rector had done, on the fallen stones or remnants of a wall.

Lily saw Arabella go by on the arm of Lord Vyse, saw Mr. Thorpe try ineffectually to distract his lordship. Arabella's laugh trilled, and Lord Vyse smiled down at her, while the London clergyman looked almost as worried as Lily felt. She was tempted to leave the rector and try to detach her cousin from Lord Vyse, but she was too close to finding out what she wanted to know. Besides, this was one of the few times that she had begun to feel comfortable with Quentin Vernon.

With relief she saw Mr. Thorpe speak to Mr. Watson, who immediately went in hot pursuit of his betrothed. To Lily's momentary distress, Arabella was suddenly no longer in sight. Where could the silly girl have gone with Lord Vyse? But she told herself she could safely leave it to Mr. Watson.

She turned again to her companion, and found that he had been watching her. "Well?" she reminded him, as he had not yet answered her question.

"I think you had better be satisfied with the reply you received from Lord Vyse," he said. His face wore an uncharacteristically stubborn expression.

"I will not be satisfied with that! There is undoubtedly an explanation and I would like to have it."

He turned to her and said, "I must remind you, Miss Sterling, that I do not owe you any explanations.

187

I apologize if my previous conduct has caused you distress, and I can assure you that—"

"Oh, you are infuriating!" she cried, quite disgusted with his evasions and with herself for having believed she could get him to tell her the truth. "I do not want your assurances. I only want—"

But a muffled scream interrupted. The other members of the party were hurrying towards the sounds, and Lily saw that they were gathering about a crumbling stone stairway leading to the cellars. It took no more than a moment for her to note that Arabella was not in sight. She rose, ignoring Quentin Vernon beside her, and ran to the others.

"What has happened?" she cried, as Violet and Mr. Hollister joined her, their breath short from running.

Mr. Watson, white-faced, said, "I believe that Lord Vyse and poor Arabella have become trapped in one of the old cellars."

Mr. Thorpe, as red as Mr. Watson was pale, said, "We were looking for Miss Forbush, and then we heard a crash like a great fall of stones. I only pray that they were not injured!"

Removing his stylishly tailored jacket and rolling up his sleeves, Mr. Watson said, "I'm going down there to see what has happened. If necessary, I shall move every stone with my bare hands!"

Lily only wished her silly cousin could see the determination on her fiancé's face. Foolish girl! Mr. Watson loved her better than she knew.

Mr. Vernon pushed through the crowd to their host's side. "Come, I shall assist you."

188

They began to wave the others away, and at that moment the sky, which had steadily been growing darker, began to drop its burden of rain. In the confusion, Lily, who could no longer bear to remain inactive, made her way to the stair.

"Arabella!" she shouted down into the dark. "Are you all right? Can you hear me?"

But there was no reply.

Some of the ladies began very inconveniently to succumb to the vapors, one or two even fainting dead away. The men therefore urged all of the fairer sex away from the distressing scene. There was little they could do for shelter, as their carriages were open and only one had a roof that could be put up, and this would take a little time.

Lily did not wish to leave, but Mr. Vernon, as he guarded the steps, somehow forbidding even in his wet clothes and with locks of hair falling into his eyes, wore an expression that told her he did not wish to be trifled with. She bit her lip, and went away to see to it that Violet was calm and well taken care of by Mr. Hollister, and then to help the signore support Olive's nerves.

But she came back to see what progress had been made. Mr. Watson and Mr. Vernon had gingerly descended what was left of the stairway, and had discovered why there had been no answer to their cries. The opening leading into the cellar was clear, but, the men reported, it was empty.

"However, there is indication that there was a gap leading farther into the cellars, and after they went

189

through it there was a collapse of the ceiling. You see, here," the rector said, his face very grim, indicating a patch of earth that had been rather moist even before the rain came, "the ground is very sunken and damp, and that must have weakened it. I fear there is a thick wall of rubble, if we cannot even hear them nor they us."

Lily saw that she could do no good there, so she walked away in the rain, racking her brain furiously. She had often clambered over these ruins. It had been a favorite picnic site when she was a child, and her father had sometimes taken the family there on a fine day to explore. He had always cautioned them, however, about the danger of the cellars, fearing just such an occurrence as had happened.

The gentlemen, meanwhile, with the help of some of the servants, were attempting to dig away at the barrier separating Arabella and Lord Vyse from them. But whenever Lily checked on their progress, her fear for her cousin's safety grew, as there was never any reply to the shouts of the men. After a while they stopped shouting, as they were afraid they would bring the rest of the ceiling down.

Lily wandered away from the others, unable to sit still, unwilling, despite the continuing rain, to stuff herself into the one sheltered carriage to be commiserated with by the other ladies, and unable to bear the sight of Mr. Watson's tense, wet, and dirt-streaked face. If only she had kept near her cousin, instead of going off to taunt Mr. Vernon! She knew it was not only to question him that she had accepted his ruse to get her away from Lord Vyse. In spite of everything, she seemed unable to resist the prospect of his company.

In her restless pacing, ignoring the rain that soaked her clothes and was ruining her bonnet, Lily passed yet another cellar entrance. She brushed a wet lock of hair out of her eyes. Of course! Why had no one thought of it before? The cellars, she was sure her father had told her, were linked by a series of corridors or tunnels. Perhaps this entrance would lead to the trapped Arabella and Lord Vyse. At least, if she were on their side of the cave-in, she could call to them and perhaps they would hear her.

Without farther thought she descended the steps, which were in much better condition than the others. Despite spider webs and a great deal of dirt, once her eyes adjusted to the darkness she could see that the tunnel was clear for quite a way. Reluctant to go in and wishing she had thought of providing herself with a light, she called her cousin's name once more, then again, louder. To her delight she was rewarded with a faint sound. She called again, and this time the reply came twice, one voice high and one lower-pitched, but very far away.

She gulped and peered, her imagination filling the dark void before her with bats and rats, and was about to begin feeling her way towards the voices in the pitch black of the tunnel, when suddenly something came down on her shoulder. She gasped and whirled around, to find Quentin Vernon beside her. She must have been so absorbed in peering into the blackness that she hadn't heard him come down to the cellar.

"What do you think you are doing, Lily?" he demanded. "Are you quite mad?"

She shook off his hand impatiently. "They are all right, listen!" and she called again. This time the voices sounded weaker. Did that mean they were hurt, or that they were inadvertently walking away from her?

There were were scratching noises and after a few moments sparks. Suddenly light flared up. "I borrowed a flint from one of the coachmen, and made a sort of torch," he said, holding up a flaring branch. "I am going to them."

"I will come with you," Lily said, following, but he put out a hand to stop her.

"You will do no such thing. Go back up with the others. It is far too dangerous."

"You cannot prevent me," she cried. "Arabella is my cousin and it is my fault."

"Nonsense. How can it be your fault?"

"I should have done my duty by her and made sure she did not go off with Lord Vyse. Instead I only thought of my own wishes and went with you."

In the uneven light of the torch she could not decipher his expression very well, but she sensed his puzzlement. Suddenly she realized what she had said, and waited for him to question her about her newly admitted desire for his company, but all he said was, "Very well, come along, but be very careful how you go."

The rector's torch casting a reddish glow on the dank stone walls about them, they proceeded cautiously, calling now and then, heartened by the sound of the replies that once more seemed to be getting closer.

Alone in the cool dank cellar with the handsome, mysterious Mr. Vernon—why, she could not have dreamed a more romantic scenario, Lily reflected during their slow progress. But there was little to rhapsodize over in this adventure. He helped her over debris and rough stones, but then quickly dropped his hand from her arm. Once when a big piece of rock fell, he pressed Lily back against the wall with his body, and just for a moment she felt a bit faint at the closeness of him.

"Are you hurt?" he asked, none too tenderly, his features looking almost wild in the flaring of the torch.

"N-no," she whispered. The flame flickered in his eyes. His gaze traveled over her. They were closer now than they had been since he had first taken advantage of her confusion, and she wondered if he would steal another kiss. But they heard Arabella's voice, nearer this time, and the moment was lost. They pressed on.

The corridor narrowed, blocked with rubble. Quentin swore, to Lily's surprise, frustrated that he could go no farther, although the voices of Arabella and Lord Vyse were ever closer.

"Give me the torch," said Lily. "I can fit where you cannot."

"I can't allow it. It may not be safe."

"I have no choice."

"But—"

Surprised at her own temerity, Lily put a finger

across his lips, and took the torch from his hand. He did not resist, only caught her hand and pressed it closer to his lips. "You are very brave and very foolish."

Lily suddenly felt amazingly cheerful, although she chastised herself. Sweet words from a man who had yet to tell her the truth about himself, she thought, meant little. Quickly, before her nerve failed her, she passed through the narrow opening. She cringed as she heard the sound of stone crumbling behind her, but the ceiling held. To her relief and joy, just a dozen more steps found her face to face with Arabella. She threw herself into Lily's arms, tears streaming down her face. "Oh, it was dreadful!"

"Come, my dear," came the voice of Lord Vyse, "It was not nearly so bad. I did my poor best to while away the time till our rescue. And you see, there were no bats after all, though I did rescue you from one or two small spiders."

Arabella gave him a weak smile, and clung to Lily.

Lily could see Lord Vyse now, and he shrugged, a sardonic smile on his face. He seemed hardly rumpled by his ordeal, and indeed, Arabella too looked well, although distraught.

"I am so glad you were not hurt. Come, Mr. Vernon and I have found another way out."

She led them out the way she had come. She had forgotten about the narrow passage, but by the time they reached it Quentin had carefully widened it and Lord Vyse, being thinner than the rector, was able to squeeze through, albeit with much damage to his attire, which seemed to leave him more discomposed than his entire ordeal. But within minutes all of them were safely above ground, and surrounded by their joyful friends. It had stopped raining, and the ladies had left their crowded shelter to welcome the lost ones back.

Mr. Watson looked after Arabella tenderly, Lily and the rector were much fussed over, and Lord Vyse subtly let it be known that in going down into the cellars he had merely bowed to a lady's wishes and to her presumed greater knowledge of the site. Arabella had the grace to look ashamed as he said this, and Lily had no doubt that it was at least partly true, but in her mind he was not entirely absolved of wrongdoing in the affair. She was certain that he had had no qualms about getting Arabella alone in close quarters, out of hearing of the others, to press his attentions on her.

The coachmen and grooms were busily drying off the seats of the carriages, and Mr. Watson announced that everyone had done enough exploring, to which no one took exception. They would now drive to a nearby inn where he had bespoken a meal for them all. His voice was tense, and glad though he appeared to have his Arabella back safe with him, the glances he shot towards Lord Vyse were most unpleasant. Obviously he shared Lily's opinion, but she hoped that the young man would not attempt to engage Lord Vyse in argument about what he had been doing with his betrothed in the cellars. Lily was sure poor Mr. Watson would come off the loser.

She said as much to Mr. Vernon on the way to the inn. To her surprise, she found herself seated beside him in the carriage, sitting opposite Violet, Mr. Hollister, and Mr. Thorpe. She scarcely remembered the rector leading her to the carriage.

"I do not doubt it," was his reply. "I fear my respected patron is somewhat careless of other men's rights to a lady's company."

This and the strange expression on Mr. Thorpe's face gave Lily pause. Did the tension between Lord Vyse and the rector have something to do with a woman? That two men of such disparate stations should quarrel over the same lady did not seem likely, but of course, she reflected, such things no doubt happened out in the world. Lily was beginning to feel very ignorant, when all these years her knowledge of life had sufficed. Mickleford was not the whole world, after all.

Their brief ride to the inn was amicably quiet. Despite the anger she had felt when Quentin Vernon had refused to answer her perfectly reasonable questions, Lily felt a deeper kinship with him than before. Perhaps their having been in danger, however slight or brief, had bound them together. In any case, she fancied he regarded her with a little more respect and it was apparent that he was more solicitous of her than before. He listened with attention to whatever remarks she happened to make, deferred to her opinion, and praised her to the others. It was almost enough to make her blush!

Violet remarked on it when they had all been set

down before the inn, and the ladies had been shown to a private room to repair the damage to their appearance that their adventures had done. "Mr. Vernon seems to admire your courage, Lily. I confess, so do I. Sensible as I pride myself on being, the thought of entering that dark, dangerous tunnel gives me serious pause."

Lily shivered involuntarily. "It *was* dreadful, Vi. But I had to. I felt it was my fault Arabella was down there with Lord Vyse."

Violet shook her head. "Arabella is not your responsibility, Lily. Mr. Watson will have to learn to look sharp if he wants to keep her. But I do understand how you feel. She is so heedless sometimes!"

Violet sighed over her cousin's behavior. Even now Arabella was huddled in a corner with two of her bosom-bows, relating in a highly dramatic manner her adventure underground, as if it had all been a game.

Lily was curious about how her sister and the young curate had spent their time, and asked, "How did you and Mr. Hollister amuse yourselves?" But Violet suddenly became reticent, only saying, "I showed him some of the pleasanter views of the abbey, and told him of the history of the monks. He was most eager to be informed. I fancy we have never had a curate quite like Mr. Hollister."

There was an noticeable heightening of her color with these words, but Lily could not question her further, as the ladies had begun to descend to the private dining parlor Mr. Watson had bespoken. When they reached the ground floor, they were dismayed to find that the rain had begun anew. Mr. Watson gazed out of the window glumly, even as Arabella meekly made her way to him without so much as a smile at Lord Vyse.

Lily felt deep sympathy for her former suitor. His wonderful outing had turned into a day of distress, and none of it was really his fault.

"I am afraid," the besieged young man announced, "that we shall have to either linger over our meal until it stops, or be very wet going home."

There was a call from the more boisterous members of the party to let the wine flow and the devil take the rain. Mr. Watson silenced them with a significant glance at the rector and the giggling ladies. "However, we cannot linger too long, or the roads may become a mire. Ah, here is our dinner. I hope all of you will enjoy it." He sat down in evident relief.

Lily found herself once again next to the rector. It was odd, she was no longer deliberately seeking him out, but he always seemed to be there. Perhaps he was sorry he had refused to answer her question.

"May I help you to some of this chicken?" he was asking her. She nodded, wondering if she dare ever broach the subject again.

"I must say that you do not look at all the worse for our adventure this morning."

"Thank you. And I also owe you thanks for your help. I doubt I would have scraped up the courage to go into that dark tunnel without light or company."

The rector smiled. "It was the least I could do, as it appears that I was unintentionally the cause of your abandoning your watch over Miss Forbush."

Lily blushed, recalling what she had blurted out in the tunnel. "Yes, and you did not even recompense me for being torn away from Lord Vyse by answering my very simple questions."

To her surprise, the corners of his lips turned up, although he would not meet her gaze.

"Let us say only that nothing you heard is the precise truth, and that Lord Vyse *was* correct. It is only a joke between gentlemen."

"But it is not a joke, sir, to Mickleford or to me!"

He sipped his wine, then turned to her. Though the room was noisy with talk and laughter, they could have been alone. "As for Mickleford, rest assured that resolving the conflicting stories you heard would make no material difference to the way it is served by me as rector. As for you, Lily . . ."

She waited, suddenly a little breathless. His face began to swim before her eyes. She was tired, and she had taken too much wine. Did she imagine the dawning of tenderness in his expression?

"As for you," he continued in a lower voice, "I would not care for you to become involved in any matter between Lord Vyse and myself. You may think my past behavior gives me little right to ask this, but let us not spoil what friendship we have built."

Lily could only stare at him. Was he once again using evasion, or was he sincere? Before she could decide her attention was claimed by the signore, who sat at her other side, and she was not able to talk to Quentin Vernon again until after the meal was over.

They assembled in the entrance of the inn, all exclaiming how fortunate it was that the rain had stopped. Lily was glad that she and her sisters and cousin had brought light cloaks with them, for dusk was about to descend on them, the air had grown chill, and there was a good three-quarters of an hour to drive before they could be home.

Once again they settled into the carriage, a little wearily on Lily's part. The others chatted desultorily as they rolled along the wet, rutted road. Lily looked about in the pale lavender light that the approaching sunset threw over everything. Buds on trees sparkled with raindrops, birds were peeping here and there, and the air smelled freshly washed. It was at times like this that an undefinable yearning would overcome her, brought on, perhaps, by the approaching season of warmth, or the freshening effect of the recent rain.

Now it was made stronger by the presence beside her of Quentin Vernon. She had not accomplished her mission, after all. He had managed to evade her questions, and to make her feel presumptuous for asking them. But although she did not understand him any better, she felt that he had been awakened to a deeper understanding of her.

Her eyes began to slide closed, and she drifted off to sleep, only to be rudely awakened by a jolt as the carriage hit a rut. She almost bounced out of her seat, but Quentin held her back. It was almost dark. She could barely see the faces of Violet and Mr. Hollister across from them. They were talking in whispers, and over the jingle of harness and the hoofbeats, the creak of the carriage, she could not make out their words. Next to them, Mr. Thorpe already slept, his head at a comical angle. Lily shut her eyes again. The rector's arm, warm and comforting, remained about her shoulders.

"You are fatigued," he said softly in her ear. "It has been a wearying day. Why not try to sleep?"

She sat up straight and murmured, "Yes, but . . ." and then the carriage jolted again, tossing her back against him.

"Allow me," and he settled them so that she was held securely in his arm and supported by him against any further tossing. She was too sleepy to protest. He was warm and smelled pleasantly of clean linen and other things she could not name, and although her conscience told her it was not exactly proper behavior, she allowed her head to fall against his shoulder and her eyes to close once more.

She felt him rearrange her crumpled, tilted bonnet more comfortably, smooth away a wayward lock of hair, and whisper something she could not make out. Then she fell asleep.

She awakened what seemed hours later, refreshed but a bit cramped. The carriage was slowing to turn, and the familiar tree-lined drive to Sterling Hall was before them, recognizable even in the dark. It had begun to rain again, and the cold wet drops on her face were what had awakened her.

Lily sat up abruptly, wondering how she had come to be held so firmly in Mr. Vernon's arms. She was glad of the darkness, for it hid her embarrassment from him. She half-expected some teasing remark, but all he did was ask her if she had had a pleasant sleep, and removed his arm as unconcernedly as if he had merely been helping her over an obstacle.

To Lily's relief, Lewis Thorpe was only just beginning to awaken. Violet and Mr. Hollister had been too engrossed in their quiet conversation to care what the other passengers did. It was only when the gravel began to rattle under the wheels that they appeared to take notice of their surroundings at all.

Lily wondered about her elder half sister's marked preference for the curate's company. Violet had always seemed such a determined spinster, and yet she was apparently encouraging the attentions of this handsome, likeable, albeit not very clever-seeming fellow. However, it was reassuring to know that even sensible Violet was susceptible to masculine charm.

Both young ladies quickly straightened their bonnets as the carriage pulled up before the house. Servants with lanterns were there to greet them, and Aunt Hyacinth stood in the doorway waiting, her posture anxious. Arabella was already being tenderly handed down by their host, and Lily could see, even in the dim light, the look of satisfaction on her aunt's face as the betrothed couple exchanged their adieux.

The steps were let down and the groom stood by to help Lily and Violet to the ground. Lily hardly knew what to say to Quentin Vernon, but he simply wished her good night, adding, "I trust you will not suffer any ill-effects from your extraordinary experiences today." She could not see his expression very well in the darkness, and this left her in some doubt as to his precise meaning. She felt him press her hand, and then she was being helped down. Violet followed, Olive and the signore were already at the door chatting to Mrs. Forbush, and the carriages were rattling away.

To Lily's relief, her aunt was busy interrogating Arabella about Mr. Watson, and she herself had to say no more than that she did not believe she had taken a chill from the rain. She would leave the explanations of her cousin's adventure to the others.

Lily spent most of the night going over in her mind each and every one of her words and actions with regard to Quentin Vernon. Had she been too forward? Too demanding? Too easily distracted by his charm? What must he think of her, she wondered, allowing herself to sleep practically in his arms? Even alone in her bed in the dark, she could feel her face flush at the recollection.

By the next morning she was exhausted and irritable. The family, for once, was almost all present at the breakfast table, and the noise and exclamations over Arabella's adventure did nothing to soothe Lily's nerves, especially when her own part in it was known.

"Oh, dear, to think what might have happened to both of you down in those dreadful cellars!" said Lady Sterling.

Lily reached over and patted her hand. "But as you see, Mama, nothing did happen, and we are quite safe."

Teague made a face at his sister. "I bet Belle *cried* when she found herself down there in the dark." He glanced at his mother as if to be certain she was paying attention. "I wouldn't have. I would have torn down the fallen rock with my bare hands!"

Arabella tossed her head. "I most certainly did not cry, and you are a silly baby if you think there was any possibility of escaping that way." She preened a little. "It was horrid, of course, but Lord Vyse told me I was very brave."

"One can only hope that Lord Vyse remembered his manners," said her mother with a sharp look.

Arabella's expression had a guilty tinge to it, but she spoke up stoutly, "Of course, Mama. Why, he was most solicitous for my comfort and safety."

Lily hurried to add, "And they were not alone for very long, Aunt Hyacinth. Why, Mr. Vernon and I found them not a quarter of an hour later."

Too late she remembered that she had wished to quench any curiosity about her own part in the adventure.

"And of course Mr. Vernon would not take advantage of the situation!" said Olive ingenuously. "Why, one can always depend on a clergyman."

Lily exchanged a glance of rueful amusement with Violet. "Don't be such a ninny," said the latter to her sister. "Lily and Mr. Vernon were much too occupied trying to rescue Arabella to even think of—" She stopped suddenly, unwilling to specify the neglected activity.

Lady Flora, who had just entered the breakfast parlor on the arm of her maid, gave a squawk of laughter. "Just so, my dear," she said, with a roguish glance at

Lily. Even though nothing improper had occurred, Lily could not help feeling uncomfortable.

Once settled regally in her chair, the matriarch demanded, "I want to hear all of it. So you were in the cellars of the old abbey with our respected pastor, eh? Well, speak up, girl."

Lily kept her gaze fastened on her plate. "It is really Arabella's story, Grandmama. She and Lord Vyse . . ."

To her relief, Lady Flora was easily distracted with this tidbit, and Arabella just as easily encouraged to recount once more her tale. Lily managed to escape the family, and hurried outside, gulping in the fresh air in relief. It was chillier than the day before, and the ground was still damp, but she took a ramble to the village with a basket on her arm, trying to put out of her mind the events of yesterday and simply enjoy ordinary things once more, but she found it difficult.

She made a few visits and hesitated as she neared the rectory. She had not had a good chat with Mrs. Philpott lately, and why should the presence of Quentin Vernon keep her from her accustomed activities and friends? But even as she entered at the door of the kitchen, she was relieved to have seen no sign of the rector.

Her visit over, Lily was leaving with some jellies Mrs. Philpott had assured her were just the thing for Lady Sterling's condition, when a long shadow darkened the doorsill. Looking up, she was startled to see Lord Vyse. How very odd of him to always be poking at doorways where one would not expect a gentleman

205

of his station to be! But there he was, and he had apparently come with the express purpose of accompanying her home.

"For our friend Mr. Thorpe told me he was just coming out of church and saw you enter good Mrs. Philpott's domain," he explained with a smile, offering his arm.

Lily resigned herself to his company and decided that she would make some use of it, although no doubt he would be as evasive as Mr. Vernon had been.

"I have been shockingly remiss, my dear. I ought to have thanked you properly for rescuing us yesterday."

"Oh, but you must thank Mr. Vernon as well. I doubt I would have had the courage to proceed alone," she told him, hoping this would lead him to speak of his protege.

"Oh, of course. Vernon is a great hero," he said with what Lily thought was a touch of sarcasm. "However, it was you who led us to freedom." He smiled down at her, then suddenly took her hand and pressed it to his lips. Lily hastily took her hand away.

"I do hope my cousin Arabella kept her head and did not succumb to the vapors while you were trapped, although I am sure the temptation to do so must have been great," she said, trying again.

"Oh, but she was most charmingly apologetic for leading me into such a dangerous place—very eager to make up for her lapse of judgment." He smiled reminiscently, and Lily looked at him sharply.

"But of course I assured her that it was my fault entirely for allowing her to go into danger. And how

206

did you and Mr. Vernon find the cellars? Amazingly uncomfortable, I thought."

Lily was a bit dazed at his sudden change of subject and at the implication that she and Mr. Vernon could have been concerned with their comfort, for whatever reason, while in the cellars. She frowned. "I do not precisely take your meaning, sir."

"Ah, you are even more enchanting when you are severe with me! Am I then to assume that this rector whom you find so objectionable did not attempt to take advantage of the situation? Come, come, my dear, I know the man well. You can safely confide in me."

The more he went on in this vein, the more angry Lily grew. True, he was right in part, for what he suggested had indeed taken place at another time, but it was his oily, insinuating manner that most disgusted Lily. To her own amazement, she found herself defending the rector.

She withdrew her arm and spoke up defiantly. "Indeed not, sir. I find your insinuations improper and your suggestions base." But she could not meet his gaze.

He stopped and put his hands in his pockets, looking more like a well-bred groom than ever. "Is that how the land lies? Well, it will avail you nothing, child. Quentin Vernon is not at all the man you think he is."

Without ceremony, he left her whistling as if he were truly an intimate of the stableyard, instead of a man of consequence. Lily was astounded at his arrogance and bad manners. How disappointed her family would be if they knew that his lordship conducted himself no better than the lowliest servant!

But what disturbed her most was that he obviously did not believe that anything untoward had occurred between herself and Mr. Vernon. She did not like the speculation in his gaze. However, one thing seemed certain. Lord Vyse had no intention of judging his incumbent's worthiness based on his amorous exploits. Whatever the matter between them was, it was not over the rector's conduct towards females. Therefore, his living was not in jeopardy. A sudden happiness that bubbled up in her at the thought that Quentin Vernon would no doubt remain rector in Mickleford.

Chapter Nine

On the evening of the Wednesday before Easter, Mrs. Philpott entered the study a bit hesitantly, carrying a small bundle. "Dinner will be ready soon, Father Vernon," she said.

"Very well, we shall be along presently," Quentin replied, without glancing up from a letter announcing that the silver baptismal font for St. Peter's, duly engraved with the arms of Lord Vyse, was ready and would be delivered the day before Easter. But he did not hear her leave and when the housekeeper cleared her throat, he finally looked up.

"Beg pardon, sir," she said, "but since you haven't made mention of it, I thought I'd venture to ask if you have the money ready for tomorrow morning." Unaware of his puzzled look, she bent to unwrap the bundle, drawing from it a little bag which she held up by a string.

Dionysus, instantly perceiving that Mrs. Philpott was offering rare sport, left his place by the fire and barked at the dangling bag. She scorned to notice him. "I took the liberty of bringing the purses that the Ladies' Society has always made."

"Down, Dionysus!" Quentin took advantage of the dog's barking to hide his own confusion, but it was difficult to pretend to know what she meant, when her words had not the slightest significance for him. "Certainly, the money . . . ah . . . precisely what money would we be speaking of, Mrs. Philpott?" She had received her half-year's wages already, so she couldn't want money for herself, and the appearance of the little purses mystified him.

The housekeeper looked surprised and a little ashamed. She was ashamed, Quentin realized, not of asking him an unanswerable question but that he should need the matter explained to him. The sinking feeling in his stomach deepened when she said, "Why, the Maundy money, to be sure, sir. Have you forgotten that tomorrow is Maundy Thursday? The poor will be in line at the church after morning service."

"So they will. Indeed, I had almost forgotten," Quentin said, recovering quickly. How could he possibly have thought that pretending to be a clergyman would be so easy? Dionysus, looking mournfully at him, had subsided by the fire once more.

"Er . . . please just leave the bags here, Mrs. Philpott. Mr. Hollister and I will see to it and bring them along to the church."

"There must be a hundred things I do not know about being a clergyman," he said to George when Mrs. Philpott had left them alone once more in the study. He examined the pile she had left. "There seem to be more than a dozen bags here, and I shall have to ask the brothers Thorpe for a donation, for I haven't brought much money with me, and I don't think the poor of Mickleford would appreciate a draft on my bank as much they would some solid coin."

George chuckled. "Won't his lordship growl when he finds that his contributions are required?"

"So he will, and it will serve him right. But I am glad that neither of them were about just now. Thorpe would jump at such a mistake, declaring it proof that I hadn't succeeded in my role as agreed upon in the wager, and Lewis would be happy for any excuse to put an end to this masquerade. By the way, where are our guests keeping themselves? I don't want to eat my dinner cold and displease poor Mrs. Philpott on their account."

George looked uneasy, and hesitated before he replied, "I haven't seen them this morning, but I have a feeling they have been sneaking about the village trying to find something to discredit you. Or at least the viscount has."

"Something to *my* discredit! After the way he conducted himself with Miss Forbush at the abbey?" blustered Quentin.

George paused and glanced up at him, as if to take better measure of his mood. "Vi—Miss Sterling, that is, told me that not only did Thorpe walk alone with her sister Lily for a good quarter of an hour the other day, but that the morning after the outing he came back to call upon them, and, finding Miss Forbush fully occupied with her betrothed, asked for Miss Lily Sterling, but she had gone to the village."

Mrs. Philpott had just entered the room again, to remind them of dinner. Quentin saw the expression on her face alter. "I'm sure it's not my place to say, sir, but that Lord Vyse was snooping about my kitchen door yesterday, almost lying in wait for that dear child, insisting on escorting her home. Hmmph!" She exited, her straight back eloquently expressing her disapproval.

Thorpe and Lily? Quentin frowned and drummed his fingers on the desk. A dangerous combination, and one which he thought he had taken great pains to break up. Indeed, by the end of the abbey outing he had wished that he might have risked being more frank with her. But the obstacles seemed innumerable. Besides, in spite of her sudden curious preference for his company, and the delightful way she had slept upon his shoulder, he was not at all sure where he stood in Lily's estimation.

He only hoped that Thorpe had not attempted to take advantage of her. He let out a long breath, and realized that he had been clenching his fists. Then he remembered that Lily Sterling could be counted upon to look after herself. There was her undoubted bravery, though foolhardiness, in the cellars. To think she had been planning a rescue all alone in the pitch dark. And then there was her proven ingenuity in outwitting gentlemen who believed themselves quite clever. Witness how she had been besting him since his arrival!

George put down his newspaper and stood up, stretching a bit too elaborately. Something, Quentin observed, was obviously on his mind. "Glad the family never had a mind to make *me* a parson—a lot of sitting about, if you ask me. Not a healthy life for a man." Dionysus stretched his paws out before him and yawned, and when George began pacing, he stood up and followed him. "Drat it, this dog of yours is a nuisance," he said, trying unsuccessfully to shake the animal from his heels.

Quentin could not help but laugh, his friend appeared so unusually querulous. "Do you not recall who thought acquiring the animal would be a capital idea? And come now, you know very well that as your father's heir you were never in any danger of taking the collar. But you are right, it isn't the sort of life I'd choose permanently—I wish Lewis joy of it!"

He sobered, and stretched out a hand. "But I have cause to be grateful to you, my good fellow, for standing by me. Especially when it was not at all necessary."

"Not another word, if you please," said George, waving away his thanks. But he grinned. "You have done me a greater favor than you know. Kept me out of town, out of trouble, and out of debt, and now I have the satisfaction of knowing how lucky I am not to have gone into the church."

"I must admit that rusticating appears to agree with you," Quentin told him. "You look remarkably rested and well, and you haven't done all that much sitting about. Every time I look for you, it seems you're off for a walk, usually up to the Hall."

At first his friend evaded his searching gaze, but then he sighed, and sat down again, twisting his hands together in an uncharacteristically anxious gesture. Dionysus came and put his head on George's knee, in apparent sympathy. "I may as well confess that although I'll be damned if I'll see Thorpe triumph over you, I have lingered here more in my own interest than in yours."

"You amaze me!" Quentin hid a smile, thinking of all the hours his "curate" had spent huddled with Miss Sterling at the Hall.

George gave the dog's head a dismissive pat, stood again and restlessly walked about, hands deep in pockets, ruining the cut of his coat, proof of deep mental disturbance. "No, it's true! I've been selfishly thinking of my own pleasure, not the wager. And now I've gone and . . . well, I've been a bit of a fool, Quentin."

Quentin murmured encouragement. In his opinion this little chat was long overdue, considering how long his friend had been dangling after Miss Sterling.

George confirmed his suspicions. "Yes, I've gone

214

and fallen in love, and I'm not good enough for her!" The tortured lover flopped once more into a chair and contemplated his booted feet stuck out in front of him. By now Dionysus, realizing that no one was truly serious about playing with him, returned to his rug by the fire and began to gnaw on a bone.

"I take it you refer to Miss Sterling?"

George sat bolt upright. "You know? Why, I had just begun to know it myself!"

"Rest easy, it is not so obvious, except to perceptive individuals like myself, and perhaps Lady Flora," said Quentin with a wry smile.

"Hope you're wrong." George shuddered. "Hate to think what that lady would say if she knew. Tell me to go off and look elsewhere for a bride, me being nothing but a poor curate."

Quentin exploded into laughter. "But you're *not* a poor curate! You're a man of fashion, a keen whip and horseman, noted amateur of the Fancy, a baronet with a landed estate and a respectable income. In short, a perfectly eligible suitor for the eldest daughter of a country squire."

For a moment George looked astounded at his good fortune as though he had forgotten the truth, so accustomed had he become to playing a role. Then his face fell. "Yes, of course I am, but how shall I tell Sir Richard that I'm not who he thinks I am? Oh, no doubt he'd give me permission to address Violet once he knew my true circumstances,

215

but in telling him I would give you away. And worse, what will she think of me, having misrepresented myself all this time? It's a wonder she hasn't discovered me already, her being so devout and knowledgeable. I tell you I feel positively ignorant beside her. And she is so gentle and wise and lovely . . ." Sir George sunk his chin on his hand and stared into space, inwardly contemplating his beloved.

Since his friend's dilemma was not so different from his own, Quentin could not but sympathize with George's anguish. It was exactly the same process he would eventually have to endure, were he to win Lily's hand.

The thought startled him. Up till now he had not entertained such high aspirations. It had seemed enough to love and want her, and hope she might realize her feelings for him. But of course he wished to marry her! His heart beat rapidly as he envisioned her as his bride, bringing life to his cold marble-bedecked townhouse, sharing laughter and love, warming his bed. And he could give her so much more than she had ever dreamed of wanting here in quiet Mickleford. He would even, if she wished, let her furnish one of his country houses, and they could live there part of the year. Right now he could think of nothing more enticing than being tucked away in the country alone with her. London's delights had faded in his memory.

He was roused from this contemplation by the

fact that George had emerged from his own reverie and had been trying to get his attention. "Quentin? It's not like you to go woolgathering like that."

"Forgive me. I have been thinking about our — your problem. It seems that unless you wish to leave without ever letting Miss Sterling know your feelings, you must wait until after Easter, perhaps even come back here alone to confess to her."

"But how will she ever forgive me?" he cried, fingers tearing through his hair.

"I don't know," Quentin replied gloomily. "One can only hope for the best." But if that were so, shouldn't he make arrangements for a happier outcome? Perhaps Lily *wouldn't* send him away with a flea in his ear if he confided his feelings to her. "Do you think I'd be able to ride to Chester and back in a day?" he asked George.

George looked up curiously. "Why, I suppose you might. Why?"

"I have a mind to go and escort Lord Vyse's generous gift back to Mickleford on Saturday, that's all." He did not elaborate on his intention, which was to transact some more personal business in the town, nor did he invite George to go with him, and in any case that gentleman remarked that he would just as soon not leave Mickleford for anything right now. "Else I'd probably lose what little heart I have and never come back."

Quentin cheerily advised him to try some optimism, and had decided to dine without his tardy guests when they finally appeared. Lewis apologized profusely, while Thorpe merely looked self-satisfied. Quentin wondered how he could discover whether the viscount had heard anything about his performance as pastor during his wanderings about the neighborhood.

"Charming girls at the Hall," remarked Thorpe, sipping his wine.

"The family, however," said Lewis, wrinkling his nose, "is very odd. Such confusion!" He chewed a cutlet decisively.

"I daresay we confused them all the more with our differing accounts of my history," Quentin remarked, recalling Lily's insistence upon having it explained.

"Fools, both of you," said Thorpe, with a scowl. "Although I don't know why I should care, as it serves me nothing to protect your false identity."

"Ah, but if mine is destroyed so also is yours," Quentin reminded him. The viscount acknowledged this with a grimace, and refilled his glass, waving away the roast beef his brother was trying to urge on him.

The Reverend Mr. Lewis Thorpe thoughtfully carved himself a slice of the rare meat, and offered, "I do not think that our little error has disturbed the squire's family, except for the very curious Miss Lily Sterling. Why, I met two of the young ladies in the village with that strange little foreigner, and they seemed to have forgotten it, if indeed it

218

had any effect upon them."

"If that lovely child Lily becomes too inquisitive," said Thorpe with a swift, sidewise glance at Quentin, "I shall deal with her."

"You will have no more to do with Lily Sterling!" Quentin was surprised by his own vehemence. He had not meant to give so much away to Lord Thorpe. He was glad that his houseguest had chosen to be a rider and not a passenger the day of the outing, or else he might have seen just where Quentin's feelings were leading him.

"I take no orders from you, Vyse." Suddenly Thorpe began to laugh. "Indeed, no, but you have taken your orders from me, Rector."

No one seemed to share his delight in the pun, so he continued, "Lily is a charming young lady, but a bit ingenuous and single-minded for my taste. What I found most refreshing about her was that she had nothing good to say about you at all, unlike most females."

Quentin forced down his irritation and curiosity, mechanically chewing and swallowing Mrs. Philpott's excellent game pie, which tasted like so much sawdust. "I am no longer the dashing man on the town, Thorpe. In Mickleford I am a respectable minister of the Church, and have nothing to do with intrigue and flirtation," he said blandly.

Thorpe raised an eyebrow. "I see. Then I suppose that is why you have disturbed the parish by resorting to the hellfire tactics so eloquently described to me by the little Sterling. That high-handed arrogance Miss Lily complained of must be but a substitute for your former ways."

"And is that all she complained of?" Quentin asked, pretending to stifle a yawn.

"I had an idea that there was something else, but the girl insisted that was all." Thorpe frowned into the depths of his glass. "Although you foiled me at the abbey, I shall have it out of her bye and bye. It will be an interesting and delicate exercise, to oversee the blooming of this particular Lily." He looked as though he relished the thought.

"Keep your hands off her," Quentin barked before he could restrain himself. He saw George shake his head and sigh, and Lewis look at him with interest.

Thorpe, however, positively beamed with satisfaction at having elicited this response. "Ah, I thought there might be something you have not told me. I have sensed a certain tension in you while in the young lady's company, Vyse."

"I mean it's bad enough you flirted so outrageously with her cousin, the one who is betrothed—"

"And therefore quite safe," Thorpe returned with glee. "As well as being born to the art, and so not taking me at all seriously. Why, even in our splendid adventure in the cellars she did naught but prattle of her Mr. Watson. She has no interest in my attentions except where others will witness them. Now the little Lily, she, I fear, might come to take one's casual attentions very seriously."

"I am ashamed of both of you," declared Lewis at this juncture. He put down his knife and fork as though to emphasize his seriousness. "It is bad enough to deceive the parish into taking a layman as their pastor, but now to involve yourselves with innocent young ladies of respectable family."

George, Quentin saw with amusement, looked guilty, as if this diatribe had been directed squarely at him. Thorpe only brushed off his brother's scold. Dionysus, who though banished from the room during dinner, had slipped inside in Mrs. Philpott's wake, nudged Quentin's leg and turned a pleading look on him.

"Greedy little mongrel!" He fed the dog a piece of meat. Deciding it was time the dangerous subject was left alone, Quentin began to question Lewis about the Maundy Thursday service. "I have learned that I am expected to distribute alms to the local poor tomorrow. And I'm afraid I shall have to ask you to help me fill the purses."

The Reverend Mr. Thorpe declared himself happy to oblige, and turned out his pockets, while promising more from a purse he had upstairs. "And you too, Geoffrey," he urged his dilatory brother. "It is the least you can do for perpetrating this fraud upon the parish."

Grudgingly, Thorpe added his mite to the collection, while Dionysus, rebuffed by both Lewis and Lord Thorpe, sat and growled softly at them.

This gratified Quentin, who called the dog to his side, and fed him again, saying softly, "You know a rum 'un when you see one, eh, boy?" Bored by the church talk, Lord Thorpe stood up and announced that he was going to the Hare and Hound where he had invited John Sterling to meet him for a game of cards.

"Take care you don't stay up all night," Quentin told him, "for tomorrow morning early you will have another excellent chance to inspect my performance as rector."

The viscount took up his hat and gloves and gave his rival a long, even look. "There are other ways of defeating you besides boring myself to death in that musty old church."

It was not at all clear what he meant, but Quentin did not trust his frequent unexplained absences, and wished that he had been able to keep closer watch on his unwanted guest's movements. But he had surprisingly been busy. He was still, despite seeing Lily's superior holiday revels, rehearsing his plodding actors in the Easter scene. He had even found himself, at first to his dismay, called upon to counsel some of his parishioners who came to him with their troubles, problems that his former life in London had never encompassed.

He had given them what seemed to him good, common-sense advice, and to his relief they did not seem surprised when he did not refer them to the Bible or some improving work. While he was thus occupied, Thorpe had no doubt been busy cultivating the acquaintance of the neighborhood in his guise of patron, gaining everyone's confidence, and trying to discover something unsavory about his supposed rector.

Quentin thought of John Sterling, undoubtedly a weak link if he had ever seen one. He only hoped that the squire's wastrel brother had been too drunk or preoccupied with his debts to concern himself with what had been happening in the parish lately. He also devoutly hoped that he would soundly trounce the viscount at cards.

In Thorpe's absence, Quentin ventured to ask Lewis, with a bit of trepidation, if there were any other seasonal duties he might be expected to perform soon. "For I am afraid I did not prepare very well for my role. Oh, a Sunday service is not beyond me, but this village seems to come up with the damnedest ancient customs and rituals, things I've never heard of."

"My dear Lord Vyse!" cried the clergyman in disapproval. "I am ashamed that a man of your station is so unfamiliar with the ceremonies of the Church of England. But it is true that some localities have developed their own little customs. For instance, in some places, the clergyman is not only supposed to distribute money to the poor, but to wash their feet, as Christ did his apostles' and as the kings once did."

"Good grief! I hope I shall be spared that at

least," he said with a laugh. Then he looked at George, who wasn't laughing. "You don't think . . ."

"I haven't heard anyone mention it, Quentin, but it does sound like the sort of rum thing these Mickleford folk would expect one to do," said his curate in a worried tone.

"And Lily Sterling would doubtless die of laughter to see me at it!" Still, he didn't really believe Mickleford could be so quaint in its habits, and so did not preoccupy himself with the thought.

Lily felt dull and listless on Thursday morning, and wished she could creep away and curl up with a book in some warm corner. However her household duties had increased now that Lady Sterling had been persuaded by the anxious aunts to retire to her rooms to await next month's expected birth, so she could hardly do as she wished. Besides that, Arabella and Olive had teased Sir Richard into at last agreeing to a ball.

"Not a ball," Violet had amended. "Just a small evening party with dancing."

Sir Richard had glanced at his eldest daughter with amusement. "Are they not one and the same, my dear?"

Violet had looked at him with mild exasperation. "Not at all, Papa. First of all, we will not serve a cold supper, but only punch and cake and biscuits. And secondly, it cannot be a ball because of Mama's condition."

"I see. But you surprise me, my dear. You have

never been very eager for such entertainments. I suppose we have to thank that curate who is constantly underfoot, hanging on to your every word. Your knowledge of theology has stood you in good stead, for it has won you a very handsome suitor!"

For the first time Lily could remember, Violet colored up almost dark enough to resemble her name. "You mistake me, Papa. Mr. Hollister is not a suitor. He is simply kind enough to listen to my opinions on church matters."

"Indeed I have often wondered if there was not something lacking in that young man's preparation for the Church," said Aunt Hyacinth thoughtfully. "He seems frightfully ignorant to me. But Violet has been a very good influence on him."

Olive interrupted. "But Papa, about our party! Aunt Hyacinth and Aunt Poppy have promised to help us prepare everything, and we can have the invitations delivered today if we hurry. Just a few neighbors, and of course the party from the rectory."

"I see that you have prepared for the unlikely contingency of my giving permission," said the baronet dryly. "It is comforting to know that my daughters have such confidence in my indulging their every whim. Very well, you may have your ball . . . er, evening party. So long as nothing disturbs your mother. She must have quiet."

So Lily had rushed from egg-dyeing to helping the boys care for their rabbit, which was rapidly gaining strength and beginning to hop again, to waiting on her mother and now to helping plan the dance for Easter Monday. She had no time to wonder if Mr. Vernon or either of the London visitors would dance with her, or if it would be awkward, seeing her neighbors and former suitors again, or if Arabella would once more snub Mr. Watson in favor of Lord Vyse, or if she and Olive would fight for Signore Marco's attentions. A brief glancing thought for each of these things, and she was off on another task.

On Maundy Thursday as many of the family as were able made an appearance in the Sterling pew. This did not include Uncle John, who had practically roused the house by coming in just before dawn, raucously drunk and shouting of his winnings. However, he did appear at breakfast, and on that occasion his sisters and nieces scolded him for having disturbed their rest.

Lady Flora was the only one who seemed to think his behavior at all amusing, and when he begged off attending worship, said, "Of course, my boy, you do just as you please. You've finally chased down that infernal draft—haven't felt it in two days—and I don't care to have you nursing your sore head and those red eyes before all the parish." She chuckled. "You must have had a rare time last night, you and his lordship."

John looked up from his cup of black coffee. "Ah, but dear Mother, it was worth it. That Lord Vyse is a clever chap, but not as clever as I am when it comes to cards." Despite his condition, the squire's brother seemed irrepressibly pleased with himself.

"Then we are to assume that you find yourself above water at last, Brother?" asked Sir Richard, presiding at the head of the table.

"Plump in the pocket again, I'm happy to say. And after Easter I'm off to London." He winked at no one in particular. "I shouldn't miss your ball for anything. Bound to be a splendid turnout."

Violet cast her gaze upwards as if to indicate her stepmother's retirement. "Not a ball, Uncle John, an evening party."

It was no wonder that Lily had completely forgotten the plans she had made for this day, until as they sat in church, Aunt Poppy whispered to her, "My goodness, there seem to be more poor folk than last year." The recipients of the Maundy were proceeding up to where Quentin Vernon waited, and suddenly she remembered what she had done.

Why had she not called off the arrangements she had made? The precise nature of her feelings for Quentin Vernon, after all that had passed between them, were not completely clear to her, but she did know that she no longer had a desire to humiliate him or punish him for the trouble he had caused her. But it was too late.

Tim Proper, as she had patiently instructed him, was bringing in the tub of water and the toweling, and the poor folk were proceeding to the chairs that had been arranged before the altar. There they sat, barefoot and some of them very dirty indeed, ready for the rector to perform his duty and to hand them their purses.

The warden of the workhouse, who knew of her family's help to the unfortunates of the neighborhood, had consented readily to her request to revive the ancient custom of the foot-washing, and had chosen a dozen worthy inmates for this honor. And now poor Mr. Vernon stood amazed as the sexton prepared a cushion for him to kneel upon, handed him a cloth, and indicated to him, grinning, that he should begin his work.

As if he could sense her thoughts, the rector's eyes met Lily's and, unwilling to let him see that she was ashamed of her attempt to publicly discomfit him, she lifted her chin and gave him a triumphant smile. That will teach him, she told herself, to think that he can taunt me with his mysteries. But she felt herself to be very much in the wrong and was almost happy when, instead of protesting or expressing disgust, he set to work with a will.

His patron, Lily noticed, was watching with extreme amazement. He had even raised a quizzing glass to his eye, as if to verify that his vision was not deceiving him. The Reverend Mr. Thorpe, on the other hand, looked well-satisfied, while Mr. Hollister the curate, seemed, from his red cheeks and the repeated opening and closing of his mouth, to be in extreme distress.

All the while, Lily observed, the rector was

calmly performing his office to the poor, talking to them in a low voice, which brought smiles to their faces. The murmuring of the congregation, which had grown loud when they saw that a long-abandoned custom had been suddenly revived, slowly settled into silence once more, and when Mr. Vernon had finished and dried his hands, he distributed the maundy purses with such grace and gallantry as to make it appear the poor folk were doing him an honor by accepting his gift.

All in all, Lily thought wryly, a great victory for the rector, and one she had not at all expected when she had first envisioned the scene. But at heart she was glad that her ill-thought-out plan had not caused further quarrels between them. Had he changed, or had she? She did not know, but, suddenly sad, realized that it could make very little difference in the end. It seemed that the parish was beginning to think of Mr. Vernon as one of its own, and there would be no escape from him for Lily, whatever wrong he had done her or however torn by conflicting feelings she was.

To her relief the ceremony was soon over, and the family prepared to leave. Mr. Vernon stood in the church porch, Mr. Hollister, Lord Vyse, and the visiting cleric at his side. Dionysus, looking as though he had spent the morning rooting through the garden, galloped up the the rector's side, with an apparent grin on his canine face, as if he knew that the parish could not be greeted without him.

Signore Marco, with a glowing Olive on his arm, rushed to be the first to speak to the rector. "Such a beautiful ceremony," he said. "So much like the one I have seen performed in my native city," he said in his lilting accent. Dionysus, Lily saw, had cocked his head and one ear flopping over, was looking at him curiously. For an instant the signore glanced nervously at the dog, and stepped back a little.

Lord Vyse now made use of the quizzing glass to inspect the foreign guest. "And from what city do you hail, sir? I do not believe I have ever heard."

For a second, the little Italian looked nonplussed. Lily exchanged a glance with Violet, who seemed to notice nothing. "Ahh . . . Genoa, signore." Dionysus, Lily observed, had approached the signore and was sniffing his boots with distrust.

Olive said, "But I thought you said your uncle was the count of Naples?"

The signore's round face turned pink, and his thick eyebrows twitched a little. "Indeed, my dear Signorina Olivia, so I did. However I have spent so many years in Genoa, on some, eh . . . business for my uncle, I think of it as home." Dionysus growled, and the little man gasped and practically jumped back. Olive said, "Hush, dog!" and bore him away.

Lily wondered if it was only her imagination, but he seemed to have lost a bit of his Italian accent. For the first time she began to wonder about the signore. It was true, they had spent a great deal of time with him at Harrogate, but there in the unfamiliar surroundings, the variety of the scene and the continual introduction of new acquaintances, the strangeness of his stories had not been so apparent.

It was only now that she saw how much he had presumed upon their hospitality in coming to Sterling Hall, because she knew she had issued no definite invitation to him. She watched him as he appeared to recover now from his fit of uncertainty, attentive both to Olive and Arabella. The latter had spotted Mr. Watson among the churchgoers but seemed to have taken up her old flirtatious habits, and remained chatting to the signore. Their guest seemed not to notice how the other man's jaw tightened in irritation. For a moment Lily thought that Mr. Watson had finally had enough and would challenge the signore, but with lightning swiftness, Lord Vyse swooped down on Arabella and removed her from the visitor's side.

Mr. Watson's looks darkened farther, but neither Lord Vyse nor Arabella seemed to notice. Lily sighed. Arabella should have learned her lesson, but none of this would have been necessary if the silly girl had had a straightforward chat with Mr. Watson about his falling off in attention. Instead she had turned to foolish games. And now Mr. Watson, instead of being forthright about his feelings, was simply sulking while his betrothed continued her flirtatious ways. Lily suddenly realized that she was as much of a fool as either of them when it came to Mr. Vernon.

She glanced from his open, candid face to that of his patron, who was leaning close, whispering something into Arabella's little pink ear. There was something altogether too sure about Lord Vyse, too practiced and sly, Lily thought. It made her wonder about his sudden personal interest in Mickleford and its rector. Surely it was unusual for a man of high station to concern himself so closely with a clergyman on whom he had bestowed a living?

As if he read her thoughts the rector turned to her. Quite as skillfully as his patron, he whisked her away from the others by the simple expedient of announcing that he must confer with her on the Easter pageant. Almost before she knew what had happened she found herself on his arm and taking a turn about the churchyard. The dog, sensing something interesting, followed them, but with a sharp command the rector sent him away. He obeyed at once, and Lily felt that she was now truly alone with Quentin, as if the animal's presence would have shielded her. She remembered the feel of his arms about her that night in the carriage as if it were a pleasant dream.

Everything, even the shrubs newly come to life which reminded her of another time they had spent there together, seemed to conspire against her. She hardly knew what to say, especially as she was half-ashamed of the arrangements she had made to discomfit him today.

But Quentin did not seem ill at ease in her company. To the contrary, he was amused. "I think this round goes to me, wouldn't you say so, my dear? Although it was an admirable attempt, admirable. I suppose you derived some pleasure, at least, from the look on my face when I saw that row of bare and dirty feet awaiting me."

Unaccountably his tone, instead of reassuring her that no harm had been done, had the effect of setting her back up. She withdrew her hand from the warm security of his arm. "What can you mean, Mr. Vernon? That ceremony is always performed on Maundy Thursday, and I am surprised you did not know it. To be sure, what a great many things there are that you do not know about running this parish," she said, and had the satisfaction of seeing sudden dismay flash in his eyes. "Besides," she continued, "how could today's service have been my doing?"

She looked up at him, her green eyes as wide and innocent as she could make them. But this had a far different effect from the one she had intended, and it was fortunate that they were now out of sight of the lingering congregation, for in one swift motion he took her into his arms and brought his face an inch from hers. "You must not look at me in just that way, you know," he murmured, and smiled straight into her eyes. "It is hardly fair to tempt a man so, when you have already been the cause of his enduring a most difficult morning."

Lily wanted to make a sharp retort, but felt her-

233

self unable to do so. Had she not been regretting her action all through the service? And now he was holding her close against him, and in spite of her danger, she could not help but wish he would kiss her again. "If I apologize," she said softly, "will you let me go? I should not like anyone to see us. Lord Vyse, for instance . . ."

Instantly she was released. "What interest does that fellow hold for you?" demanded the rector, in fashion most disrespectful to the man who was his supposed patron.

"Why," she replied, surprised at his vehemence, "I merely mention his name as an example of someone who seems interested in your doings. You must not fret; I set him down sharply for insinuating that in the abbey cellars you and I . . . well, that we had anything on our minds but rescuing him and Arabella."

"And didn't we?" His look was teasing.

Lily was gratified to see how his demeanor changed at this news. However, she ignored his provoking remark. "And now I am sorry that I told him how much trouble you have caused here, for I have decided that I do not at all like him," she confided on an impulse.

"Do you not?" Suddenly Quentin was grinning. "I applaud you. I did not think, despite your wishing for a heroic lord to save you from the wicked rector, that his lordship would be to your taste."

"Pray do not allow this indiscreet revelation of

234

mine to swell your head, sir," she retorted, still puzzled as to why he so disliked his patron. "My opinion of you has not measurably changed." She knew this was a lie even as she said it, but her pride would not allow her to admit to a change of feeling where the rector was concerned. True, he had seemed to be jealous of Lord Vyse's attentions to her, but perhaps he was only troubled by her having complained to his lordship about his rector's behavior. If only she could know the truth!

But it appeared that she and the rector were no nearer to being honest with one another than before.

"I regret to hear that I have not risen in your esteem, my dear," Quentin was saying. "But perhaps such an eventuality is too much to hope for on my part." He looked deep into her eyes for a long moment, as if searching for something. Lily found that she could not meet his gaze, after a while. Something in it stirred her to the depths, exciting, but frightening depths that she dare not think about.

He took her hand and placed it upon his arm again, and led her around the church back to where her family and his guests waited, calmly chatting of the pageant as if they had been discussing the matter all along. Still amazed by his capacity for pretending, she simply nodded, affecting not to notice the several pairs of interested eyes that rested upon them as they came into view.

Once it would have pleased her to anticipate how

235

her Easter pageant, compared with his faltering play, would show the rector in a bad light before his patron and everyone else. Now the prospect seemed unimportant, and the whole idea very dull. It was more urgent that she discover the truth about Quentin Vernon, for Lily feared very much that he was rapidly becoming the most important thing in the world to her, and to leap blindly into such a love was to risk being hurt very badly indeed.

"Ah, there you are, my child," said the squire, observing his daughter's return on the arm of the rector. "Before we go, I did want to have a word with the rector. It seems my daughters' hearts are set on having a little ball."

"Evening party, Papa," reminded Olive and Violet in chorus.

"Yes, well, evening party then, with dancing," continued the squire with a smile, "on Easter Monday, and we would be delighted if you and your guests would join us."

Lily glanced up at the rector and perceived a swift change of expression across his mobile countenance, first amusement, then anxiety, but finally he said, "But of course, Sir Richard, we would be honored." He bowed to the Sterling ladies, including Lily, and as he came up bestowed a wry glance upon her. "I hope I may have the pleasure of dancing with all of your daughters on that occasion, sir."

Sir Richard chuckled. "Why, don't apply to me for that permission, young man. I suppose the girls

236

will do as they like. They always do." He glanced at his wayward niece. Mr. Watson had apparently acquired the necessary fortitude and was engaged in a battle to separate his fianceé from Lord Vyse, and though the two gentlemen seemed polite, there was a steeliness to their expressions that was alarming. The cause of their rivalry, however, was plainly delighted.

"Come along, Arabella," called her uncle, and the girl reluctantly took her leave of both gentlemen. Lily went to hurry her cousin away, and Lord Vyse vouchsafed her a mocking smile. As she firmly bade him good day, he passed a glance over her and something in his eyes made her want to cringe. She led Arabella back to the rest of the family party, intercepting an exchange of looks between Quentin and his patron, and was once more left wondering about the hidden undercurrents that had begun to flow in Mickleford with the arrival of the new rector.

Upon their return to the Hall, Lily found it her task to entertain the children before dinner, since the others were either assisting with preparations for Easter dinner and the Easter Monday dance, or had conveniently disappeared.

So she went out with the boys to the edge of the garden where they had placed the rabbit hutch made for them by an obliging estate worker. "Goodness, he is getting big!" Lily cried. For the creature, only days ago looking wretched and weak, was now

237

plump, its eyes alert, whiskers twitching as it gobbled up the scraps the children delightedly placed before it. Its white coat was clean and shiny and its leg, though still bandaged, seemed to cause it no pain.

"How kind Mr. Vernon was to rescue it and bring it to us!" cried William.

"Yes, I like him," announced Steven, solemnly watching the rabbit. "Even if he is awfully severe with us in church."

"Indeed, it was thoughtful of the rector," was all Lily could say, though she thought the rector had been thinking less of the boys' pleasure than of his own reputation. "Now, you have not named your bunny yet. What will you call him?"

Various names, some silly, some simply too ponderous for a rabbit, were brought forth, until Teague made a suggestion. The older boy, though affecting disdain for the children's pets, had followed them down to the hutch in the hopes that an airing in the garden would make his cheeks rosier. He tentatively poked a piece of lettuce through the cage and said, "Why don't you call him after the rector, then?"

"Yes, let's call him Vernon!" cried Steven.

Lily laughed to think of what the proud rector would say when he knew himself namesake for a rabbit, but agreed. Soon tiring of watching the bunny eat his dinner, little William demanded to be allowed to hold the animal. "I won't hurt him," he promised, looking up with pleading eyes to his older sister. "Please, Lily."

Lily could not resist, especially when Steven and Teague also joined their voices to the William's, for they wished to hold the rabbit, too. "Very well, but be careful not to squeeze him too hard, or drop him, because he is still not fully recovered, and if he runs off he may very well hurt himself again."

"Or perhaps that dog, Dionysus, will attempt to savage him again," suggested Steven, wide-eyed.

Lily smiled, knowing that the dog seemed to do nothing without the rector's express permission, and said she doubted it very much. Meanwhile William lifted the rabbit and held it while the others stroked its ears. Suddenly, the animal made a break for freedom. Its legs, even the wounded one, were apparently more powerful than they seemed for it sprang out of William's arms and shot off across the garden, to disappear under the shrubbery.

The children shouted and ran after it, not heeding Lily's warning that they would only frighten Vernon into running farther away.

"Vernon, Vernon!" they cried, peering under shrubs and searching every corner of the garden, but to no avail.

Lily was busy consoling poor William, who wailed that it was his fault the rabbit had run away, and for a while she did not notice Lady Flora, who had apparently come out to take the air. But when she had sent her little brother off with a hug, she

239

turned and saw her grandmother standing near the gate, her look abstracted.

As Lily approached, the old lady was murmuring, "Vernon, Vernon . . . something familiar about that name. Why can't I remember? Being old is shockingly tiresome! Oh, there you are, child. Your Aunt Hyacinth wants your advice on the simnel cakes — actually, she is driving Cook mad, so you had better go and smooth them both down. Now what was it about that name that tickles my memory?"

"Do you mean Vernon, Grandmama? The children had decided to name the rabbit after the rector, only he escaped — the rabbit, I mean," she said with a chuckle.

"Confound it, girl, I know it's the rector's name, but I have just realized after all these weeks that there's something else I ought to remember about it." She shook her head. "Never mind, then. Off with you to the kitchen, before Cook gives notice, and then we shall be at the mercy of Aunt Hyacinth. Too many women in this house, that's what's wrong here!"

Lily obeyed, and when reaching the kitchen found that it was her duty to remind Aunt Hyacinth that their simnel cakes — rich plum cakes, their crusts colored with saffron — had always been brushed with egg after being boiled in a cloth and before being baked hard. Cook looked triumphantly at the interfering Mrs. Forbush, and thanked Lily.

"Now don't forget we need plenty to send the

neighbors for Easter," Aunt Hyacinth reminded her, not willing to allow another the last word, "and an extra one for the rectory."

Lily smiled as she wondered what Quentin and his elegant London guests would make of the hard, solid, almost inedibly sweet cake. They should be prepared, she knew, to receive many such gifts from the parish at Easter.

"Perhaps," suggested Aunt Poppy, who had recently arrived to observe the preparations, "we should send over some hot cross buns tomorrow morning too, as it's Good Friday. I'm sure Mr. Hollister would do justice to them."

"I fear, dear aunt," said Lily, leading her out of the kitchen before more harm could be done, "that Mrs. Philpott would be hurt. You know she can make very good buns, and is no doubt readying her dough as we speak." Lily smiled to herself over poor Mr. Hollister, who would no doubt be faced with a pile of treats during the holiday, all baked by his lady admirers.

Just then Violet came in, tying an apron round her dress, but stopped short when she saw her sister and her two aunts. "Oh! I . . . I thought I would make a tansy pudding."

"I shall do it, miss," Cook reminded her, arms folded across her chest. "Just as I have been doing this twenty year and more."

Lily laughed at the downcast expression on Violet's face. Don't worry, my dear. I'm sure Mr. Hollister, fond though he might be of tansy pudding and buns and cake, will forgive you for not making him one with your very own hands."

Violet blushed and looked away, unusual behavior for her, Lily thought. "I don't know what you mean, Lily. I always like to make a pudding for Easter."

"I shan't tease you any more, Vi," Lily promised, drawing her out of the kitchen. "But it has become obvious that Mr. Hollister has eyes for no one but you."

"Oh, Lily, I wish I knew what to do! I thought I was too old for courting, but now . . ."

"Too old!" Lily cried. "Why, that is nonsense." With a swift gesture, she pulled off the little cap that covered her sister's hair. "There, it is you who have made yourself too old. Now you look much more the thing — an eligible young lady who is barely six and twenty, and who has captured the heart of the curate, who is not good enough for you!"

That afternoon they were closeted in the sitting room, mercifully empty. Violet picked up and put down some work she had left there, and looked at her sister miserably. "I am very much afraid that Mr. Hollister is going to speak to Papa, Lily, and that Papa will not think it a good match. To be sure, he *is* only a curate, and not a very good one either," a fond smile came over her face, "but when I am with him I feel happy, and there is something about him that is not like any of the young men I have met before. A few times I was certain he was going to tell me of his feelings, but then such a look came over his face, as if he were utterly miserable! I cannot think what to do."

Lily spent a few minutes trying to console and encourage her sister, but they were interrupted by Lady Flora, and started guiltily as she turned her sharp eye upon them.

"No need to jump so, my dears. Unless, of course, you are up to some mischief." The old lady tittered, obviously pleased with herself. She sat down in the most comfortable chair in the room and summoned her two granddaughters with a regal wave of the hand. "Come here. There is something very important that we must discuss."

Lily looked anxiously at Violet, but her elder sister seemed outwardly calm, except for a conscious little gleam in her eyes. She had not put back the cap that Lily had taken off her head earlier, and Lady Flora's still sharp eyes noticed it at once.

"Hmm, so it's as I supposed," she murmured brushing a hand over Violet's blond curls. "Just as well. I never dreamed you'd see sense and take off that silly thing. You're far too young, and I think Mr. Hollister will be pleased to see you out of it."

Violet's composure dissolved, and her grandmother hastened to reassure her. "Oh, don't worry so, child. You know that there's precious little that goes on here that I don't see. And, of course, if the curate should offer for you, and you feel you must have him, I shall do everything in my power to convince your father." She sighed. "Though I had hoped to look higher. Never mind. At this late date he'll do."

"Oh, Grandmama!" wailed Violet, while Lily watched anxiously, certain her turn was not far off. Meanwhile, the matriarch went on. "Of course I'm bound to tell you that at times he just doesn't seem like a curate." She shook her head. "No more than that Quentin Vernon seems an ordained minister of the church! I've finally remembered why that name nagged at my mind. I may be old, but I haven't lost all my faculties yet!" she announced proudly.

"What do you mean, Grandmama?" asked Violet, uttering the very words Lily's dry throat could not produce.

"I'll tell you, but it mustn't go farther than this room," said the old lady. She fixed her eyes on Lily, and shook her head. "You haven't confided in your old Grandmama lately, my dear, but I can tell from your eyes when you look at him that the rector has turned your head. At first, I admit, I encouraged the idea, but now I'm not so certain I was right."

Lily was bursting with impatience, and could not pretend to be calm any more. But she still was not ready to admit to anyone her feelings for Quentin. "I do not know what you mean, Grandmama. But if you have some information about the rector, please tell us, for I have been suspecting that there is something decidedly odd about him, and the sudden appearance of Lord Vyse."

The old lady settled back in her chair. "All right. Do you remember when the children were calling that rabbit, having named him Vernon after the rector? I told you the name Vernon rang a bell in my old brain. Well, Vernon, as I finally remembered, is the family name of Lord Vyse."

Lily and Violet, stunned, simply stared at her. "Lord Vyse? But that must mean . . ." Violet was too confused to go on.

"It must mean," Lady Flora said, frowning at being interrupted, "that the rector is the illegitimate son of someone in that family. Perhaps he is even Lord Vyse's natural half brother! What better way to assure his future than to give him a family living, in a place where no one knows the family well?"

To Lily's amazement, the prospect made no difference to her. Did it matter to her if Quentin was the product of an unblessed alliance between the old Lord Vyse and some unknown female? He was still, after all, Quentin.

But she could see that the notion of the rector being the natural son of Lord Vyse had taken hold of her grandmother's imagination, and that Violet, too, was perturbed by it. Just then the room started to fill with Sterlings gathering before dinner, and the girls picked up their work and changed the subject.

The next day the children were still inconsolable

over the loss of the rabbit, Arabella wept with repentence over a note from Mr. Watson, accusing her of being faithless, and even the weather cooperated in gloominess so that Good Friday was appropriately sad and solemn. Lily stayed home from church attending to her mother, who was tired and uncharacteristically fretful.

"I like to have you with me, my dear," said Lady Sterling, as she sat in her boudoir hemming a diaper, with Lily beside her. "Your aunts are kind and mean well, but they worry me to death, always telling me not to do this or that—as if I hadn't already been through this many times! And your Grandmama is far too forceful a person to be around a lady in my state." She sighed. "I only wish I could come down and help—there must be so much to do! And now your father tells me he has given permission for a dance on Monday."

"I hope it does not displease you, Mother," said Lily. "I promise it will trouble you not at all. Perhaps you can come down and sit for a while and watch the dancing."

"Oh, no," replied Lady Sterling. "Not once I have been confined. Everyone would think it very odd indeed. And you must not think I am displeased. I only wish for you and the other girls to enjoy yourselves now while you are yet young. And it is an excellent time for a dance, with so many young men about. Why, just think, perhaps Lord Vyse himself will dance with you!"

246

"Yes, perhaps he will," Lily replied, trying to repress her instinctive reaction of dismay. She wondered what it would be like to dance with Mr. Vernon, and decided that he would probably take delight in standing up with her before everyone, fueling speculation and causing her embarrassment. But she would not allow him to do so, she decided. She would take advantage of the situation, and challenge him to reveal his great secret, even if it might be the one her grandmother suspected. She was not sure if she was ready to hear it, for had he not said that she would despise him for it? But affairs could not be allowed to proceed any further until she had discovered the truth.

Chapter Ten

"I tell you I shall not permit it! I have carried on well enough till now and I will not have you ruin it all for a silly scruple." Quentin slammed his glass down, spilling some of his wine on the polished mahogany table.

He was not a little amazed at his own vehemence, for Lewis Thorpe had made his suggestion in a spirit of friendship and concern. But he was miserably out of sorts, and knew he would remain so until he could settle what had become the central question of his existence these days, his feelings for Lily Sterling and hers for him. That morning he had rented a miserable hack at the local inn and ridden to Chester, where, in addition to overseeing the shipment of the silver font, he had made what he now realized had been a rash purchase. No doubt Lily would throw it back at him if he dared present his ring to her. But he must not abuse poor Lewis because of it, he reminded himself.

Faced with the clergyman's tactful silence, he rubbed his aching head. "I'm sorry. That was uncalled for. I know you are only doing your duty, but foolish as this whole wager has been, I have so far acted my part well, and the thought of you taking over the Easter service is like admitting failure."

"But you have not failed, Lord Vyse," replied Lewis soothingly. "You have certainly won the wager—even my brother would admit it—"

"I don't care a damn about that," interrupted Quentin. By now it was not the wager Quentin was concerned about; it was Lily's discovering from anyone but himself that he was not the man he pretended to be. It would be just like Thorpe, he thought, to use his absence from the pulpit on Easter as an excuse to reveal both their identities. Little he would care for the anger of the neighborhood! He could simply enjoy the mischief he had caused and leave Quentin and Sir George to explain. There must be no chance of Lily hearing the story from any lips but his own.

Quentin thought he knew Lily well enough to anticipate her reaction. She would not be especially pleased to discover that she had won the admiration of a lord and not a humble parson. No, he thought with a secret smile, his Lily cared nothing for such things as rank. Besides, Thorpe was a lord and and the girl had frankly admitted she disliked him, he thought wryly.

Aware that Lewis awaited an answer, he gathered his courage together and came to a decision. He had hidden behind this identity long enough. It was

249

time he faced the consequences of his folly.

"Very well," he told the delighted Reverend Thorpe. "You take Easter service. As of tomorrow I am no long Mr. Vernon, Rector of Mickleford, but once more Lord Vyse."

"I am happy to hear you say so, sir," said the clergyman, pressing his hand. "And you have my earnest assurances that I will support you in this matter, no matter what my brother might say. I will even stay on a few days to perform the christenings, now that your 'patron's' gift has arrived," he ended with a twinkle in his eye.

Quentin raised his eyebrows. "My congratulations, Lewis. I did not know you had it in you to stand up to your brother." He began to laugh. "I wonder if the neighborhood will not be more angry with him than with me, for pretending to be the long-awaited Lord Vyse! At least when they discover who *I* am, local curiosity will protect me somewhat from their wrath. And you may tell your brother that if he wishes to argue over the terms of the wager, he can have my grays and be welcome. He may not be a top-sawyer, but at least he's not so cow-handed that he'll ruin their mouths. Besides, I want nothing to do with that flashy curricle of his. I'm after a better prize."

Leaving the Reverend Mr. Thorpe's curiosity over his sudden change of heart unsatisfied, he left in search of Sir George. "Ah, there you are," he said as he caught sight of that gentleman preparing to

250

leave the rectory. "Off to the Hall once more?"

George paled. "I was going to . . . going to take my leave of her, Quentin. I can't support this masquerade any longer."

Quentin clapped his friend across the back. "Faint heart! I have come to the same conclusion, but with a different intent. Come, let's walk." And in a turn around the rectory garden, he told his friend what was in his heart and mind. "And I'll take the chance of her despising me, but she must know the truth," he finished, enjoying Sir George's open-mouthed amazement.

"You're a close one, Quentin. Never realized how strongly you felt about young Lily. Then again I was entirely preoccupied with my own problems." He grinned sheepishly. "But I want to wish you all the luck in the world."

Quentin grimaced. "I'll need it, I fear, and so will you. There's something smoky about Thorpe lately. He was undoubtedly surprised to find that we had done so well at our task, but he won't give in so easily. I only hope he doesn't do something to ruin our chances before we are able to reveal the truth in our own ways."

"But when? Don't want to wait too long — I'm bursting with impatience already."

"I'm going to tell her as soon as I can contrive to see her alone, but I shan't go up to the Hall. That would be to risk creating a distressing scene."

"You mean in case she throws you out," George

prompted gloomily. "I suppose you're right. That will mean waiting till they come here." He brightened. "After service everyone is sure to be busy watching the mumming."

"Exactly my thought. And take heart, my friend. Even if Miss Sterling sends you away with a flea in your ear, you can always come back and try again."

"I shan't leave off trying till there is no hope left," proclaimed Sir George stoutly.

Quentin smiled, wondering if Violet Sterling would be any more receptive to the news that she had been fooled than he expected her sister would be. "By the way, you must know that I am no longer playing clergyman. Lewis is going to conduct the service tomorrow."

George protested. "People will be bound to suspect something havey-cavey."

"Not necessarily," replied Quentin. "Everyone will imagine I am indisposed." He smiled. "In fact, *you* will tell them so at the church door. And as for Lord Thorpe, I'll see to him. As far as I am concerned, the wager is over. I want my name and my life back again."

Easter morning, after the congregation had paused outside to watch the joyful burning of the Jack 'o Lent on the green by a gang of lively youths, they filed into church and were very surprised to be greeted with the news that the rector was indisposed. Even the splendid job the Ladies' Society had done in filling the church with flowers, the sight of the big white Easter candle in its gilded stand upon the altar, and the shining church silver and embroidered cloths did not distract the festive worshipers from the oddity of the rector's absence.

The buzz of gossip grew louder when the word was passed that the visiting Reverend Lewis would take the service. Miss Finch and Miss Hicks were dismayed, Ned and Bert grumbled, and Tim Proper looked gloomy.

"Does this mean," the two spinsters asked a nervous Sir George, "that we are not to perform our play?"

"Not at all," he assured them. "you shall do it just as we rehearsed it, directly after the sermon." Lewis had agreed that it should be done. Thus reassured, the players took their pews as did the rest of the congregation.

The squire's family, all attired in their best, arrived a bit late, and Lily felt a lurch in her stomach when she looked up at the pulpit and saw not Quentin, but the visiting clergyman in his place. Throughout the service she brooded. Perhaps he was really ill, as it was whispered, though it seemed unlikely. Perhaps he had simply left, and Lord Vyse would appoint the Reverend Mr. Thorpe instead, which seemed even less likely. Had she driven him away? If only she had not been so foolish, tormenting him at every turn, making things difficult for

253

him. What matter if he had pretended to be stern and self-righteous, covering a soul just as prone to error as everyone else's? She was certainly no better.

In all, she scarcely heard a word of the service, and even the sincere, but halting performance of the play the rector had so painfully rehearsed failed to bring so much as a smile to her face, though she heard smothered chuckles from some corners of the church, and the squire himself was obviously making a heroic effort to maintain his composure at the thought of Miss Finch as Mary Magdelene, and at Tim Proper's expression as he pretended to regard the risen Savior.

It was only when she was outside and the band of mummers she had organized were gathering about her that Lily was able to throw off her dejection. She helped them form up the procession, led by local musicians and with the brightly dressed village children joining in. They paraded to the applause of onlookers until they gathered across the green.

She stood a little apart from the crowd, watching her players anxiously, and to her relief the performance went smoothly, and the audience appeared delighted. Even the clergyman from London, she noticed, watched it without so much as a yawn. It did disturb her, however, to note that Uncle John was standing apart with Lord Vyse, and that the two appeared to be in deep converse. She knew her uncle to be a good-natured but careless man, and wondered what their sudden friendship portended. Just then she felt a light touch at her elbow. Turning, she saw that it was Quentin. No one else seemed to notice him. The crowd was absorbed in the antics of one of the mummers as he went about collecting money, and the cider, ale, and cakes were being distributed.

Quentin tugged a little at her arm, and she withdrew with him under the trees, out of sight of the celebrants. He was dressed much more finely than she had ever seen him, and looked most unlike himself. An unfamiliar, exquisitely tailored blue coat fit his form so snugly that it appeared to move with him like his skin. His neckcloth was artfully tied beneath his chin, and above it he held his head proudly. There was a clarity and determination in his eyes that had not been there before, even in those moments when he had looked upon her with passion. Some pretense that had used to color his every speech and movement, she realized, had now disappeared.

But his voice was as warm as ever. "Do not look so surprised, my dear. I was sure that you, of all people, would not believe that faradiddle about my being ill."

"You are right; I thought you had deserted us."

"Deserted you, or deserted Mickleford?" he asked, gesturing to the scene before them. She looked at him and saw what looked like guilt in his eyes. Then she looked away, at the assembled villagers.

Confused at his appearance and tone, she wondered what he wanted of her, and took refuge in observing the activity on the green.

The refreshments almost consumed, attention on the green was being turned to the the great egg rolling. The eggs that Lily and Violet had dyed under Lady Flora's direction had been brought to church in baskets and blessed by Mr. Thorpe, and now the children contested to see whose egg would remain unbroken. Lily saw William and Steven gaily join the village children with their own eggs, which she and Violet had specially decorated by drawing their names and pretty designs upon them in hot wax before dipping them in dye. Noting that she was not observed by anyone, she turned reluctantly away from the festivities and back to Quentin. His figure seemed to loom beside her like her very fate.

"Come, before they see us." He took her arm.

Lily stood still. "I do not know why I should go with you," she said to him, pretending truculence, when what she really felt was fear. She told herself she shouldn't allow him to spoil her feast day, for which she had worked so hard. But she knew in her heart that she was simply too weak to be alone with him again.

His eyes looked candidly into hers. "Please."

It was only one word, but it was complete in its sincerity. His request touched her in spite of herself, and she let him guide her away from the boisterous celebration, across the green and back to the rectory. She wondered what he meant by this sudden urgency and knew she should have been angry with him for spiriting her away. But just then he reassuringly squeezed the hand that was resting on his arm, and all that seemed to matter was his presence beside her, his arm bearing her along.

She looked up at his strong profile, admiring in spite of herself the line of his jaw, the curve of his mouth, and the way he carried his lithe body. Her agitation was betrayed by the trembling hand she brought up to straighten her new spring bonnet. The silk ribbons danced as she attempted to set the rose-colored bonnet straighter on her head as they reached the gate.

Quentin took her hand down and held it gently between his own. The trembling stilled but she could not look at him. He led her into the deserted rectory, and she followed, as if in a daze. "Please, sit down," he said, and drew her down beside him onto a sofa in his study. She stared unseeingly at the desk, the bookshelves, the masculine clutter that had defied Mrs. Philpott's efforts at tidiness.

His words startled her out of her dreamlike state. "I must tell you that it is necessary for me to leave Mickleford," he said.

"I . . . I am sorry." What had come over her? Weeks ago she would have been loath to admit such a thing, but now out of the storm in her heart came the truth. She *was* sorry, bitterly so.

Lily could not look at him, but his voice went on, deep, serious. "You must not be. I know that you suspect it is because of you that I am leaving, and in a fashion you are right, but—"

She could not be still any longer. "I will not upbraid you for what passed between us. I was as much at fault as you," she blurted out. On looking up at him she was surprised by the pain in his eyes.

"Dear sweet Lily, do not apologize, not to me." He took both of her hands and pressed them to his lips. "It is my place to apologize. I am not what I have claimed to be. I have deceived you."

So Lady Flora had been right! If that was all, she could readily forgive him. "Oh, Quentin," she said impulsively, holding his hands tighter, "you must not fear that we look down upon you because of your birth. Why, no one need know that you are not Lord Vyse's legitimate son. And if you only took orders because the family wanted you out of the way, why, perhaps Papa can—"

"My dear Lily, what is all of this?" he asked incredulously. "I had no idea that there was any such speculation about me."

Lily stepped away, wishing she had said nothing. "It was Lady Flora, you see. She finally remembered, after she heard the children calling their rabbit, which they had named after you, that Lord Vyse's family name is Vernon, and so she at once realized who you must be." Lily was startled to see the corners of his eyes crinkle with laughter and a

258

smile spread across his lips. Very well, she thought with annoyance, it was nothing to be ashamed of, but must he laugh at his illegitimacy?

"I fear," he said with a gentle smile, "that the truth is much worse than Lady Flora's very interesting theory. And please remind me, before I leave, to thank the children for naming the rabbit after me."

Reminded of his intention, Lily hung her head. "It too, has gone away. We have not been able to find it for three days." But by now, though she was ashamed of having jumped to a false conclusion, she trembled to think of what the truth might be that was worse than the stain of bastardy.

"But you must let me go on," he continued "My name is Quentin Vernon, yes, but I am no clergyman. *I* am Lord Vyse. The man who introduced himself here as Lord Vyse is Thorpe, an old rival of mine, who two months ago offered me a wager that I could not pose successfully as a clergyman."

Lily, shocked, withdrew her hands. "A *wager!*" She felt soiled and disgusted. That two men of rank should make a mockery of the village in such a way was something she could not comprehend, or forgive. No doubt they had enjoyed further sport wagering whether one of them could not seduce some innocent country girl. And here she had begun to extend a comforting hand to this very man, thinking that he was ashamed of his birth. She felt her face burn, and hardened her heart.

259

"Then I suppose you have won your wager, sir, though much good it will do Mickleford," she said bitterly, turning her head away from him. "You are despicable."

His voice in reply was harsh. "Did I not once tell you that you would despise me? But still I am surprised at how much it pains me to hear it confirmed from your own lips."

Lily's anger flowed and mingled with the pain of having been betrayed, by him and by her own heart. "You can hardly expect me to believe that it is in my power to cause you any pain," she cried, facing him once again, eyes ablaze, "when you have so little opinion of me as to make me a party to this absurd masquerade. From the first moment we set eyes on each other you have been making a game of me."

He recaptured her hands and placed them against his chest. "You are wrong. It is love, sweetheart, that has made a game of me. Oh, I was arrogant and thoughtless, I admit it, so accustomed to flirting with every pretty face that I almost forgot my foolish mission here when I first beheld you. But I knew it would be cruel to both of us to continue, so I tried to ignore you."

He was smiling now, as if reminiscing on their battles, and Lily's chest began to feel tight. Beneath her hands pumped the deep and steady rhythm of his heart, and she did not pull away. "But at every turn this beauteous Lily sprang up to rebuke me with her wonderful eyes as green as verdant nature herself. I tried every way I could to give you a disgust of me, though it failed to save me from my own passion."

"And so you did give me a disgust of you, sir," Lily forced herself to reply, resisting being lulled by his soft words and ardent gaze. For answer he stroked her cheek, which made her shiver. "I beg you to forget now that I am anything but your Quentin—not the rector, not Mr. Vernon, not Lord Vyse—just a soul at your command, a heart at your feet."

"I . . . I cannot," she choked, pulling her hand away and rising up from the bench.

He rose and gathered her into his arms, and though she knew it would be safer to run away she found herself instead resting her head against his broad chest. "To have been so taken in . . ." Her tears broke and he held her closer, pushing back the bonnet, already askew, and smoothing the wild waves of her hair.

"Each one of your tears is a blade piercing me. I blame myself, over and over, for inflicting any unhappiness on you, Lily, but now I am in a position to make up for the hurt I have caused."

She looked up, startled, her eyes still wet, her lips moist and slightly parted. Before she knew it she was being kissed most thoroughly, and if there had been any doubt of the power of his passion for her before, it was removed at one stroke. But the ques-

261

tion tormented her. How did he intend to make up for what he had done? He could not possibly suggest that she become his mistress; any man who claimed to love her should know her better than that. But that he would offer a more honorable suggestion she could scarcely credit. Yet it soon became apparent that was indeed what he intended.

Lord Vyse sat down with her again, releasing her with palpable reluctance as he spoke very softly to her. "I most sincerely beg, my dearest Lily, that you will permit me to call formally upon your father and ask his permission . . ." He stopped, touched her face again, almost worshipfully, and said, "Oh, the devil take his permission! Will you be my wife?"

An instant pounding of her pulse seemed to urge Lily to shout "yes" at the top of her lungs, but a moment's sober reflection, gained only because he was no longer holding her so closely and thus disturbing her senses, gave her pause. Despite the apparent fulfillment of her dreams of being swept away by just such a lover, it would be the greatest folly to agree to marry a man about whom she knew so little, and who had deceived her.

She told him as much, her voice gradually growing more forceful. "I know nothing of you, Lord Vyse. I thought I knew Quentin Vernon, and that it was my misfortune to . . . to have fallen in love . . ." She had to pause, for on her pronouncing the word he took her hand and pressed it to his lips. ". . . with a man who seemed set out to frustrate

262

my every plan, and who, it became apparent, had a different nature than that he showed to the world."

"I will show you who and what I really am, my love, if you will only give me the chance," he said earnestly. "And I have something for you." He took out of his pocket a little green velvet bag and handed it to her.

Numbly, Lily opened it to find a tiny, exquisite egg in silver filigree, studded with tiny emeralds and diamonds. She caught her breath, watching the sunlight sparkle and reflect off it. "You must not—" She attempted to give it back to him, but he firmly pressed it into her hands.

"At least open it, and give me the pleasure of knowing that your eyes have looked on my gift. Whether you will accept it or not is up to you."

She saw that there was a tiny catch at one side, and as she pressed it half of the egg flew open, revealing a black velvet bed on which rested the most beautiful ring she had ever seen. It was a thin gold band, engraved in an intricate pattern of leaves, and set in a bed of sparkling emeralds was a perfect diamond.

"I wish you to know that this is no attempt to impress you with my wealth or rank or any of the other things for which you don't give a fig, but a symbol of my most earnest desire to cherish you forever. If you will but allow me to do so, you will make me the happiest man in the world."

As she stared at the ring, Lily was torn. In itself

263

it was but a beautiful bauble, and though she owned nothing like it and no doubt never would in her present situation, it meant nothing without the assurance of his love. Her feelings were urging her to let him do as he wished and prove it to her, but how?

She began to think about the uproar the revelation of his real identity would cause. What would her family say? Certainly her aunts would think him a wonderful catch, masquerader or not, but her gentle mother and honest, upright father might very well be shocked and disapproving. And what of the rest of Mickleford? She would be betraying the village that had been in her family's trust for generations: people she had helped and cajoled, shared good and bad times with since her childhood. Worse, what if she was merely a novelty for this Lord Vyse, the landlord who had never troubled to show his face in the neighborhood before until it suited him and his frivolous amusements to do so? She with her country ways and simple tastes would never fit into his fashionable life.

"I cannot," she repeated. "Please, I must go."

He slowly let her go. "Very well. I did expect this. But you will see me again. I will do whatever is necessary to convince you of my sincerity. In the meantime, will you keep the ring as a token of my promise? It binds you to nothing, and even if you refuse ever to receive me again, I shall be happy knowing that it is with you, though I cannot be."

264

For a moment, looking into his clear blue eyes that held nothing but love, she was ready to accept him, but he had already acted one part very well; he could be acting one now. How could she ever trust him?

She turned the ring over in her hand, and was about to give it back to him, when as she extended her hand she saw his vulnerability in the set of his mouth and the steady, expectant way his gaze rested on her. On impulse, she slipped the ring back into its little egg, and said, "Very well. I will keep it. But I will not wear it. Until . . ."

His tension visibly lightened. "Until, I hope, you will allow me to put it on your finger."

She slipped the egg into her reticule, gave Quentin one last, wondering glance, and left the rectory. Slowly she walked across the green to join her family. The crowd was just breaking up, and William was jumping up and down holding aloft his bright green egg.

"I won, I won!" he cried.

Absently, Lily ruffled his fair hair, and to the questions of her sisters and cousin, she offered no explanation.

"But indeed it was very odd of you to disappear like that during all the fun," Arabella persisted. "Fortunately, no one but the family remarked on it."

Lily, relieved that no one had actually seen Quentin spirit her away, listened with surprise as Olive said with a sly glance at her elder sister, "And

Violet was spirited off by Mr. Hollister!" she said with a sly glance at her elder sister. She giggled. "Perhaps Lily had a tryst, too."

Signore Marco chuckled. He seemed to have regained his former ebullience, and was obviously devoting himself exclusively to Olive. "A holiday is a fine time for courting, as you know, my dear signorina, so do not be severe with your sisters." He squeezed her arm and she blushed.

Lily glanced sharply at Violet, who had a brooding look about her, but her half sister did not offer any explanation of her tête-à-tête with the curate.

When Sir Richard offered the gig to his daughters, saying he would walk home with the boys, Violet and Lily climbed in gratefully and Lily took the reins. As they drew out of sight of the village, Violet put her hand over her sister's, and said softly, "I know."

Startled, Lily almost dropped the reins. "How can you?"

"It was Mr. Hollister, that is, Sir George. He told me of this wager that was on between Lord Vyse—the real Lord Vyse—and Lord Thorpe and that his lordship was going to reveal himself to you, as George did to me, because . . ."

She choked back a sob. "Oh, Lily, he says he loves me, but I am so mortified! To think I have been so taken in . . ."

"And I, too," said Lily. Quentin had not even troubled to tell her that Mr. Hollister was part of this ludicrous masque, but of course, how could he not be? And now Violet, too, was suffering as she was. She barely paid attention to the horse; it knew its way home. Instead she stared out over the countryside, green and shining on Easter morn. But in her heart it was dank February, like the day she had met Quentin Vernon for the first time.

At home the Easter dinner was uncustomarily quiet. The squire watched over the holiday board, his eyes resting occasionally on the troubled faces of his daughters. Violet was outwardly calm, but her emotions betrayed her in that she ate hardly anything and failed to reprove Olive, who was in high gig, laughing merrily at every sally of the signore's. As for Lily, she tried to assume her usual manner, but her thoughts intruded and she surpassed even Aunt Poppy for vagueness when she had to be asked three times if she desired another slice of roast lamb.

The rest of the family appeared preoccupied as well. The children were flushed from their morning's holiday amusements, but had begun to recall the loss of their rabbit, and twitched in their chairs, wanting to be excused to go and look for it again. Arabella was looking exceptionally pretty and no longer spared a glance for the signore, as both Lord Vyse and Mr. Watson had promised to dance with her on the morrow.

Lady Flora cast a suspicious eye at her son John, who left off his usual teasing manner with his young nieces and now simply stared at them and smiled, shaking his head occasionally, in between swallows of wine. "And what has put you in such fine fettle, my boy? Thinking of leaving us and going off to Town?"

"Of course not, Mama, at least not until this famous dance of ours tomorrow. Why, the entire neighborhood is looking forward to it. Such a fitting way to celebrate the holiday."

"Hmmph," Lady Flora replied. "Don't you try to bamboozle me, because it won't wash. You are up to something, because you have that same look you always did when you were a boy and about to get into mischief."

But Uncle John would confess nothing, he just smiled and called for more pudding. Lily wondered again what her uncle was about. Now that she knew the real identity of the supposed Lord Vyse, it occurred to her that he might have communicated the story of the wager to her uncle. If so, Uncle John was showing remarkable discretion. It was something he would ordinarily take great pleasure in revealing, just to enjoy the reaction it would elicit.

After dinner as the ladies of the family prepared to withdraw, Lily saw Olive press Signore Marco's hand fervently, and they exchanged a speaking glance. Could the little visitor have made her sister an offer? Unaccountably, she was worried. What, after all, did they really know about him? But she trusted her father to deal with the problem.

Still, she was not prepared for Olive's excited announcement as they retired to the drawing room. "I must go up and tell Stepmama—she will be so happy—but first I must tell you all what has happened," she declared, when they had barely seated themselves and found some needlework or books to occupy them. Arabella, who was at the pianoforte, turned expectantly.

"Why, what is it, my dear?" asked Aunt Hyacinth, who had been too preoccupied with the possible ruin of her daughter's engagement to pay much attention to her niece's cavorting with the foreign visitor.

Aunt Poppy twinkled and looked knowing. "Does it have something to do with the dear signore?" she asked.

Olive blushed. "Oh, and I thought we were so discreet! But it is true. Signore Marco has asked me to be his bride!"

The aunts and Arabella gave their wholehearted congratulations, but Lily and Violet were more subdued. Violet apparently shared Lily's mistrust, perhaps because of their recent experiences, and even attempted to temper her sister's transports.

"Are you certain, my dear, that you know the signore well enough? After all, he being a foreigner, we know nothing of his family or his reputation."

"But we know of his Uncle the count!" protested Olive, shocked.

"Of course," Violet said calmly. "But what we know is only what the signore has told us, and you have to admit that it all sounds rather far-fetched."

"Besides," added Lily practically, "his Italian accent is very erratic. Sometimes I think he sounds distinctly English."

Olive's eyes grew moist. "You are all jealous of my happiness, and are only trying to spoil it for me."

They hurried to assure her that it was her future happiness that concerned them, and that they had only been advising her to wait a bit before making her decision, but she would not hear them.

Just then, a distracted-looking signore burst into the room, his neckcloth askew, his hair plastered across his head, and his full face very red.

"My dear," he said without a trace of accent, "you must speak to your father! Tell him—" He saw the sharp glances the ladies exchanged and suddenly continued in his former mellifluous tones. "Bella Olivia, it seems that your esteemed Papa, the squire, has . . . he has refused his permission for me to address you!"

"It seems far too late for that," commented Aunt Poppy with unexpected shrewdness.

As if she were a bubble pricked by a pin, Olive collapsed, and it took her sister and one of her aunts to support her, weeping, up to her chamber, while the agitated signore, ignoring the others and all his former good manners, strode over to the

270

table where the brandy was kept and poured himself a large glass, which he downed in one gulp.

"Signore?" said Arabella tentatively.

He seemed to come to himself and almost dropped the glass guiltily. "I . . ."

"Never mind; just tell us why you are pretending to be the connection of an Italian nobleman, and what we are to do about poor Olive," said Lily in a neutral tone, at which her aunt, cousin, and grandmother stared at her as if she had three heads.

"I . . ." Again the man opened and closed his mouth, looked at the faces around him, and sighed. In so doing, he seemed to shrink down, until he was not an exotic, eccentric foreigner but simply a disappointed little man in a funny waistcoat. "I am sorry." "I've been a bit of a fool." He spoke in educated, respectable English with a distinct Northern twang. "I know I should have confessed at once, but how else was I to make anyone take notice of me amongst all that great crowd at Harrogate but by pretending to be different?"

"Your uncle is not a count at all, is he?" said Arabella with the air of one discovering a great mystery.

Lady Flora snorted. "Of course not, idiot girl. Come here, young man. Sit down—but first pour yourself another brandy and bring one for me—and you shall tell us of this foolish masquerade of yours."

To Lily's surprise, her grandmother seemed to be

271

enjoying herself. She supposed it was due to relief that the fellow wasn't one of the despised foreigners after all, but simply a silly Englishman. No less silly, she thought, than another pair of gentlemen who had come to the village this spring. Despite her misery, it almost made her smile. To think that Lord Vyse and the "Italian" visitor he had laughed at had so much in common!

"Now," Lady Flora continued, sipping her brandy with relish, "you will, if you please, tell us who you are and what all this nonsense is about."

The "signore" looked less distraught than formerly. Whether this was due to the brandy or because it had become clear to him that he was in no immediate danger of being ejected from the house in disgrace, Lily could not tell. Now he obligingly told his story.

"My real name is Mark Murray. My father is the owner of an ironworks near Sheffield, along with some other manufacturing enterprises."

"Aha!" cried Lady Flora, while the others gaped in amazement. "I begin to see. But go on, young man."

The newly revealed Mr. Murray resorted once more to his brandy, and thus emboldened, continued. "I spend some years in Italy, in Genoa, to be precise, managing trade for my father and uncle, his business partner."

"Formerly known to us as your uncle the count I presume," murmured Lily with a smile she could not repress.

Mr. Murray looked rueful. "Precisely, Miss Lily. I shudder to think now of the way I have imposed on all of you, but when I saw you at Harrogate, such a fine family, obviously well-bred, born to the land for generations, not . . . not mushrooms, like the Murrays." He hung his head for a moment.

"But you mustn't be ashamed!" cried Aunt Poppy, obviously wishing to comfort him. "There is nothing disgraceful in being in trade." But she said this with with a smidgen of doubt.

"Perhaps not, ma'am, but all my life I have had what Papa always called ideas above my station. Oh, I never aspired to be one of the fashionable set, or a Pink of the Ton."

Glancing at his gaudy attire, Lily wanted to giggle. But she was beginning to feel sorry for him.

"I just wanted to be one of you."

Arabella looked at him in amazement. "One of us?" she said incredulously. "Why, we are not very rich, nor are we particularly fashionable. Uncle Richard will not hear of us spending a season in London, or being presented at court."

"No, but have I even that choice? True, I am wealthy, much more wealthy than you might imagine, but I don't *belong* anywhere the way you do. I am an upstart, a jumped-up Cit, and although it doesn't trouble my father or my uncle, it does me. So I thought the best way to achieve my ends was to . . ." he hesitated, seeing that they all hung on

273

his words, "to marry into that class to which I aspire. As there was no way I could make you believe that I was an English gentleman of fashion and leisure, rather than a man of business, I pretended to be an Italian gentleman related to the aristocracy. I thought I could get away with it long enough to find some lady of good birth who would love me, and then I could make her understand . . ." He stumbled a little, then held up his hands. *am* very very rich, you know." He spread his hands. "And I *do* love Olive, though I doubt she would believe it after this."

Lily wanted to laugh, but the young man's torment was all too real. She could hardly comprehend that there was such foolishness in the world as had been exhibited to her in the past few days. She wondered what Quentin would say about it, then a sudden spasm in her chest reminded her that he was gone from her life. She brought her mind back to the immediate problem; Olive, although not knowing her suitor's real identity, was apparently in love with him, and her father had refused to countenance the idea of a marriage. Probably he had long ago taken the visitor's measure, and if she and Violet had not been so distracted, they might themselves have seen through him before this.

"What is to be done, Mama?" asked Aunt Poppy, patently distressed. "Poor, *poor* dear Olive! Why, her heart will be broken. And you, signore—I mean, of course, Mr. Murray—I do believe you when you say that you love her. Oh, what are we to do?"

"Don't be nonsensical, Poppy," retorted Lady Flora, who had been thinking deeply, chin sunk on her age-veined hand. "They will be married, of course. No one else has offered for the girl, though she's getting to be more than a girl. And I like this young man."

Poppy, Arabella, and Lily gasped. "You . . . you *like* him, Grandmama?" asked Lily uncertainly.

"Certainly. He may be a mushroom, as he admits, and have soiled his hands in trade, but he has plenty of bottom, and though his idea was pitiful," she cast him a slightly scornful glance, but not without sympathy, "he did fool us all for a long time. Come, it's not so bad. I don't know what Dickey is thinking of, to refuse you. As you say, you are very rich. My son ought to be pleased."

Mr. Murray looked as though he scarcely dared to hope. "But my family . . . my father's business . . ."

Lady Flora waved these objections away. "Piffle. Nothing for it but to quit and set yourself up somewhere in the neighborhood. Couple of good houses, with land, going to decay, not more than two hours drive from here."

Mr. Murray looked appreciably cheerier than when he had first come in, in fact, almost like his jovial Italian alter ego. Then his smile fell. "But Sir Richard refused me even when he thought I was still Signore Marco. He may be pleased that I am

275

rich, but what will an honest man like the squire think of my deception?"

"I shall speak to him," proclaimed Lady Flora, rising majestically from her chair. "Now you wait here, and I shall be back directly after I have explained everything to my son." And, spine straight, step determined, she went in search of the squire.

Arabella giggled. "I hope Uncle Richard will appreciate Grandmama's explaining everything to him."

"I wish she would have let me speak to Papa," Lily said. "I think I could have made him understand. But Grandmama will only set his back up."

"True," agreed Aunt Poppy. "She will very likely order him to give his blessing to the match. Poor Olive! Who is going to tell her this sad news?"

Their gazes all fell on the erstwhile signore. He shrank away at first, but at length he straightened up and put down his glass. "Of course it is my responsibility to tell her. I only hope she can find it in her heart to forgive me."

"I shall go and tell her you wish to speak with her," offered Lily. "Go and wait in the sitting room. I do not know what she will say, Mr. Murray, when she hears the truth, but she must know so that she can decide. If she really wants to marry you . . . Well, I think you have been very silly but that you truly do care for her."

For a moment he resorted to his put-on continental manner, and, kissing her hand gratefully, hurried from the room to await Olive.

"His manners are very good for a man in trade," remarked Aunt Poppy, gazing after him with renewed interest.

"And if he is very rich, just think of all the carriages and clothes, parties and pin money cousin Olive will have!" said Arabella eyes dancing. "And perhaps they will have a house in London, and invite us all to stay."

Leaving the others to these grandiose dreams, Lily made her way upstairs to Olive's bedchamber, where the girls' maid and Violet were restoring her with handkerchiefs soaked in lavender water and eau de cologne, vinaigrettes and burnt feathers.

But as Lily came in, Olive sat up in bed and waved away all these efforts, took the cup of tea Violet held and began to sip it. Lily had prudently taken some ratafia biscuits with her, and she approached the broken-hearted Olive she offered them. "Here, my dear, you must keep up your strength. Your suitor begs the favor of a private interview in the sitting room."

Olive sniffed and put down her teacup, clattering it into the saucer. She accepted a biscuit and began to nibble tentatively, then finished it in another bite. Already there was more color in her face. "Does he? I suppose I must go. Only I am afraid of what he will say. And Papa—"

Lily sat down on the bed. "I'm afraid that you will have to endure one more bit of shocking news, but it is not all bad, so you must be very brave and listen to what the signore has to say to you."

Violet administered more sweetened tea, and finally Olive got up, rearranged her hair with the sisters' help, straightened her gown, and went down to the sitting room. Lily and Violet accompanied her as far as the door, where they gave her an encouraging hug, and sent her in. From the doorway they could hear the pacing feet of Mr. Murray.

To their dismay, squeals and cries could soon be heard emerging from the room, but there was no telling from these sounds exactly how Olive was accepting the story, and from the low, rumbling tones of Mr. Murray, there was no telling if he was as expert a lover in English as he was in Italian. Fortunately, their suspense was put to an end very soon. The door opened and Olive emerged. Her face was pink and shiny, her eyes moist.

"Oh!" she cried. "I have never been so taken in in all my life! A very good joke indeed, wouldn't you say? I always suspected there was no count, you know. And did you know that darling Mark is very rich? And he assures me that he loves me. Papa must be made to listen to reason."

"Grandmama has gone in to him," Lily told her, stunned at her sister's lack of sensibility, but relieved. "She may just bring him around to her way of thinking. She told us that she likes Mr. Murray, and admires his spirit. A thing that surprised us very much indeed, I can tell you!"

Just then Lady Flora emerged from the squire's study. "Well, girls, what do you do hanging about here? Why are you not keeping watch over that Mr. Murray? He's so jumpy he's like to get away if we don't hold him. And he had better not. I have spoken to your father and made it all right," she said with satisfaction. Lily imagined that it had been a struggle of wills, the kind that Lady Flora liked best, but that in the end the squire, who only desired peace, had been bested.

"Oh, thank you, dear Grandmother!" cried Olive. "Mr. Murray has told me all about his silly little masquerade—but I confess I do not know why he should be so modest about himself. As if I wouldn't love him without his having an uncle who is a count! Mrs. Murray . . ." she said dreamily. "I like it ever so much better than Signora Marco."

Violet attempted to bring her sister's thoughts to more practical matters. "But dearest, are you sure? I mean, he seemed very sincere, once he had gotten round to telling the truth, but after all, we still know very little about him."

Olive was scornful. "He's still the same man, whether he calls himself Signore Marco or Mark Murray, isn't he?" Just then her betrothed emerged, a bit sheepishly, from the sitting room, to hear the good news, and rejoicing, the pair went into the study to receive the squire's blessing.

Lily was left wondering whether her sister was not right after all. Was not Quentin Vernon still himself, whether he played at being cleric or not? The things she had come to love about him had nothing to do with his performance as the rector of Mickleford. It was in his voice, his hands, his eyes, the way his slow smile would emerge when he looked at her. It was not his name or in his clothes, but some indefinable thing that made him Quentin Vernon and not some other man. Had she been a fool for sending him away? She surreptitiously patted her pocket, where she carried the little filigree egg and its precious burden. She was glad she had kept it. Perhaps he would come to the dance tomorrow.

Chapter Eleven

The squire surveyed with resignation the chaos that reigned in his household on Easter Monday. First he had been bullied into giving his reluctant assent to Olive's betrothal to Signore Marco, who had turned out to be the son of a Sheffield ironmonger. Now he was faced with the results of his own folly in having given permission for a dance.

His sisters, daughters, and niece were scurrying about, conferring on the refreshments and the girls' gowns and coiffures. The servants were busy moving rugs and furniture from the drawing room, polishing mirrors and silver, setting out punchbowls and glasses. Having spent a relatively peaceful half-hour sitting with his wife, the squire now turned from the confusion in the hall to the refuge of his study only to be brought up short by his mother, who instantly demanded his attention.

Lady Flora was once encased in shawls. "Dickey, must I ask you again to see to that draft? Our guests will come down with congestion of the lungs!"

In truth, the squire himself felt a keen blast of chill

air flowing past his ankles, but was in no mood to think about the reason for its reappearance. "I thought John had seen to it, Mama," he said, edging towards the study door, hoping to get away before the storm broke over his head.

But Lady Flora stepped between him and safety. "Well, it has returned. It rushes through the whole house, but it's worse in the dining room. And where is your brother? I know he's been hobnobbing with that Lord Vyse lately, but he could at least keep to home today of all days." Lady Flora seemed as agitated as the girls at the prospect of that evening's entertainment.

Sir Richard smiled. "I sincerely doubt, Mama, that my brother has left his bed yet, or that Lord Vyse would deign to make a social engagement at the unfashionable hour of eleven in the morning."

Lady Flora appeared to mellow. "You are right, my boy, of course," she said, patting his shoulder as if he were still a youngster and not a grown man and father of his own large family. "My wits have gone begging today, what with all this to'ing and fro'ing, and the girls of no use at all. They have let this quite go to their heads. You would think they had never danced in their lives!"

"Even Violet, Mama?" asked Sir Richard with a smile.

"Even your eldest," she confirmed. With a conspiratorial gesture, she motioned him closer. "Do you know, I believe that curate fellow is going to offer for her."

Sir Richard frowned. "What? Yet another unsuitable match? I don't think I can countenance it."

"Nonsense. You have three marriageable daughters, and none of them getting any younger. Mr. Hollister is undoubtedly a gentleman, and who knows? He may receive preferment from some powerful friend, as Mr. Vernon has."

"About that rector of ours. The girls have whispered it about that there is something between him and Lily," said the squire with the air of a man who is rapidly losing control of his family.

"And if there is?" replied Lady Flora smartly. "I should think you'd be delighted."

"Delighted? Another poor clergyman, dependent upon the whims of a fellow like Lord Vyse?" The squire was growing red in the face.

Lady Flora looked sly. "Well, I think the connection there is closer than we assumed." She repeated to him her suspicions of the rector's origins, at which his frown grew even deeper.

"I don't think that's any recommendation," said Sir Richard. "Mind you, he's a decent enough fellow, and unless I miss my guess there *is* something between him and Lily, though I'll be damned if I can figure out what it is. But to have her wed to the natural son of some profligate peer—"

"Hush!" cried his mother, for Lily was coming down the corridor, a large vase in her arms.

"Ah, here she is, the only one who has at least some of her wits about her today," continued Lady Flora in a quick change of subject. "Now I wish you will go and rest after you do the flowers, my dear. You must look

283

especially pretty tonight, you know."

Lily's smile was a bit abstracted. She wanted nothing better than to nap, but the excitement of the household, her mother's condition, and her own problems prohibited any immediate rest, mental or physical. Nevertheless she replied, "I shall, Grandmama, if Mama does not need me."

"Oh, to be sure," murmured Lady Flora, as if only now recalling that her daughter-in-law was shortly due to present her with another grandchild. "I shall go and sit with her. I must take her some of that special cordial of mine and make sure she drinks it."

Lily, knowing how little to her mother's liking this visitation would be, sent her father a speaking glance. The squire sighed, foreseeing the loss of at least an hour of his precious freedom, but he knew where his duty lay. "Hmm! Well, I shall just go into the dining room to investigate that draft."

At which Lady Flora completely forgot her original intention and was determined on accompanying him. Lily smiled gratefully at her father, sorry to have put him to the trouble, but her first duty at this time was to protect her mother. She was a little worried about her condition.

Although as an unmarried girl she was expected to be ignorant of such things, she had been old enough when her youngest siblings were born to have learned something of the process, and to her eyes her mother did not look well. Yet she had no solid evidence on which to base a recommendation to her father to cancel tonight's entertainment. To be sure, her mother made no complaint, but she was no longer very young, and though Lady Sterling was no stranger to the discomforts of impending motherhood, this was the first time Lily had seen her so tired and restless. Lady Sterling, however, insisted nothing was wrong and that she would prefer not being fussed over till it was absolutely necessary.

Putting aside her anxiety for a moment, Lily set to work filling vases with flowers, some seasonal ones from the Sterling's own garden and a great many hothouse-grown blooms sent by a kindly neighbor. In the bunches that had been delivered by cart that morning, there had been a small posy of primroses tied with green ribbon, with a card tucked away inside. It had been handed to her with a smile and a wink by the boy driving the cart. She had slipped it carefully into the capacious pocket of her apron and tried not to look conscious, but she somehow knew that the bold handwriting on the card was Quentin's. When she was alone, she took it out and her guess was confirmed. The card said only, "May I beg the honor of a dance this evening?" and was signed with his initials. In spite of her distress over his revelations she could not help but be gratified.

Apparently, he was not going to give up easily, although she thought she had been as plain as possible with him yesterday. She had hardly slept last night, thinking about his intentions. At times his sincerity seemed so obvious as to make her feel foolish to doubt it. But after what had happened, she could not easily put her trust in him.

She trembled to think of the consequences if everyone else found out the truth about him. And yet, she knew that when he asked her to dance that evening, she would accept, and not only because it would look rude to refuse. Pausing in her work, she dreamed a moment, imagining herself dancing with him, touching his hand, feeling his arm about her waist, seeing him smile down at her.

Her musing interrupted by yet another claim on her attention, she hurried through her remaining tasks, managed to fit in a half-hour nap from which she awoke with some of her old vigor restored, and set about dressing.

Violet, who was the first one ready, came to help her. Her eldest sister looked younger and prettier than she had in years, in a coral pink silk gown trimmed with cream-colored rosettes and deep flounces, the cut showing off her still excellent figure and ivory skin, while her golden curls were held in place with combs.

"I am so glad you chose the green," she said to Lily, helping her drape the folds of her the gown about her. "It almost matches your eyes, and they look bigger than ever."

"Oh, she looks like a fairy princess!" cried Olive, who entered at that moment, radiant in silver-trimmed pale blue.

Lily stared into the looking-glass, and had the satisfaction of seeing that they were right. Ordinarily she was not overly concerned with her appearance, though it pleased her to wear pretty gowns and to be complimented, but tonight she felt she must absolutely look her best, if only to bolster her confidence. Now that she knew the truth about Quentin Vernon it was going to be a difficult task to face him again in front of everyone.

In the slim gown of misty green crepe, with its gauze overskirt and gold embroidery, she felt like a princess indeed. It embraced the curves of her figure gently, and the slightly dipped décolletage and tiny sleeves showed what seemed to Lily a shocking expanse of smooth, golden-tinted skin. She had hardly noticed this effect during her hurried fittings, squeezed in between errands.

Just then Arabella, in gleaming yellow silk with a beaded bodice and pearls in her hair, entered and, taking in Lily's appearance, drew in her breath. "Oh, my! And now you must let me do your hair."

Waving away the hovering maid, she sat her cousin down, took up brushes, combs, pins, and heated curling tongs and with a skill that her cousins knew well, transformed Lily's freshly washed golden brown locks into a soft mass of waves and curls, caught up by the cluster of primroses in a tiny jeweled holder lent by Lady Sterling. Lily was glad that no one expected her to explain the posy, and that they assumed she had gathered the flowers herself. For a moment she felt a flash of gratitude to Quentin for not embarrassing her with a large display of roses or something extravagant that would cause distressing comment.

Since revealing the truth about himself he had been all humility and consideration. Was that the real Quentin Vernon? Recalling their minor battles and their moments of startling passion, it seemed that a hint of the real Quentin had always lurked behind the pretense.

Wondering if she would ever understand him, she went in to her mother, who was sitting in her boudoir knitting and enjoying the indulgence of a fire in her little grate, for the evening had turned cool. Lady Sterling admired Lily's gown and coiffure, and glad that she had a few moments alone with her before the others came in, Lily pulled a branch of candles closer and sat down next to her mother.

Lady Sterling's delicate features seemed swollen, the circles under her eyes darker than before. She shifted uncomfortably in her seat. All of this Lily had seen before, but this time it unaccountably worried her.

Her mother said, "Oh, dear, I know it is foolish, but I find I am wishing that there was not quite so much time to go before . . ." As if suddenly realizing who she was speaking to, she stopped. "But never mind," she said firmly, pressing her daughter's hand. "You must not think of me, but have a wonderful time, and dance with everyone. Poor dear, you do work hard, even if occasionally you are not to be found precisely when you are wanted," she said with a smile that Lily returned. "But you are a good girl, and I would like to see you happy."

"I *am* happy, Mama," Lily assured her.

Lady Sterling fixed an unusually shrewd gaze upon her eldest daughter. "Are you truly, my love?"

For a moment Lily was strongly tempted to pour out her troubles into that understanding bosom, but she refrained, knowing that to burden her mother at this time would be wrong. With an effort, she smiled and kissed her mother's cheek. "Of course," she replied. "I have the best family in the world, I'm wearing a beautiful gown, and I am going downstairs now to dance the night away. What more could I wish for?"

"What more indeed?" murmured Lady Sterling with a smile. She got up and walked with Lily to the door, stretching wearily, hand on her lower back. For a moment a startled expression crossed her face, but then it disappeared, and Lily thought nothing of it. Promising to come to see her in the morning and tell her all about the dance, she left.

Downstairs, the girls paraded before an appreciative Sir Richard and Uncle John, while Mr. Murray, although he complimented all of the young ladies, had eyes only for his betrothed. When the two went off to coo in a corner while awaiting the guests' arrival, Uncle John chuckled. "Glad to see one of you is off the shelf. Perhaps with a good night's work we can dispose of a few more unmarried females," he said with knowing glances at Lily and Violet, glances that caused them both to blush.

"Hush, sir," said Lady Flora, speaking more harshly than she usually did to her favorite son. "It is extremely vulgar of you to talk so. We are merely entertaining our neighbors, not setting up for a marriage mart."

"Yes, Mama," said John Sterling meekly, but his irrepressible grin took in his two nieces again.

Lily was by now more certain than ever that her

uncle knew more than he should. Yet she was powerless to say anything to him. She merely prayed the evening would pass without any trouble, for when her uncle was even a trifle disguised, his manners were all too apt to suffer.

The guests began to arrive, and passing through the hall where they were relieved of their wraps, they went upstairs to be welcomed by the family at the entrance to the drawing room. Lily greeted her neighbors, including her former suitor Mr. Smythe, enthusiastically, and basked in compliments. Although it was a fairly small party altogether, there were enough young people to make up a set of ten couples down the center of the long drawing room.

The musicians were getting ready, the dancers were tapping their toes, and everyone had arrived except the party from the rectory. Olive and Mr. Murray, whose engagement was going to be announced that evening, were to open the dance, but Lady Flora insisted they could not begin until Lord Vyse arrived with the rector.

Lily had promised the first dance to one of her local admirers, but she was too anxious to take any pleasure in the prospect as yet. Until she had seen Quentin, and observed his demeanor towards her after their last conversation, she could not relax. Violet, standing nearby, seemed to share her trepidation. Surreptitiously she squeezed her sister's hand, and Violet gave her a weak smile. Lily hoped her Uncle John would keep to himself whatever he knew, but when she looked for him, she saw that he had slipped away.

Finally the rectory party made their entrance, and Lily almost gasped. She had never seen Quentin in full evening dress. In his white breeches and black tail coat, satin waistcoat, white silk stockings, and immaculate linen, he moved into the room like a prince, his head held high. For a moment she scarcely saw anyone else, so dazzling did he appear. Briefly their eyes met and although his expression was warm, he gave an almost imperceptible bow. She only hoped no one had noticed her stare.

When the whole party had been greeted by the squire and Lady Flora, they passed on to the other members of the family, and relief surged through Lily when she saw that Quentin was not going to draw any attention to their situation. He merely bowed and greeted her politely as he did her sisters, inquired about the dance she had promised him, and moved on. Before he did, however, Lily was sure he had noticed the posy of primroses in her hair, and that he had allowed a brief look of pleasure to cross his face. She was sure no one else had seen it.

Beside her, she felt Violet bringing her trembling under control as Sir George approached. He, too, looked unusually elegant, and his greeting was as quiet as Quentin's had been, but he immediately bore Violet away with him to the dance.

This part of her ordeal being over, Lily gladly relinquished her hand to her first partner and performed her part in the dance perfectly, smiling and making such conversation as she knew was expected of her. With extreme effort, she kept from allowing her gaze to rest on Quentin, who stood on the side watching the dancers, his gaze occasionally following her.

Somewhat less tense now and sure of her own ability to keep up appearances, Lily danced a second dance and then accepted the offer of her latest partner, who happened to be Mr. Smythe, to get her a glass of punch. It looked as thought Quentin might have changed his mind about dancing with her, for he had not yet approached her. She was surprised at her own feeling of disappointment, for it was bound to have been a difficult experience.

After Mr. Smythe brought her the glass, they stood near the window overlooking the lawns, illuminated by an almost full moon. For a while they stood and chatted comfortably, as her former suitor seemed to have totally lost his awe of her. Lily was relieved to hear that he was now courting another young lady.

Allowing her gaze to drift once more to Quentin, Lily noted to her dismay that he was looking straight at her, even as he stood talking to some other guests. Her heart began to thump harder, though she told herself it meant nothing. Unconsciously she touched the flowers in her hair, and looking up, she saw him watching yet again. He was now only a few yards away, and his slow half-smile made her feel like melting. Hurriedly she looked away. The music stopped and Mr. Smythe began to lead her back to where her grandmama sat enthroned, talking to her cronies and watching over her granddaughters.

When they were almost there Lord Thorpe intercepted them. He, too, wore fashionable evening clothes, but to Lily's eyes the careless way he carried himself could not compare with Quentin's elegant bearing. Even his deep bow seemed insolent, his smile seemed to be musing on a private joke. "May I have the honor of the next dance?"

Lily wondered how to refuse him gracefully. She noted many pairs of eyes on them, because as of yet the man whom everyone thought was Lord Vyse had not honored any of the young ladies with his company. To refuse would look churlish. Just then a shadow fell across the floor. Quentin stood at her side.

"I believe Miss Lily was already promised to me for this dance," he said quietly, and took her hand upon his arm. Strength seemed to flow into her and Lily glanced up, trying to hide her relief, for by now all eyes were upon them. She thought she could hear the gossip beginning to buzz already. Quentin pressed her hand almost imperceptibly closer.

Courage renewed, she said, "That is so, sir. I beg you will excuse us."

Swiftly Quentin escorted her into the set which was forming. Strongly aware of the curiosity of her family and neighbors, she felt herself begin the familiar figures of a country dance almost without thinking.

"Smile," Quentin whispered as they took hands and passed shoulders. He was right, she thought. She must not draw attention to herself, but behave normally. After all, no one should be surprised to see the rector having a dance with the squire's daughter.

Eventually she simply began to enjoy the music and the steps, and the happiness of the other dancers became infectious. Too, it was such a pleasure to watch Quentin move. His dancing combined masculine grace and power with a courtly air towards his partner, and in his eyes there was a hint of his thoughts as he looked across at her, which made her feel very warm.

Her suspicions of these thoughts were confirmed, as he held her around the waist on a turn and whispered into her neck, "You are beautiful."

She looked away, blushing, wondering if their near neighbors had heard. But the other couples seemed to be engaged in their own little flirtations, or else dancing too energetically to pay attention. Out of the corner of her eye she saw Violet dancing animatedly with Sir George, and Arabella on the arm of her betrothed. Quentin grinned at her and at the next opportunity murmured, "Don't worry so. We are the picture of propriety," which made her laugh in spite of herself.

By the time the dance had ended, Lily was more confused than ever. Could she be wrong? The feelings Quentin elicited from her were so powerful that she could not shut them out. He had been in her thoughts almost constantly from the moment they had met, but now that things had come to what in other circumstances would be their natural conclusion, she was paralyzed with doubt.

A little breathless at the dance's end, she allowed Quentin to lead her to the table where refreshments were set out, and they stood sipping and staring wordlessly at one another over the rims of delicate crystal glasses. In his blue eyes was once more that assurance that she was truly cherished and desired. It was like a powerful drug, and affected her most strangely. Her head began to feel light, and she hastily put down her punch with a slight laugh.

"Oh! I shall have no more of that," she said, swaying a little.

Instantly he reached out to support her with an arm around her shoulders, and the heat of his hand on the bare skin made her wobble all over again. He seemed to understand, and steadied the small of her back instead. But his eyes told her that he wanted to touch her skin again. Hastily she pulled her wits about her. "I am all right now, thank you."

"Are you? You didn't look very well just now. Perhaps you would rather not dance with me again." The look he gave her was almost a challenge.

"Again?" Lily was very surprised to discover that she had been wishing he would say just that thing. "Would that not cause comment?"

He shrugged. "Perhaps. But if I am to go away and never see you again, it will soon die down. And if I do see you again after tonight . . ."

He left his thought unfinished, but Lily knew precisely what he meant, and took a deep breath. What matter if people saw the rector favor Lily Sterling with two dances tonight, if she was later to accept an offer of marriage from him?

Her will was weakening. It was, she decided, the proximity to him that was doing it. She hardened her heart, and said to him very deliberately, "I do not believe I can accept another invitation to dance, sir. It would not be . . . wise."

He bowed. "I am disappointed, but I understand." He truly did look less hopeful than he had when he first approached her, although not as resigned as he should, thought Lily. Obviously, he was not ready to give up. From then on, however, he talked only commonplaces with her until they were approached by Violet and Sir George.

Lily suddenly realized she had not seen them since the last dance. Sir George looked deliriously happy, his red and smiling face seeming ready to burst. Violet looked quietly radiant, but a little frightened. Lily was shocked, as she had never seen her eldest sister anything but confident and quite certain of her own good sense. Could Violet have succumbed? Had she chanced her happiness on a man who had been living a lie for two months? It seemed that she had. A sudden sadness swept over her. She could not look at Quentin, who seemed to have observed his friend's success and was smiling.

Quietly, Violet admitted that she had just become betrothed to Sir George.

Lily congratulated her sister. "But what will Papa say?"

Sir George grew a bit pale, but said stoutly, "I shall, of course, speak to the squire."

"Whatever he says," said Violet with unaccustomed determination, "we are going to be married. I am certainly old enough to know my own mind."

Lily wondered if anyone else could guess what had happened simply by the expressions on the faces of the newly engaged couple, but on the heels of this revelation came the formal announcement of Olive's betrothal to Mr. Murray. Lily was warmed by the joyful way this news was received, considering that at least some of their neighbors had heard there was an Italian gentleman staying at the Hall, and might wonder who, instead, was this Mr. Murray. But seeing Olive's happiness, she vowed she would stand by her, whatever confusion might arise from her adventurous betrothal. It was a shame that her own affairs could not be so simply arranged.

The music began again, and Sir George was offering his arm to Violet, while Quentin leaned closer to Lily with an expectant light in his eyes. But at that moment John Sterling, walking with a familiar tilt, approached them. Over his head Lily could see Lord Thorpe watching with ill-concealed amusement. The squire also stood nearby, getting a glass of lemonade for one of the ladies, while Lady Flora sat in her chair of state not far away.

"Why good evening, Lord Vyse, Sir George," said John Sterling quite clearly to Quentin and his companion, his exaggerated bow almost causing him to topple over. "Sorry I wasn't here to greet you earlier. Enjoying our little village fete? Not up to any entertainment you might get in London, gentlemen, but the girls are deuced pretty, eh?"

The squire stared at his brother. "Have you gone mad, John?" he said in a fierce whisper. "Why are you calling the rector Lord Vyse?" Enough people had noticed that now the room's attention was turned on them. Lord Thorpe drew closer, his smile broader.

John Sterling exchanged a triumphant glance with Lord Thorpe and laughed. "Not mad, brother." He tapped his forehead. "Canny. Allow me to present you to Lord Vyse—the *real* Lord Vyse, and Sir George Hollister. Didn't know they weren't who they claim to be, did you? Capital joke they've played on us all. It was a wager these gentlemen contrived, and very clever I think it was." His listeners' shock patently amused him.

Lily's gaze flew to Quentin's white face. His mouth was a thin line of rage, and he was looking at her uncle as though he would mill him down right there upon the slightest excuse.

Aunt Poppy and Aunt Hyacinth, Arabella and Olive wore expressions ranging from bewilderment to hurt, while the erstwhile signore, Mr. Murray, was obviously trying to hide a smile. Lily could hardly blame him for being delighted to find that men of rank could indulge in the same game as he.

The squire, seeing that Quentin and George made no move to deny John's assertions, approached them. "You had better explain yourself, and damned quickly," he said sotto voce, but leaving no doubt that he would be satisfied with only the truth. His frown encompassed not only his brother but Quentin, Sir George, and Lord Thorpe, who was the only person besides Uncle John who seemed to be enjoying the situation. In fact, he was the first to speak.

"Allow me to correct the false impression we have found it necessary to give. Lord Thorpe, sir, at your service," he said to an even more amazed Sir Richard. His grin seemed to stretch from ear to ear. The squire merely stared at him, as did everyone.

Calmly he continued, "I'm afraid you've all been hoodwinked, but no harm done. My friends and I have merely engaged in a little wager, and sadly, I must now concede that Vyse here has undoubtedly won. Try as I might, I could find no one who was not thoroughly convinced that he was indeed a clergyman, albeit a strange one. And what better proof than your shock at discovering that he is not who you thought he was? He made an excellent rector, did he not? I confess I did not think he would manage to last a week, considering that in London he hardly ever sees the inside of a church. No, his common haunts, I am afraid, are gaming clubs, race courses, and other such places of amusement." He stuck out his hand to Quentin. "Well done, Vyse."

Lily burned with indignation at the way the viscount cleverly bound himself and Quentin together, making that much more difficult his escape from the wrath of the duped people. And yet, had they not conceived the plan together? Still, looking from one to the other, the superiority of Quentin over the scheming Lord Thorpe could not but be obvious to her. Quentin contemptuously ignored the outstretched hand.

By now the entire drawing room had been shocked into silence, and Thorpe's ringing tones carried, so there was no one who did not hear every damning word. After a chilling moment, Quentin turned to her

299

father and spoke.

"I should like to apologize to you, sir, and to the entire village. I can assure you, my imposition was not conceived with any malice in mind towards this neighborhood or its church. And now, Sir Richard, I beg the indulgence of a few private words with you." His voice was clear and steady.

Lily held her breath, but looked pleadingly at her father. Suddenly it was immensely important that he did not turn Quentin away without giving him a chance to explain himself. The squire, his mouth in a hard line, looked into Quentin's face for a long moment. Finally he nodded. "Very well. Come with me."

He followed the squire out of the room and did not look back at Lily. She had an idea that his pride would not allow him to do so.

At first she was silent, taking in the reactions of the others. Lady Flora for once was almost speechless. Her face was a ghastly shade of gray.

"Brandy!" she choked, and Mr. Murray hurried to her side with a glass. She drank it down, and her daughters and granddaughters hovered solicitously over her, forgetting for a moment their own shock. But when the matriarch had recovered, Aunt Hyacinth said, "Well, I always knew there was something odd about that young man! Did I not tell you, Poppy, he stumbled in the prayers?"

"Oh, my!" said Aunt Poppy, looking at a red-faced Sir George as if he were a traitor. "How could you!" she cried. Sir George looked miserable, and Violet at his side gave no sign of support. Lily wondered how she could stand there and say nothing. But she saw that her sister was thrown off balance by the vehemence of people's reactions. Some of their guests were crying, "Shame!" and a slightly befuddled Billy Smythe was offering to draw the counterfeit rector's cork for him. All around there were calls for Quentin Vernon's head, the more angry as they knew that there was no real recourse.

If only, thought Lily, Uncle John had not been prompted by who knew what imp to divulge the secret in front of their guests! Even now he was joking among them, laughing about the wager, though none of them appeared to find it in the least amusing. Some, in fact, had already called for their carriages. By tomorrow the village would be ready to tar and feather Quentin and Sir George. But not, Lily decided, Lord Thorpe, for he would surely find some method of eluding their anger.

Even now, no one approached him or appeared to associate him with the deception, though he had been the author of it and the one who had revealed all its details to them. Lily supposed it was because they had not taken him into their midst as they had Quentin. He was an outsider. Quentin had become one of them, and Mickleford felt betrayed.

Thorpe sat to one side drinking, and by the look of deep satisfaction on his face it was obvious that he had been the instigator of Uncle John' untimely revelation. How could she not have seen it? He and her uncle had been rather thick lately. A win at cards, a night of drinking, and Uncle John could be persuaded to spill

301

the secret at the time most inconvenient for Thorpe's enemy. No doubt he knew both of Quentin's interest in her and Sir George's passion for Violet, and enjoyed the added benefit of having spoiled these courtships.

Rage burned in her and she knew it was time she spoke up. She moved into the center of the buzzing group of guests and stood quietly, until they saw that she had something to say and fell silent.

"You are angry," she began. "And it is natural. Yes, we have been deceived. I cannot condone Lord Vyse's masquerade, but I beg you will be moderate in your treatment of him. I think that he was on the point of confessing the deception himself, and that he was rudely forestalled. Besides, I firmly believe that he meant no ill towards us, and you must concede that no actual harm has been done to the parish."

There was murmuring among the guests. "My cousin is right," said Arabella, emboldened by too much punch. "Why, did we not have the best Easter pageant ever?"

"And we have a new baptismal font," piped up Aunt Poppy, whose soft heart had already been swayed.

"It has certainly been as entertaining a Lenten season as I've ever spent," volunteered Lady Flora, looking on her irate granddaughter with pride.

"In addition," continued Lily, sensing a change of heart in her listeners, "those of our neighbors who are tenants of Lord Vyse will have the satisfaction of knowing that now that he truly knows Mickleford, and will be more awake to its needs. I, for one, am ready to forgive him."

There was a sudden murmur that swept over the room and heads turned. Lily followed their gazes and saw that Quentin and her father had returned. It was apparent that they had stood there listening to her harangue, for Quentin's face seemed to be a study in amazement and hope. She could not look at him very long, however. When on the squire's orders the musicians struck up a country dance, he grinned at her as if daring her to demonstrate her faith in him, and again asked for her hand in the dance.

Head high, cheeks and eyes bright, Lily laid her gloved hand on his arm and they took their places at the head of the set. Slowly, beginning with Violet and Sir George, and Olive and Mr. Murray, and although several guests had left, a few other couples followed and joined the dancers.

"Did you mean it?" Quentin bent his head to ask her a they joined hands.

Lily's face was flaming, and she did not look up. "If you mean do I forgive you, I suppose I cannot lie now. The answer is yes."

"And the other answer? The one for which I have been waiting?"

His voice was hushed and tender. Lily finally looked up and saw his eyes intent on her face. She hesitated, and then the movements of the dance took them apart. They danced in silence until they reached the end of the set, and then Lily saw a servant hurry over to her father. In a hushed rapid voice he said something which caused the squire to start and cast his gaze up towards the ceiling. He nodded, went to speak with his sisters, and quickly the three left the drawing room.

The dance was just ending, but Lily ignored the pleading look in Quentin's eyes and her own need to talk to him, saying, "I'm sorry—I believe it is my mother. I must go."

Her hand in his trembled a little, and his expression changed at once to concern. "Of course, but please let me at least see you upstairs—you are very agitated."

She agreed, and the two of them flew up as if they were on wings, only to be stopped at the door of Lady Sterling's rooms by her Aunt Hyacinth. "No one is allowed in," she said firmly, "especially you girls." Lily thought she heard a muffled sound from inside, and Aunt Hyacinth swiftly bundled them away.

Quentin pressed her hand once more with sympathy, and discreetly stepped out of hearing. But his presence a few feet away in a shadowed corner was somehow comforting to her, as she heard her aunt tell her that it appeared the baby was coming sooner than expected, and that this time there seemed to be something wrong. "I won't go into detail, for it wouldn't be right," said Mrs. Forbush, but Lily could tell from her voice that she was indeed worried.

"Oh, please, let me go to her," she begged, but her aunt took her firmly by the shoulders and turned her away. "It isn't proper. Your Aunt Poppy is with her, and the midwife."

"The midwife already?"

"Yes, it appears the pains began just as the dance

was starting, and your dear mother did not want to disturb anyone, so she sent her maid down to send the footman out to bring her. But now . . ." For once, Lily saw her strong aunt falter. "I think we need the doctor."

The doctor! Nobody on the squire's estate saw a doctor unless they were well on the way to dying. Between the apothecary in the village and Lady Flora's herbal recipes the family, servants and villagers were kept in fair health.

"But the nearest doctor is out along the Chester road!" cried Lily.

At this it became apparent that Quentin had overheard most of the conversation. He hurried over. "I have ridden there. I know the quickest way. Please allow me."

Aunt Hyacinth looked at him in amazement. "But Mr. Vernon, I mean, Lord Vyse . . . in your evening clothes? We can send a servant, I assure you."

"I can manage it, if the squire will be so good as to lend me his fastest horse and tell me in which house I might find the doctor."

The squire had emerged from his wife's room at that moment, his face pale and heavy. "I shall count it a great favor, sir, if you would. The servants are hysterical or drunk—I found they've been celebrating in the kitchen while we entertained our guests—and I fear Lady Sterling is—" He broke off, and put an arm about Lily's shoulders, as if for support. She forced herself to stand steady, frightened as she was. Her father had always seemed so strong, and now he

305

needed her.

"I'll go at once then." Quentin's gaze held Lily's reassuringly.

The squire seemed to pull himself together. "I'll give the orders." He turned to Lily. "But you, my dear, must go downstairs and see to our guests. You may quietly tell them that your mother is not well. I'm sure they will appreciate the circumstances. And the dance was almost over anyway."

Before anyone knew what had happened, the squire's fastest hunter was prepared for Quentin, and, removing his tight coat, he rode off for the village, his skill surmounting the difficulty of riding in evening clothes. The guests, meanwhile, had heard the news as it filtered down, and decorously, for the most part, took their leave, thanking Lady Flora for her hospitality and leaving kind messages for the squire, who was above, pacing outside his wife's rooms.

After the guests had gone, Lily and her sisters huddled in a corner of the drawing room. It was still warm from its recent occupancy by a crowd, but all the candles except a few branches near them had been blown out. The tables were littered with dirty glasses, empty chairs sat crookedly along the walls, and the room seemed to echo with the music that had recently set them all dancing.

"What a night!" cried Olive, voicing the thoughts of most of them. Mr. Murray had tactfully taken himself off to bed, satisfied at least that his engagement had been made public before disaster had overtaken the party. Arabella was too excited and tired to stay up and keep watch, for she had made up the quarrel with Mr. Watson and he had pressed her to name a day for their wedding. So it was only Lily, Olive, and Violet who sat and listened to the silent drawing room and waited to hear the arrival of the doctor.

Lily did not realize she had fallen asleep until the sound of horses and mens' voices below startled her. She leaped up and went to the window. An unfamiliar gig was revealed in the lanterns held by the housekeeper at the door, and a man in a dark greatcoat was getting down, a large bag in his hand. She did not see Quentin.

Her impulse was to rush downstairs, but Violet, who had also awakened, put a restraining hand on her arm. "Best to let him go up to your mama right away. We can do nothing but wait."

Lily only hoped that it was not too late. She now and then heard quick footsteps from above, but no urgent sounds. While she waited, she thought of Quentin. It appeared that he was not coming back tonight. But she knew he would be back tomorrow, for she had not given him his answer. It was useless to deny that she was deeply in love with him. But she could not think about how she was going to tell him she had changed her mind. There was still tonight to be endured. But the thought of him lay comforting and warm in the back of her mind.

Violet jogged her arm, waking her from another doze. "Go to bed, dear. Olive has already gone, and Aunt Poppy was here to say the doctor is still with her."

"The baby?" asked Lily sleepily.

Violet shook her head. "Not yet."

Wearily she dragged herself up to her room. Passing the door to her mother's chamber she heard hushed voices and a moan. For a moment she longed to be there, to reassure herself, but she knew she would not be permitted. Once in her room, she undressed wearily and got into her nightgown. But before she went to bed, she went to her jewel box and unwrapped the sliver filigree egg from its velvet bag. She held it in her hand, got into bed, and fell asleep at once.

When children's voices outside in the garden woke her the next morning, she was still loosely holding the egg. Smiling, she put it down on her dressing table, but at that moment she heard a baby's lusty cry. She hurried into her dressing gown and sped down the hall to her mother's rooms. Without knocking she burst in and saw her mother sitting up in bed, looking down at a tiny, wailing, red-faced bundle she held in her arms.

"Oh, Mama!" Lily wanted to throw herself on the bed in relief, but the sight of her mother's white, exhausted face stopped her. Lady Sterling looked up and managed a weak smile. "Come and meet your new sister, darling."

Lily softly went over and bent to kiss her mother's cheek. "We were so worried. But the aunts wouldn't let us in. Oh, Mama, I'm so glad you're all right." Lily blinked back tears of relief, and her mother reached a hand up to touch her face.

"Of course I am, my love. Just very tired. I'm afraid I shall be in bed a good long while." She sighed and readjusted the bundle on her arm. "Will you take her, dear? Doctor said I should sleep."

Indeed, her eyes were already closing, so Lily gently disengaged the swaddled infant from her mother's arm and held it. Its milky blue eyes looked briefly at her and promptly closed. Lily smiled down at her baby sister, touching the soft little cheek gently, and then handed the bundle to Nurse, who stood waiting for it.

"It's glad I am to have another little one to look after, miss," the woman said to Lily. "T'other little miss is almost toddling after Miss Blossom already, and won't be needing me for very long."

Lily assured Nurse that the family could not do without her, and went back to her room to dress. Her heart was full. And when she went down to breakfast, it became even more so when her father told her that if it were not for Quentin the doctor would not have arrived in time.

The squire cleared his throat. They were alone in the breakfast parlor, the others either having breakfasted already or still abed after their late night. "That young man, Lord Vyse . . . we had an interesting chat last evening, he and I."

Lily glance up and saw that her father was watching her curiously. "I suppose he explained about the wager."

"Yes, he did. Pack of young fools! Never could stand those Town dandies when I was that age."

"Lord Vyse and Sir George are hardly dandies, Papa!"

The squire smiled at her ready defense. "No, I

309

suppose not, but what they did was inexcusable. That's not to say I don't like Vyse as much as I did when I thought he was only Mr. Vernon." He began to chuckle. "I must admit that he did an excellent job. Even fooled your aunts and that Ladies' Church Society!"

"And Violet," Lily reminded him slyly.

"Yes, Violet too. She has informed me, with great spirit, that she intends to marry a fellow called Sir George Hollister, lately a curate of this parish." He chuckled. "Almost too many surprises for a man my age! But it is you I am concerned with now: you and Lord Vyse. He asked my permission to address you. However," he said, giving her as shrewd a look as Lady Flora herself, "I have an idea that it was after the fact."

Lily was silent, looking down at her hands folded in her lap. Suddenly full of decision, she lifted her head. "I believe I have decided, Papa. Believe me, I felt as betrayed as anyone when Lord Vyse first revealed to me his real identity, but . . ."

Her father held up a hand. "No need to explain it to me. I know I'm a good judge of men, and whatever silly games young Vyse has indulged in in the past, it's plain he is as sound as they come. Besides," he grinned, "your Grandmama will have my head if I don't give my permission. She wanted him for you even when she thought he was his own illegitimate brother! Now come and kiss me."

Lily obeyed, and feeling as if a huge weight had been lifted from her, she went about her duties. Quentin, she was sure, would call that morning, so she gladly stayed within reach of the house, keeping the filigree egg and its ring in her pocket. Sure enough, when she brought the children back from their morning walk, Aunt Poppy intercepted her.

"It is Mr. Vernon—no, I mean Lord Vyse. Oh, I vow I am so confused I do not know who I mean. In any case, my love, he is here to see you, and your papa says that you may see him alone in the morning room." Her aunt looked hopefully at her, obviously awaiting enlightenment regarding this unusual command on the squire's part, but Lily, feeling her hardwon calm instantly crumble, was too intent on sustaining her composure and planning what she would say to Quentin to indulge her aunt's curiosity.

"Thank you, dear Aunt Poppy," was all she said. Without stopping to so much as remove her bonnet, she set off for the morning room. Still she did not know exactly how she would let him know about her decision, but she hoped he might make it easy for her. After all, he really had only to look at her in that particular way to bring the truth to her eyes where she could plainly read it. Unless . . . her heart nearly stopped at the thought—he had changed his mind. Poised at the closed door of the morning room, Lily took a deep breath and gathered her courage. At this unfortunate moment Lady Flora chose to drag her errant younger son down the corridor.

"It is coming from the dining room, I tell you. Now, will you see to it, or must a lady of my advanced years get down on her knees and poke about the floorboards looking for drafts?" she demanded.

John Sterling, showing the aftereffects of last night's overindulgence, and retaining none of that satisfaction that had come to him from enlightening the neighborhood on the rector's true identity, yawned and clutched at his temples. "Good grief, Mama, please do not carry on so! My poor head!"

Lady Flora snorted. "Hah! Your poor head indeed, my boy. Who told you to drink so much last night? And I have not yet had a word with you about that disgraceful performance of yours last evening. You shamed us, John, shamed the family before all the neighbors."

John bridled. "I? What about Vyse and Hollister? They were the ones pulling the wool over everyone's eyes. It was Lord Thorpe that confirmed it. Dashed good fellow! Won a pony from him, and likely more where that came from."

"Dunderhead!" Lady Flora tapped her son none too lightly across the back with her walking stick. "Can't you see he made use of you to do his dirty work for him? It's obvious he is no friend to Lord Vyse. He cared less about the wager than about making him look a fool before the everyone. And you fell right in with his plan."

Mr. Sterling, upon reflection, suddenly seemed to realized the truth of this assertion, and grew sulky. "Doesn't matter anyway. Bound to have found out soon."

"Yes, I would have told you all the truth—today, in fact. I did not wish to spoil either your Easter holiday

312

or your evening with such a story," came a calm, even voice.

Lily, who had been waiting impatiently for her grandmother and uncle to pass by, was startled to find that Quentin had emerged from the morning room and stood close behind her. She started, and saw looks of astonishment on both her grandmother's and her uncle's faces.

"Indeed, sir?" asked Lady Flora, a trifle more haughtily than usual.

"I assure you, Lady Flora," said Quentin, approaching her, "it pained me greatly, not to have my perfidy revealed, but that the manner of its revelation should cause you and your family so much distress."

Her face relaxed. "Of course. Call yourself what you will, I don't think it makes any difference. And after what you did for us last night — why, we owe Lady Sterling's safe deliverance to your dispatch. Others," she said, turning a stern glance on her son, "were too drunk to ride for the doctor." She nodded approval at Quentin, while Lily looked on, bemused. "A good man to have about the place in an emergency."

John Sterling sneered. "Perhaps Lord Vyse can assist you in the matter of the draft, Mama, since he is such a paragon."

Just then from downstairs there were childish cries of glee, pounding feet, and hysterical barking. In a moment the boys, heralded by the bounding leaps of the dog Dionysus, came up to the landing, both shouting at once.

313

"What is this mongrel doing in my house?" Lady Flora laid about her with her stick, fortunately with little accuracy. Dionysus merely lolled his tongue at her and bounded down the hall.

"After him!' cried William, and, followed by Stephen, he raced after the dog.

"What on earth—" began Lily.

Quentin smiled. "I'm afraid the creature followed me here this morning, and, meeting the boys outside, I asked them to entertain him for me while I paid a call. But I see that he is a bit too much for them."

"Where is the wretched beast off to?" asked Lady Flora.

"Shall we follow and see? Knowing his keen nose, there may be a bit of a surprise waiting for us at his destination."

Lady Flora smiled, and accepted the offer of his arm. "I shall never say no to an adventure, sir. Lead on."

Lily exchanged a glance with Quentin. His eyes promised that when they were alone he would have something of import to say to her. She realized, as he did, that as long as they were surrounded by people they would not be able to get away until the dog was found and had been packed out of the house, together with children, Uncle John, and Lady Flora.

But for now there was no recourse but to follow the odd procession along the corridor, and, judging by the direction of the children's cries, to the dining room.

By this time the squire had been roused from his study by the noise, and joined them at the door.

314

"May I ask what in heaven's name is going on here?" he asked.

"Hush, Dickey, we are following the dog. Vyse thinks he might be on the scent of something." Lady Flora shook of Quentin's arm and strode into the room, her stick tapping on the floor.

The squire groaned. "I must be going mad."

"Have patience, sir," advised Quentin. "I think at least one of your troubles is about to come to an and."

"Whatever do you mean?"

"Have you noticed a pronounced gust of chilly air coming through the room?"

The squire frowned. "Yes, as usual."

Lily shivered, drawing her pelisse tighter about her. "It's grandmama's draft, and it's worse than ever."

Quentin looked at her. "May I escort you within, Miss Lily? I believe we shall now discover not only the source of the draft that has so incommoded your revered Grandmama," he said with a mischievous look in his eyes, "but something even more interesting, knowing that dog's nose."

Lily took his arm, her nervousness in his presence gone. John glumly followed, and the squire marched behind. Once inside, Quentin followed the sounds of barking and small boys and gallantly led Lady Flora into the pantry off the dining room, the entrance to which was covered by a folding screen. There in the corner was a large movable cupboard, underneath which the dog's stubby tail could be seen protruding, wagging as if it would fall off his little body.

"Dionysus!" At Quentin's call the dog deserted his

315

watchpost and came to heel, looking up at his master proudly, as if waiting to be praised for his cleverness.

The boys, too small to move the cabinet but too big to burrow under or behind it, jumped up and down with excitement as Quentin pushed it away form the wall.

In the wainscoting behind the cabinet was a large hole from which chill air was pouring. On the floor was scattered small piles of straw which had apparently once filled it. To Lily' astonished eyes, it seemed that one pile in the very corner of the pantry, some distance from the hole, was moving.

Amidst the general outcry of surprise came Lady Flora's dismissive tones. "A fine job you did, sir! I see I ought not to have trusted you to take care of it," she said, glaring at her no longer favorite son. "Stuff a bit of straw in the wainscoting and have done with it, eh?"

John shrugged. "I did away with the draft, didn't I? Someone must have disturbed it, else it would still be serving the purpose now."

"Not someone," said Quentin, bending to look closer. "Some*thing*." He held up a piece of dirty straw and indicated the pile which had caught Lily's eye. A scrap of fur wriggled out of it. "I think we have found my missing namesake."

The children and Lily peered closer. There to her amazement was the rabbit, surrounded by straw and numerous progeny. "Look, it's Vernon!" cried William. "And there are a lot of little rabbits with him."

"With *her*, you mean," said Steven in a superior tone. He rolled his eyes as if to indicate that his

316

brother was too young to know better.

When she met Quentin's eyes, Lily went from amazement to laughter. "*What* a surprise! I should never have guessed that Vernon was really a Mrs. Vernon and about to present us with a whole new warren of pets."

"Neither should I," said Quentin. "And regarding that, I wonder if you will like having a rabbit for a namesake as much as I do?"

Lily blushed, but the children appeared not to notice as he put her arm around her shoulders and smiled down at her.

Uncle John gave them a swift, curious glance, and was about to speak, but he saw the look in his mother's eye, and swallowed his words. "Foiled by a bunny, by God!" was all he said.

Sir Richard was the only one not amused. "Vernon? Surely you mean *vermin!*" He rang to summon a servant. "These creatures must be removed at once."

Among the children's protests, Lily and Quentin slipped away, through the hall and back to the morning room, his arm tight about her waist. "I hope, after your spirited defense of me, my love, that your heart has not failed you, for I must formally beg once more that you grant me the honor of becoming my wife."

Slowly, Lily drew out the filigree egg, opened it, and removed the ring. She handed it to Quentin.

At first his face fell, but her smile was so tender that he could hardly mistake her meaning, and when she held out her left hand, his face broke into smiles of pure joy. Taking her hand in his, he slowly slid the ring onto her third finger. The ensuing kiss lasted until it became once more necessary to breathe.

Afterwards as they sat close together on a settee, her head resting on his shoulder, Lily told him, "I could hardly deny that I have come to realize that I was wrong after what I said about you in front of everyone last night. But all at once, when Uncle John exposed you, and people began to say horrid things, I knew I could not bear it."

Quentin faced her, pulling her so close that she could see every green fleck in his eyes. "Does that mean . . . ?

Lily looked at him, her lips parted. How could she have been so foolish as to wait this long? "I do love you," she whispered.

For an answer he kissed her again.

Dear Reader,

Zebra Books welcomes your comments about this book or any other Zebra Regency you have read recently. Please address your comments to:

Zebra Books, Dept. WM
475 Park Avenue South
New York, NY 10016

Thank you for your interest.

Sincerely,
The Editorial Department
Zebra Books

GOTHICS A LA MOOR—FROM ZEBRA

ISLAND OF LOST RUBIES
by Patricia Werner   (2603, $3.95)
Heartbroken by her father's death and the loss of her great love, Eileen returns to her island home to claim her inheritance. But eerie things begin happening the minute she steps off the boat, and it isn't long before Eileen realizes that there's no escape from *THE ISLAND OF LOST RUBIES*.

DARK CRIES OF GRAY OAKS
by Lee Karr   (2736, $3.95)
When orphaned Brianna Anderson was offered a job as companion to the mentally ill seventeen-year-old girl, Cassie, she was grateful for the non-troublesome employment. Soon she began to wonder why the girl's family insisted that Cassie be given hydro-electrical therapy and increased doses of laudanum. What was the shocking secret that Cassie held in her dark tormented mind? And was she herself in danger?

CRYSTAL SHADOWS
by Michele Y. Thomas   (2819, $3.95)
When Teresa Hawthorne accepted a post as tutor to the wealthy Curtis family, she didn't believe the scandal surrounding them would be any concern of hers. However, it soon began to seem as if someone was trying to ruin the Curtises and Theresa was becoming the unwitting target of a deadly conspiracy . . .

CASTLE OF CRUSHED SHAMROCKS
by Lee Karr   (2843, $3.95)
Penniless and alone, eighteen-year-old Aileen O'Conner traveled to the coast of Ireland to be recognized as daughter and heir to Lord Edwin Lynhurst. Upon her arrival, she was horrified to find her long lost father had been murdered. And slowly, the extent of the danger dawned upon her: her father's killer was still at large. And her name was next on the list.

BRIDE OF HATFIELD CASTLE
by Beverly G. Warren   (2517, $3.95)
Left a widow on her wedding night and the sole inheritor of Hatfield's fortune, Eden Lane was convinced that someone wanted her out of the castle, preferably dead. Her failing health, the whispering voices of death, and the phantoms who roamed the keep were driving her mad. And although she came to the castle as a bride, she needed to discover who was trying to kill her, or leave as a corpse!

Available wherever paperbacks are sold, or order direct from the Publisher. Send cover price plus 50¢ per copy for mailing and handling to Zebra Books, Dept. 3330, 475 Park Avenue South, New York, N.Y. 10016. Residents of New York, New Jersey and Pennsylvania must include sales tax. DO NOT SEND CASH.